FLUKE

ADRIANA LOCKE

Fluke

Cover Designer: Kari March

Cover Photo: iStock

Content Editor: Marion Making Manuscripts

Copy Editor: Editing 4 Indies, Jenny Sims

Proofreader: Michele Ficht

Umbrella Publishing, Inc.

PAPERBACK ISBN: 978-1-960355-01-0

To Michele Ficht,
Everyone should be lucky enough to have someone like you in their corner.
With love.

BOOKS BY ADRIANA LOCKE

Landry Family Series

Sway

Swing

Switch

Swear

Swink

Sweet

The Gibson Boys Series

Crank

Craft

Cross

Crave

Crazy

Mason Family Series

Restraint

Reputation

Reckless

Relentless

Resolution

Carmichael Family Series

Flirt

Fling

Fluke

Flaunt

Flame

The Exception Series

The Exception

The Connection

The Perception

Honey Creek Series

Like You Love Me

Dogwood Lane Series

Tumble

Tangle

Trouble

Cherry Falls

608 Alpha Avenue

907 For Keeps Way

Standalone Novels

Sacrifice

Wherever It Leads

Written in the Scars

Lucky Number Eleven

Battle of Sexes

The Relationship Pact (Hollis's story)

The Sweet Spot

For an email every time Adriana has a new release, sign up for an alert here: http://bit.ly/AmazonAlertAddy or text the word adriana to 21000

DEAR READER

What can I say? I thoroughly enjoyed writing this book. The levity, banter, and shenanigans gave me a break from the heaviness that can be everyday life. I hope they do that for you too.

My goal for this story was simply to put a smile on your face for a few hours. The Carmichael men are swoony and steamy, while also being a little silly.

It was just what my heart ordered.

Thank you for choosing to read this book. I know you have a million choices out there, and I'm honored that you decided to give Fluke, and me, a try.

I hope you enjoy.

With love,

Addy

SYNOPSIS

SEEKING AN EX-HUSBAND

I need a *fake ex-husband*.

Let me explain ...

I may have let it slip to my new coworkers that I have an ex-husband. Now they're fascinated with the details, specifically with him.

Why wouldn't they be? He's gorgeous, has exceptional skills in the bedroom, and is determined to win me back.

But there's a problem. *He doesn't exist*.

The bigger problem? I have to produce him to save my job.

This is where you come in.

I'm seeking someone to play a smitten ex-husband for two weeks. You'll need to remember our love story—details matter when it comes to romance! I need you to be prepared to travel in-state at a moment's notice. We may be in close proximity; sharing a bed may be required.

One more thing—kisses are essential for optics as necessary.

If this sounds interesting or, at the very least, entertaining, let me know.

Signed,
Your Future Ex-Wife

Buckle up for a steamy adventure between friends-turned-lovers in this new "fresh twist on a favorite trope" take on fake dating, close proximity, and romance in the workplace from USA Today Bestselling author Adriana Locke.

1

PIPPA

"Seeking a fake ex-husband."

My words fall into the air, sounding just as ridiculous as I imagined they would. I sigh and lift a brow at Kerissa, my best friend and troublemaker extraordinaire, sitting across the table from me. The mischief in her eyes complements the smug grin on her face, and I know, beyond the shadow of a doubt, that I need to rethink this attempt at crisis management.

"I can't do this," I say, slamming my notebook closed.

"And why not?"

I level my gaze with hers. "You've come up with a lot of bizarre things in your life, but this one takes the cake."

"Takes the ... *wedding cake*?"

She laughs at her joke—one that I don't find especially funny under the circumstances.

How do I get myself into these situations?

I grab a couple of Cajun fries—the whole reason we came to Shade House for happy hour—and pop them in my mouth. Tables around us begin to fill with patrons ordering drinks and appetizers. I side-eye my root beer float and consider breaking down and ordering an amaretto sour. The only problem is that my problem-solving abilities go down with each drink. At this point, I need all the help I can get.

"We could use this as an excuse to throw a divorce party," Kerissa says.

"Kerissa—"

"Will you just think about it? Hear me out." Her eyes twinkle. "We'll go to Savannah and get a room at Picante."

I sigh happily. "I do love that hotel."

"*Right*? We can hit up a Georgia Hornets game, get a massage, and shop. Maybe find a couple of unassuming bachelors to ravage for the weekend."

"Well, I did see that Lincoln Landry is the general manager of the Hornets now." I wiggle my eyebrows. "I'm thinking about buying a Hornets shirt with Landry on the back."

She laughs. "They don't have shirts with the GM's name on them."

"Oh, no. *They do*." I point at her. "You can get them online. I've already looked."

"How did you know all this, Miss I Hate Sports?"

"Because Lincoln Landry transcends baseball. He went viral last season for nothing other than a smirk and the way he licked his lips." I shrug. "Who am I not to follow a fan account dedicated to giving me delicious videos every morning? LandryLover0808 works hard at her craft, and I support content creators, *thank you very much*."

Her laughter grows louder. "Sometimes I wonder if I even know you."

I laugh too.

"There's this little place called Judy's down the street from Picante," Kerissa says. "We can grab breakfast there."

"Yes, and maybe we can ..." I stop as reality knocks me sideways. "Wait a minute. *I'm not actually getting a divorce*, remember?"

Kerissa frowns.

I flop back in my chair, the legs rattling against the tile floor, and huff.

Ten minutes ago, I was frustrated that I was a fake divorcée. Now I'm irritated that I'm not a real one.

Why am I the way I am?

Kerissa leans forward, folding her hands on the tabletop. "Is it wrong if I say I'm sad you don't have a marriage in trouble?"

I can't help it. I giggle.

"I'm kidding," she says, although I'm not sure she is. That's okay because I'm not sure I am either.

A trip to Savannah sounds like the perfect antidote to the mess at work. But taking trips to avoid my problems is almost as unhealthy as working with Chuck "the Schmuck" Collins.

My jaw clenches at his name rolling around in my head.

I shouldn't let him get to me. I'm a grown-ass woman who should be able to bite her tongue and let douchebags be douchey. But I was born lacking a filter to prohibit myself from snapping back at assholes.

It's not one of my finer qualities and certainly doesn't do me any favors. If I wanted to play the blame game, I could credit it to having two uber successful, brilliant parents who embodied the definition of hubris. The only way to survive surgeons as parents when you grow up wanting nothing to do with the medical field is to learn to stand up for yourself. It took me a long time to learn that.

Ten years later, I'd say I've mastered it—maybe a little too well.

"Now that you're calm-er," Kerissa says, "tell me what happened today."

Ugh. I take a deep breath. "My boss, Bridgit, wants to expand Bloom Match again. Originally, it was a small online matchmaking service. Then they got the idea to make it a regional thing where we blind-match people from this area, set up the dates, host mixers—all that stuff."

"Right."

"Business has been going well—exploding, even. Bridgit asked everyone a couple of months ago to brainstorm ways to take the company further. We all proposed our ideas, and it's come down to me and Chuck the Fuck."

"We hate him."

"We do." I nod, my blood pressure rising. "I dislike him on a good day. Even if I got up on time, had the perfect latte, and a great hair day, I'd still hate Chuck. If I had to nominate someone for the Hunger Games, it would be him. I wouldn't even have to think about it."

She snorts.

"I hit the alarm three times this morning, Muggers screwed up my latte, and my hair looks like this." I point at my head. "I woke up emotional, which makes me ragey itself because emotions are inconvenient and make me feel weak."

Kerissa rubs a hand against her forehead. "This does not bode well for Chuck."

My teeth clench as I remember the smarmy look the jerk gave me.

"So we're going back and forth about our ideas, right? The whole office is in the conference room listening to us weigh the pros and cons of our proposals. I wrap up my little impromptu presentation *—which I nailed, by the way*. He must've felt threatened or something because he leaned back in his chair, his arms behind his head like he's proudly displaying his sweat stains in his armpits, and says"—I pause to channel my inner Chuck voice— "'*I'd like to point out that we're taking relationship advice from a woman who has no verifiable experience with them.*'"

The top of my head might blow up.

"*He did not*," Kerissa says, eyes wide.

"Everyone was staring at me. I had flashbacks from high school when everyone found out about my mom's chandelier debacle. I just opened my mouth and spewed … I don't even know what I said, Kerissa. *I was so pissed off*. Something about being touched he pays so much attention to my private life but that I had been married before." I stop to drag in a hasty breath. "Then, because I'm petty and I know from office gossip that he and his wife are having problems, I said that at least I knew when to walk away, unlike others who live a loveless life in misery."

Her jaw drops.

"Not my proudest moment," I say, shifting in my seat.

"Well, silver lining—at least you put it in past tense. You could've said you *are* married. That would've been way more awkward."

I stare at her.

"What? I'm trying to help here," she says.

"What would've helped is if you'd gone to work with me and clamped a hand over my mouth. Because everyone started jabbering about how they didn't know that about me. I stood there with red freaking cheeks, constructing a fake marriage that we ended after a couple of years when we realized it wasn't right for us. *Oh*—he's still smitten with me, too, because why not? If you're creating an ex-husband, you might as well make him worth the fake marriage, right?"

Kerissa chuckles as I groan.

It's fine. Everything is going to be fine.

Hannah, our server, slides up to the table. A wad of pink gum snaps between her teeth.

I rest back against my chair and take a long, deep breath. I had big plans for today after work, including a walk on the beach and making a cold tomato soup with tarragon crème fraîche for my new neighbor. It's been a long time since I made something for anyone besides Kerissa, and she has the palate of a child. I was excited to take my sweet new friend a bowl of soup and listen to her stories about years gone by.

"You ladies look like you're in the middle of a serious conversation, but I wanted to make sure you don't need anything else," Hannah says.

Kerissa cups her chin in her hand and smiles at Hannah. "I'm fine. Pippa told her coworkers that she was married. For the record, she's never sniffed a wedding veil."

"I'm sitting right here."

"I know," Kerissa says. "I saved you the trouble of explaining. You're welcome."

Hannah grins. "That sounds like a prickly situation."

"How do you mean?" I ask, fiddling with my straw.

"Well, don't you work at a matchmaking company in Lakely?"

I nod.

"What if someone asks who you were married to?" she asks. "What do you say then? He's just someone from out of town? Because Lakely is a good forty-five minutes from here, and while there's not tons of crossover, someone might ask just to see if they know them."

I know. Dammit.

Kerissa sits up and laughs. "No, because that would've been too easy. She told them that she has dinner with him once a month."

I glare at her. "I said *sometimes*, not once a month." I shrug. "He still loves me. I can't help it. I'm lovable."

Kerissa rolls her eyes.

"I'm sure you are," Hannah says, cackling. "But I think you should plot out the rest of your story before you return to work tomorrow. You don't want to be caught with your pants down ... unless your ex-husband is coming around. Maybe he was good in bed."

"He was. I might've mentioned that too."

Kerissa and Hannah laugh at the heat in my cheeks.

"You both suck," I say, joining in the laughter.

"I'm with you on this," Kerissa tells Hannah. "I told her she needs to find a fake ex-husband to have on hand just in case. I know people who have done this kind of thing, and it worked out very, *very* well."

"Well, good for them," I say, holding my head in my hands. "I'm glad they found their knight in shining armor. But I have no interest in finding a man to deal with for the rest of my life, nor am I super excited about having a fake one either."

Hannah taps on the table. "Let me know if you need anything. I have a couple of new tables to check on."

Kerissa takes my notepad and slides it across the table as Hannah leaves.

I love my job, and Bridgit, more than any job I've had before. And while a part of me knows she would understand my predicament—especially since I think she dislikes Chuck too—I don't want to give her a reason to think poorly of me.

I don't want to disappoint her.

"Okay, I think this was a solid start," Kerissa says. "Just look at it.

You'll feel better if you have an option in your back pocket."

She's right. Options are good.

She turns the notepad around, and together, we read.

SEEKING AN EX-HUSBAND

I need a *fake ex-husband.*

Let me explain ...

I may have let it slip to my new coworkers that I have an ex-husband. Now they're fascinated with the details, specifically with him.

Why wouldn't they be? He's gorgeous, has exceptional skills in the bedroom, and is determined to win me back.

But there's a problem. *He doesn't exist.*

The bigger problem? I have to produce him to save my job.

This is where you come in.

I'm seeking someone to play a smitten ex-husband for two weeks. You'll need to remember our love story—details matter when it comes to romance! I need you to be prepared to travel in-state at a moment's notice. We may be in close proximity; sharing a bed may be required.

One more thing—kisses are required for optics as necessary.

If this sounds interesting or, at the very least, entertaining, let me know.

Signed,

Your Future Ex-Wife

"See?" I take the notepad and stuff it into my bag. "That's ... *no.* Funny, but no."

"Suit yourself."

I twist to hang the bag on the back of my chair. "I think I'd rather find an actual husband than post that. I ..."

As I start to turn back, my eyes latch on to a pair of the greenest eyes I've ever seen.

Screw. Me.

2

PIPPA

Lord have mercy.

Pheromones ripple through the air as my gaze collides with the man sitting behind me. The corners of his lips curl into a smirk, sending shivers snaking down my spine.

Jess Carmichael is nothing short of a dream.

Thick, sandy-colored hair styled in a crew cut with tapered sides gives him a boy-next-door vibe. His smile—complete with full lips ready to be kissed.

Or maybe that's just me.

His jaw is sharp, and his shoulders tell tales of lifting heavy things all day. The scruff dotting his cheeks—begging to scratch my inner thighs—only draws more attention to his fantastic green eyes that twinkle like they hold a lifetime's worth of secrets.

Or, again, maybe that's just me.

It's amazing that God continued to make men after he wrapped Jess. He'd already crafted perfection.

"Did I hear you say that you're looking for a husband?" he asks, rubbing a finger along his bottom lip.

"You heard no such thing."

"Are you sure? Because I'm pretty damn certain I heard you say that you want to find a husband."

I grin. "You heard me say that I'd rather find a husband than go through with Kerissa's silliness."

His smile incinerates my insides. "If you change your mind, I'm up for the job."

I shove his arm and immediately regret the decision.

The contact is akin to touching a piece of metal after shuffling across the carpet in clean socks. Despite the jolt of energy, my hand remains on his solid bicep for a moment longer than necessary.

Jess laughs, the sound taking up the space between us as I withdraw my touch.

I've known Jess and his brothers most of my life, thanks to my brother, Greg. Dad didn't give his only son much of a choice. He was going to carry on the family legacy and become a wrestler. It turns out that wrestling is a very, *very* small world, and the Carmichaels were a permanent fixture in that landscape.

I spent countless weekends traveling to tournaments as a young girl, watching Greg do his thing. As we grew older, my brother and Jess became best friends. And when we all graduated from high school, Greg went to college on a course for med school, and I followed the year after. Jess stayed behind.

Since then, I've loosely kept up with the Carmichaels through social media and saying hello on occasions when we bump into one another somewhere. But because I made it a point not to come back to this area, mostly to avoid my parents until I moved back last week, I haven't had an opportunity to really talk to any of them in a long time.

"When did you get here?" I ask, imploring my cheeks to cool.

"We've been here—what? Ten minutes?" He looks across the table. "Is that about right, Banks?"

A shorter, darker-headed version of Jess shrugs. "Probably. Hey, Pippa."

"Hi, Banks."

"Kerissa," he says, nodding warily.

"*Banks*." She lifts a brow and turns her back to him.

Jess and I laugh at the two of them still holding a grudge that's years in the making—even though I'm almost positive that if Kerissa would give up her end of the beef, so would Banks. He's stubborn, but fighting probably takes away from the attention value he could get from actually being able to talk to her.

If I remember one thing about Banks Carmichael, it's that he loves attention.

"What have you been up to?" I ask, ignoring the strong pulse of my heart. "I haven't seen you in ages."

"Not much. Working a lot."

"Do you still work for your dad?"

He nods. "I'm running a crew now, and my brother Moss is running the other. The old man is keeping us pretty busy."

"What about you, Banks?" I ask. "What have you been up to?"

"Looking for a new best friend. Are you in the hunt for one?"

Kerissa's head whips around to his. "*No*. She absolutely is not."

"I didn't ask you," he says, narrowing his eyes at her.

She narrows hers right back.

Banks does the only thing to make things worse—he grins. This only causes the flames shooting out of Kerissa's head to grow hotter.

"I'm going to the ladies' room," Kerissa says, giving Banks a final glare. "I'll be back, Pip."

She storms off toward the back of the building.

"That's funny," Jess says, tipping his beer toward his brother. "Banks was just about to go to the truck to get his wallet."

Banks flinches. "I was?"

"*You were*." Jess lifts a brow. "So *go get it*."

"Fine," Banks says, sighing dramatically as he gets up from the table. "I'll go get my wallet even though it's not like I'm going to pay anyway."

I can't help but laugh as he heads toward the front of Shade House, leaving the two of us behind.

The air shifts, engulfing me in the scent of *man*—sweat and dirt and just enough exotic spices to elicit a chemical response from every woman within twenty yards. Despite the overt stare from the gorgeous woman at a table next to us, Jess focuses on me.

It's a heady feeling to be the center of this man's curiosity. He could give it to any woman in this restaurant, and they would soak it up. He's the kind of guy who walks into a packed room, and within a few minutes, everyone seemingly knows he's there.

And they want to talk to him. Why? Not just because he's handsome but because he's present. He looks you in the eye and responds with comments as if he's actually listening.

People don't do that anymore.

"Can I sit with you?" he asks.

"Yeah. Sure."

He stands, towering over me with his six-foot-plus frame. His jeans are stained and ripped; his black shirt is torn at the hem, clinging to his muscled frame. It takes everything in me not to drool.

"You are a sight for sore eyes," he says, sitting across from me. "How have you been?"

"I'm good. Working, unpacking—boring life stuff."

"Unpacking?"

I grin. "Yeah. I just moved to Kismet Beach."

His eyes widen. "Is that so?"

"That is so."

His smile pulls mine along with it.

"Did you move *alone*?" he asks, prying.

I laugh. "Are you asking me if I'm single, Carmichael?"

"Yes, Plum. *I'm asking if you're single.*"

My lips press together as I give him a look. *His response*? He chuckles.

Jess has asked me out at least once a year for the past fifteen years. I only saw him once last year—at a mutual friend's birthday party—and he managed to slip in a dating proposal in the four hours we were together.

Sometimes it surprises me that we've never been an item. We get along famously. He is the definition of a catch. Our chemistry isn't lacking in any way, shape, or form. But when we were younger, I knew my parents would murder me if I brought home anyone who wasn't on track to have fancy letters after their name.

Now that we're older—now that my parents have basically excommunicated me, and *I* control my own life—hooking up with Jess hasn't been a viable option.

Not that I would take the option if it were possible.

He licks his lips, and I shiver.

Doesn't hurt to imagine, though.

"You know me," I say, leaning back against my chair. "I'm never attached to anyone."

As if he can't take the added distance between us, he leans forward. His hands fold on the tabletop next to the carousel of condiments.

"What's wrong with you? Why are you always single, anyway?" he asks, his head tilted to the side.

"Because boys are trouble."

"Good thing I'm not a boy, then. I assure you—*I'm a man*."

Slowly, like he knows I need time to process those three words, he settles back in his seat. The fabric of his shirt shifts, lying flat against his stomach. A slip of skin at his hip where his shirt bunched glistens.

It's akin to walking inside a donut shop while cutting carbs.

Pure torture.

"What about you?" I say, redirecting the conversation away from my private life. "Who are you seeing these days?"

He stretches his legs out beneath the table. His foot swipes against mine, and I know he notices. He rolls his tongue around his mouth.

"I don't have time to see anyone," he says. "I work ten or twelve hours a day and spend the rest of it eating, sleeping, or keeping Banks out of my house."

I snort. "What's up with that?"

"Maddox got married last week, and Banks is beside himself."

"Banks doesn't like Maddox's wife?"

"Oh, he likes her fine. We all love Ashley. But she effectively stole Banks's best friend. Maddox won't let Banks sleep on his couch anymore or hang out at his house twenty-four seven. It's a thing, and Banksy is driving me fucking nuts."

I laugh. "So is Banks homeless now?"

"Hell, no. You know where we live, right?"

"Yeah, I think so. Aren't you all just before you get into Kismet Beach if you're coming from Sunnydale?"

He nods. "Mom and Dad bought all the houses along Honeysuckle Lane—one for all six kids. Obviously, Mom has codependency issues."

We share a smile.

I remember Damaris Carmichael from Greg's wrestling days. She was always so warm, so sweet—always ready with a smile and a sandwich if anyone in the gym was hungry. *Such a contrast to my mother*.

"So what brought you back to town?" Jess asks.

"Unless I want to live in a bug-infested condo in an area that requires mace at night, it's cheaper for me to live here and drive into Lakely every day. The housing prices are astronomical."

"If you ever buy a reno project, hit me up. I know a guy."

"Oh, you do, do you?"

He laughs. "I do. He can probably get you a good price too. He has connections."

"*Right*," I say, grinning so hard that my cheeks ache.

"If you throw in a couple of dinner dates, I bet you could knock off a few grand."

I can't help it—I burst out laughing. "My presence isn't worth a couple of grand, Mr. Carmichael."

"Speak for yourself."

I shake my head and try to tell myself he's this flirty with everyone, but I know that's not true. I've witnessed him in many situations over the years, and he always flocks to me. He builds me up, making me feel really good about myself. Sure, he's respectful of other women in conversations—I've watched him from afar enough to know this is true. But with them, he's not like he is with me.

And there's an unspoken intimacy—like we share a secret—that feels special.

Maybe we do. Maybe that secret is that we both want each other. I just happen to know that someone else would be better for him than me.

That sucks, but it's true.

"You're good for the ego. You know that?" I ask, grinning.

"And you're bad for mine since you always shut me down."

"Trust me, you don't want to date me."

Jess snorts. "Okay."

"*You don't*. You're marriage and daddy material. I'm not into that."

He leans forward, his voice dropping a few levels. "Trust me, Pip, *you'd be into that*."

His eyes darken into the deepest green that I've ever seen them. A chill races across my skin, leaving goose bumps in its wake.

I'm absolutely certain I'd be into *that* with him. How could I not be? Hell, I've imagined him many nights when it's just me in bed and I need relief.

But when I can already sense the complications that would arise with Jess, and we're only friends, that's enough to keep my head on straight. There's no sense in wasting our time. Although, any orgasm Jess Carmichael delivers would be spectacular.

But I'll never be all the things he'd want me to be.

And I'm fine with that.

"Are you afraid you'll fall in love with me?" he asks.

I giggle. "No. Not even a little bit."

Kerissa pulls out her chair beside me and sits, looking over her shoulder and scanning the room.

Jess and I smile.

"Banks isn't back yet," Jess says.

Her shoulders slump. "Good."

"Why do you hate him so much?" I ask. "It's been so long that I don't even remember."

Kerissa looks surprised. "He dated my sister. Remember?"

Oh yeah. That's right.

Kandace was devastated when she and Banks ended things. It wasn't like they dated for a long time, but the girl acted like a kicked puppy. Everything reminded her of him. She moped for weeks, crying and pouting and acting ridiculous. We spent most of that summer with her, trying to take her mind off it at their mother's command. It was a messy ordeal, but I barely remember what started it.

"Yeah." She glances at Jess. "Your brother broke my sister's heart so completely that I will never, ever forgive him."

Jess shrugs. "Hey, you're not going to hear an argument from me. The little shit does stuff all the time that I find unforgivable."

"Like what?" I ask.

"Well, like the fact that I've spent the past two fucking weeks finding stickers with his face on them stuck to everything in my house."

My jaw drops. "You're kidding?"

"Nope. He ordered one thousand of them and broke in and plastered them on every surface. Cups, the floor, condoms—my toothbrush. They're in the bottom of my shoes. I went to use my debit card the other day, and there he was."

"You should kill him," Kerissa says. "Do the world a favor."

Jess looks down at his phone and laughs. "Speaking of the devil, I need to go. He picked me up from a job site, and I rode over here with him. He's ready to leave—he even paid our tab—and if I don't go out there now, the fucker will leave me."

His gaze lands on mine once again. It's like being held—a contactless form of support that I've rarely found in the world.

It's probably because I've known him for a long time.

"It was good to see you, Jess," I say.

He pushes away from the table and says goodbye to Kerissa. Then he walks over to me.

My heart thumps as he bends, lowering his lips to my ear. "Pip?"

I hum, staring straight ahead and trying to ignore the heat of his breath on my skin.

"I'll let you call me daddy if you want," he whispers.

A surprised laugh sputters from me as I turn to swat at him. He laughs, darting out of the way before my hand contacts his shoulder.

"Bye," he says, walking backward.

"Bye."

He gives me a little wave, then turns, opens the door, and leaves.

"What the hell was that?" Kerissa asks.

I stare at the door and grin.

That was trouble if I don't watch it.

Sexy, dirty, six-foot-three trouble all wrapped up in a sinful package.

3

JESS

"Imagine the worst thing in the world that could happen to you."

My youngest brother, Banks, closes his eyes. He rests the back of his head on my couch, his forehead wrinkling as if he's deep in thought—something I'm certain he's incapable of, but whatever.

"Okay," he says. "Got it."

"That's how I feel when I think about letting you move in."

His eyes pop open, and his jaw hits the floor. "That's ... really hurtful, Jess."

"Oh, *please*."

He grabs the remote off the coffee table and turns down the volume on the television.

I never should've let him in my house tonight. I knew better. But my mind was on Pippa as I climbed out of the truck, and my defenses were down just enough to leave me vulnerable.

It's as if Banks senses my weakness. I swear the guy could be across the planet and still know when there's an opening for him to manipulate. I don't get it. I'm also kind of jealous of his abilities, but I have no idea how he does it.

"You act like you don't even like me," he says from across the living room. Moonlight streams through the window beside him.

"I do?" I hum, bringing a beer bottle to my lips. "That's interesting."

"*You like me*," he says as if he's trying to convince both of us. "I'll even go out on a limb and say we've bonded over the past couple of weeks—really cementing our new two-man wolf pack—"

I choke on my drink, spraying bits of alcohol through the air like tiny pieces of surprise confetti.

"What?" Banks turns his palms toward the ceiling innocently. "What did I say?"

"Did you just say our *two-man wolf pack*?" I clear my throat, blinking back tears. "Is that what I heard?"

"Yeah. That's what we are now, right? I mean, Moss has a girlfriend. Maddox got married last week," he says, rolling his eyes. "So it's just you and me now. Well, there's Foxx, but he's not the wolf-pack type. He's more ... lone, possibly rabid wolf."

I stare at him. *What would it be like to be in his head? Is it lonely in there? Can he hear gears grinding when he thinks too hard?*

I stretch out in my recliner, my feet dangling off the edge.

My body aches from a long day of tearing down drywall. My head hurts from an afternoon spent with Banks. Worst of all, my stomach is all tied up after seeing Pippa Plum.

That woman has been my crush since I was fourteen years old. One day, she was Greg's little sister. The next, she walked into the gym early on a Saturday morning, and everything was different. Her legs were longer in her black workout pants. A yellow top hugged curves that I'd never noticed before. The hidden layer of mischief in her grin didn't feel childish anymore. It was curious. Secretive. *Hot.*

And she's only gotten hotter.

"Back to our wolf pack," Banks says. "I—"

"We *are not* a wolf pack."

"Then our brotherhood."

I eye him, and I almost—*almost*—feel bad for the guy. Instead, I reach toward him. "Hey, come here."

"Why?"

"I think you have a piece of glitter stuck in your hair."

He ducks my half attempt at smacking the side of his head and glares at me.

"What?" I ask, snickering. "Too soon?"

"It will *always* be too soon."

"You can dish shit out but not take it?"

He lifts a brow. "*Jess*. You rigged my house with six buckets of glitter."

"*You* put your face on one thousand fucking stickers and stuck them on every surface in my house that doesn't move."

He smirks. "Nah, some things moved."

I punch him in the arm, earning a yelp from the little asshole.

Banks has an overwhelming case of youngest child syndrome—even though he's *not* the youngest child in our family. When our parents brought our only sister home, Banks dug in his heels and refused to give up his spot as the family's baby. As a result, he's spoiled, craves attention, and is willing to take unnecessary risks with his life and liberty.

He also hates being alone.

This hasn't bothered me because he's always had Maddox. But now that Maddox is married, he's on his own—whether he likes it or not.

"Can we focus here?" he asks, gripping his punched arm with his other hand.

"On what?"

"On our living arrangements."

I take a long, cold swig of my drink. "Did you come here just to convince me to let you move in?"

"I don't want to *move in*, move in."

"Good. Because you're not."

He sighs. "I just need a place to hang out."

"Sounds like a *you problem* to me."

"You're not even thinking about it."

"There's nothing to think about, Sparkles." I pause to enjoy his irritation at my new pet name for him. *Worth it*. "I know you're having a quarter-life crisis because Maddox stopped letting you suck his tit, but that has nothing to do with me."

He starts to respond, but a sports news break sidetracks him.

I twist my bottle between my fingers and close my eyes.

As much as Banks is the youngest child in his glory, I'm the proverbial middle child. I value my independence over everything. The idea of having someone around all the time makes me feel claustrophobic. I like to keep the peace, but I won't be stepped on or manipulated—and if anyone, namely my siblings, wants to go to battle, I'll win.

Period.

And that's what this is with my youngest brother—a battle of wills.

"Just hear me out," Banks says, ignoring my groan. "You and me tearin' it up. Bad boys for life. Hanging out in the garage, ordering pizza, turning some wrenches."

"What you mean is we can hang out in *my* garage, *I* can order, and *I* can pay for pizza, and you can use *my tools* to fuck around with whatever project you have going on?"

He slowly blinks. "I mean, I can order it if you want."

"*Banks* ..." I watch as he rests his head on his hands. "You have your own house."

"Why does everyone use that as an excuse? '*Banks, you have your own house.*' Like I don't know that, but it's not the point."

I roll my eyes.

"I'm tired of hearing '*Why are you in my house, Banks*?' I want to feel like I'm supposed to be there."

"Well, you're not. So there's that."

A knock raps on the door.

"Who is it?" I shout.

"Foxx."

"Come in," I yell.

"Hey." Our eldest brother Foxx stands in the doorway. "What are you two doing?"

I give Foxx a look. He nods, understanding the situation at hand.

"We're negotiating," Banks says with a tired sigh.

"We are *not* negotiating, Sparkles," I say.

Banks glares at me.

"A negotiation is a give-and-take," I say. "That's not what's happening here, no matter how hard you try to force it."

"Fine." He looks at Foxx. "He's right. I'm giving, and Jess is *not taking.*"

"I haven't been present for the entirety of this conversation," Foxx says, hiding a grin. "But I'm certain that's not the case."

"How would you possibly know that?" Banks asks.

Foxx is amused. "I just came from Mom's. Do you know what she was doing?"

Banks shakes his head slowly. He senses the trap our brother is laying for him but knows it's too late to avoid it now.

I sit back, crossing my arms over my chest, and enjoy the show.

"She was going to hose down the house this evening. She spent an hour looking for her power washer," Foxx says.

"Why'd she do that? I took ... *it. Shit.*" He takes in our smug grins and holds up a finger. "It's not like that."

"Oh, Banks, *but it is*," Foxx says. "The only thing you give anyone is a fucking headache."

I snort.

"Well, how about this," Banks says. "I have a proposition, and Jess won't even hear me out."

"Banks, Foxx would rather talk about his emotions than listen to your proposition."

"Accurate," Foxx says.

"You guys are mean," Banks says.

Foxx crosses his arms over his chest and peers down at our brother. "If you need to be coddled, go see Mom. *I'm not the one.*"

"I expect this from *you*," Banks tells him. "I just thought maybe Jess would be in a more amicable mood tonight since we ran into Pippa Plum."

The relief the alcohol has afforded me is gone. In its place is a tension that makes it hard to sit still.

Knowing she's back in town—less than ten minutes away regardless of where she lives in Kismet Beach—fucks with me. It's like there's a magnet hidden in town, and I can't rest until I find it.

I'm thrown back into the cycle I find myself in every time I encounter Pippa; it's been this way since I was a teenager. I see her, talk to her, spend a few minutes with her, and suddenly, she's all I can think about for days. If I'm seeing someone else casually, I lose interest—which I know is wholly unfair to them. But I can't help being the asshole secretly wishing I was with Pippa instead.

At least I'm not enough of an asshole to stay with someone else while thinking about another.

The memory of Pippa has ruined more than a few good hookups.

"I remember her," Foxx says. "Short. Brunette. Highly intelligent."

Banks snickers. "You are the only person in the world who gets three adjectives to describe Pippa, and you choose *intelligent*."

"I'm with Sparkles on this one," I say.

Short, brunette, intelligent.

Funny, sexy—exceptional.

"You two are heathens," Foxx says. "There's more to women besides their cup size and hip measurements."

"True. But none of us know if she can suck a dick," Banks says.

My jaw clenches.

"You're a disgrace to our family," Foxx says.

Banks laughs. "No, I'm not. I was just seeing how pissed that would make Jess."

"Regardless of whether it would piss off Jess," Foxx says, "it's inherently rude. Please, grow up." He turns to me. "I'm stopping at Shade House for takeout, then I'm leaving town for a few days. Can you get my mail?"

"Sure."

Banks peers around me. "You're not eating in your truck, are you?"

Foxx just stares at him.

"You won't let *me* eat in your truck," Banks says.

"Banks, I won't let you *in my truck* if I can help it."

"Why? What harm would I do?"

Foxx settles his sights on our brother. "Let's take your last appearance in my vehicle, shall we?"

Banks sees where he's going with this and cringes.

"It was three in the morning, and I was picking you up *from jail*," Foxx says. "Dried blood was on your shirt from crushing a man's face. Trust me when I say you'll never be in my truck again."

"Sounds like a challenge to me," Banks says.

A part of me would like to kick back and watch this play out. No one can put someone in their place like Foxx, and he gets entirely too much enjoyment out of dressing down our youngest brother. But another part of me, one I'm kinda pissed about acknowledging, that *almost* feels sorry for Banks.

"Where are you headed?" I ask Foxx to keep him from tearing into Banks.

"I just have a few things to do. You know how it is."

"Yeah," I say. But even though I'm sure I know *how it is* more than anyone else in our family, I don't have a fucking clue *how it is*. While I'd say I'm the closest to Foxx, we might as well operate on different continents.

I spend my days working for Dad's company, Laguna Homes. Foxx spends his days working, for sure. He has plenty of money and travels often. But what does he *do* for employment? I have no idea.

And I've realized over the years that I don't want to know. It feels safer somehow.

"Guess we'll see ya when we see ya," I say.

"I'll be back the first of the week," Foxx says.

"Be safe," Banks tells him.

Foxx turns to the door. "Goodbye."

"Later," I call after him.

The door closes with a soft thud.

I turn to tell Banks it's time for him to go home when my phone buzzes in my pocket. I pull it out and look at the screen.

Unknown: An underwater city built by octopuses called Octopolis was found in 2009.

"What the hell?"

"What's wrong?" Banks asks.

"I just got a text from an unknown number about an octopus city."

Banks smirks. "Is that code for something?"

"What? No. I mean it. It says, 'An underwater city built by octopuses called Octopolis was discovered in 2009.' What the fuck is that?"

"Wait. Moss and Maddox both said that they get random texts too. I can't remember what about, but it's not octopuses."

Me: Who is this?

I wait for a response, but nothing comes. *Weird.*

"I feel left out," Banks says. "I want random texts too."

"Want me to send them your phone number?"

He sighs. "No, because I don't want octopus facts. I want car facts or something."

"You don't get to pick, it seems."

Banks yawns. "I think I'm going to grab a shower."

I pull my legs down and sit up in the recliner. "Time for you to go home then."

"You have an extra bathroom upstairs that—"

"Go home."

"*Jess* ..."

I get to my feet and stretch. "I'll tell you what. If you go home now and don't come back, maybe I'll hang out with you Saturday."

"Really?" He stands. "Deal." He turns toward the door. "I'll go see what Dad's doing."

I shake my head and follow him to the doorway. As soon as he's outside, I lock it behind him.

The house is quieter than I remember. Even with the television on, it feels empty. I don't know if it's because I've had a people-filled day or because two of my brothers were just here. But, for whatever reason, I'm unsettled.

I gather the empty bottles from the evening and carry them into the kitchen. My mind wanders to the pretty, *intelligent* brunette I crossed paths with today.

"You have to get a grip, Carmichael," I say aloud. "You can't sit around thinking about Pippa all night."

Instead of focusing on another topic, all I can think of is how her eyes lit up when I whispered in her ear.

"Nope," I say, adjusting myself and heading for my bedroom. "I'll stand in the shower and think about her instead."

4

PIPPA

"To the left," I say, motioning with my hands. "No, *your left*, Kerissa. The other left."

She drops the picture to her chest and looks at me over her shoulder. "This project is turning into a Beyoncé song."

I snort.

My new apartment in Kismet Beach is everything I hoped it would be.

The balcony off the living room has a small glimpse of the ocean, but the building between us blocks much of the coastal wind. The walls are thick enough to block out my neighbors' sounds. And, best of all, it's clean—and cheap.

Well, cheaper than every safe neighborhood in Lakely and available rental in Sunnydale.

"There has to be a hack for this," Kerissa says, climbing off the sofa. She sets the piece of art I bought at Seachella a few years ago down on the coffee table. "There's a hack for everything these days."

"I wish there was a hack to losing weight."

"It's just mathematics—"

"Don't," I say, shaking my head. "Don't start with it's just addition and subtraction of calories in and out."

"But ... it is."

"And ... we're talking about a hack. As in—I don't want to do the math. Math sucks. Give me a way to suck calories out of pizza, not an easier way to do algebra."

She laughs. "It's basic arithmetic, not algebra, you dork."

I flop on the couch. "If you're not a math person, all numbers are algebra."

"Well, don't hold your breath for a calorie hack. Crap like that is how these scammer companies make millions."

"Speaking of making millions, did you see the kid that makes millions a year playing with toys online? He gets them sent to him, his parents film him playing with them, they post it, and voilà! Money." I frown. "I need to be sponsored."

Kerissa sits down beside me and scrolls through her phone. "Who would you get to sponsor you?"

Good question. I look around the room and take in the eggshell-colored walls and ceiling fans that probably remember the late twentieth century. It's not like the marble countertops and crystal chandeliers that I grew up with or the modern, sterile unit I occupied in Lakely ... and I really kind of like it.

All the updated rentals in Kismet Beach are occupied and have a waiting list behind them for when they're not. If I wanted an ocean view for a realistic price, my only choice was to move into something that needed work. I was nervous about it at first, but now I understand the pull some people have to places that need to be renovated.

I'd love to do so many things with this place—things I won't do because I don't own it. But if I did, I'd paint the walls something warmer and less uninviting. I'd remove the wall between the kitchen and living room so I could hang out with people in one bigger space. This place would turn into something cozy and comfortable. It would be a place like I've never really lived before.

"Hmm ... I'd take one of those architectural shows that come in and renovate your dream home. Or a car company so they can send me new cars every year, and I can just drive them around and video myself. Or if I'm being practical, the insurance company. I feel violated every time I see that payment clear."

She hums in agreement.

"What about you?" I ask. "Who would you get to sponsor you?"

"I don't know. I'd be happy with a sugar daddy at this point in my life."

I laugh.

She puts her phone on her lap. "I'm serious. We're almost thirty freaking years old, Pip. I'm tired of doing this all by myself. I'm actively lowering my standards in hopes I can find some rich old guy who just wants arm candy in exchange for paying my bills."

"That sounds terrible."

"Terrible? *Why*?" She holds out her hands. "I've not given up on finding an actual soulmate—if such things even exist. And for the record, I'm not sure they even do. But I'm starting to wonder if *soulmate* is a social construct designed to make people actually believe they're supposed to be with their mate to quell the divorce rates."

I shake my head.

"I mean it." She picks up her phone again. "I wonder if people around the world believe in soulmates or if that's just an American thing."

"No clue."

"What about you? Do you believe in soulmates?"

I rest my head against the cushions and close my eyes.

Kerissa's question is one I don't like answering. It feels like a trap even though I know she doesn't mean it that way.

In the depths of my heart, I think everyone on the planet has a perfect match somewhere. But the odds of haphazardly bumping into that person are slim.

That's one of the reasons I love working for Bloom Match. Being surrounded by people who believe in love—that would put themselves out there like our clients do for a chance to meet their lobster—is uplifting. It's fun. It's heartwarming, and I love everything about it.

Except for Chuck. Fuck Chuck.

"Probably," I say, looking at her. "If you take the number of people on Earth, it's logical to believe that one of those eight billion people would be a perfect fit."

She smirks. "*Ooh*. Did you just do math?"

"No. That was logic. Anyway," I say, tucking my legs beneath me, "just because I believe they exist doesn't mean I think you'll necessarily ever meet them."

"I wouldn't have pegged you to be the romantic out of the two of us."

I sigh. "I like the idea of love. It's a beautiful concept. And for the people who are lucky enough to scan the globe and find that needle in a haystack, I'm happy for them. I just think a lot of people scramble around and assign the word *love* to things that probably aren't love at all."

My body fills with an energy that propels me to my feet.

Talking about love makes me feel like a fraud. It's a large part of why Chuck's stupid comment bothered me so much today.

For someone who believes in the four-letter word and works in an industry based around the idea, I don't know that I've ever been loved.

By anyone.

Kerissa is my friend, and I'm sure she loves me in that way. My brother tolerates me. My parents maybe feel *an obligation* toward me. Then again, maybe they don't even feel that.

I heave out a breath. The heaviness in my chest is hard to shake.

"What in the world do you mean, Philippa? You aren't going to medical school? That's the most ludicrous thing I've ever heard."

"It's just not for me, Mom. I'm miserable. I can't see myself as a surgeon or a doctor. I don't want to."

My father's face fell. "You are the biggest disappointment of my life. I hope you know what you're doing." He turns to Mom. "Let's go, Andrea."

When my boyfriend of one year dumped me because of my future aspirations, he used similar words now that I think of it.

I sigh. *Maybe I am a love fraud. Maybe Chuck is right, and I don't know shit about it.*

Ugh. Chuck and right should never be in the same sentence.

"What did you think about Jess Carmichael today?" she asks, looking up at me with a smirk.

My cheeks flush at the mention of his name.

Seeing him again was like seeing an old friend—it *was* seeing an old friend. But the way my stomach flutters when I think of him feels more like old friends with potential benefits.

Which can't happen.

"I wondered how long it would take you to bring him up," I say, sitting beside her again. "We could talk about Banks instead."

She growls. This time, *I* laugh.

"Banks isn't a bad guy," I say, raising my brows as she starts to argue. "I know you don't like him, and I know Kandace was really sad when they broke up."

"*Sad*? She didn't leave the house for a month."

"But Kandace wouldn't have found Ryan if Banks had stuck around. And don't we love Ryan for Kandace?"

Her disgust softens. "We do love Ryan for Kandace."

"See? It worked out."

She crosses her arms over her chest. "Fine. But I'm not going to be friends with him. I probably won't even talk to him. *Ever*. Because I'm loyal."

I pat her shoulder and giggle.

"I have a question for you, though," she says.

"Shoot."

"How in the hell do you sit next to Jess and not try to ride him like a pony?"

My giggle turns into laughter.

"Pip, *I mean it*," she says, laughing in disbelief. "He's the whole package. Drop-dead gorgeous. He has confidence that's not quite cocky but just arrogant enough to give him bad-boy vibes. And those eyes ... I can't even with those eyes."

Yeah, me either, friend.

"As much as I can't stand Banks, I'd lick every inch of his brother," she says. "Any of them. Have you seen the other Carmichael boys in a while?"

I shake my head.

"*Girl* ..." She sighs dreamily. "I ran into the eldest one, Foxx, the other day at the gas station. Holy mother of all. He must be in his midthirties by now and this motherfucker gets hotter as he ages. It's unfair."

"I can imagine. Their dad was always pretty hot."

"Right? And then there's Moss. I saw him at Muggers a while back, and he bought my coffee for me. I thought for sure it was foreplay. Turns out, he was just being nice."

I laugh again.

"Maddox's face is all over town since he's a real estate agent. And let me just say this—he really should charge the town of Kismet Beach a fee because that face undoubtedly brings in female tourists. I'd stop here."

"Stop it," I say, holding my stomach. "What's wrong with you?"

"Me? *What's wrong with you*? You have the best one of them all practically begging you for attention, and you play it off like he's another dude from the bar."

A warmth settles over me as I consider what she's saying. Even though I'm not interested in pursuing anything with Jess, knowing he's into me isn't terrible for my self-confidence.

"Jess is the kind of guy who will want to marry someone and settle down. Have a houseful of kids," I say.

"Yeah. So?"

I wrinkle my nose. "So that's not my idea of a good life."

"You still really don't want kids? Ever?"

My lack of a desire to have children is as true as the fact that I have brown hair and hate math.

I was never the girl who played with dolls or wanted to babysit. Kids grossed me out ... and they still do.

I'm okay with that.

I've accepted my choice and I'm not about to change that for anyone ... and it's been a deal breaker in the two relationships I've had that have *almost* gotten serious—both heart-wrenching conversations and heart-wrecking decisions. They were both very quick to dismiss me as if I mattered little once the talk of the availability of my uterus came into the equation.

Could you really love someone and let them go so painlessly?

The only way I'll *maybe* ever try my hand at a relationship again is if the man is absolutely, one thousand million percent in the same headspace. Because if there's one thing I don't want more than children, it's having my soul crushed over it.

Which is precisely why Jess is a no-go.

Unfortunately.

"No. *Never*," I say.

She shrugs. "Cool. You can be my kids' aunt someday."

"I'll be the best damn aunt in the universe. I'll spoil them rotten with all the candy and sleepovers and trips to the beach. They'll love me."

I sigh, needing a way out of this conversation. If I leave it to Kerissa, we'll sit here and talk about Jess all night. While that wouldn't be an ugly conversation, it wouldn't be productive either.

"Are we putting this picture up or not?" I ask, gazing down at the picture on the coffee table.

"Shit. I forgot to find a hack. Let me look."

"You do that, and I'll get us a drink."

"Deal."

I make my way into the kitchen, my mind on Jess Carmichael. The simplicity in his smile and the kindness in his eyes ease the turbulence in my stomach.

I remove two glasses from the cabinet.

"Did I hear you say that you're looking for a husband?"

"No, Jess, I'm not. The only thing I apparently need is an *ex*-husband."

A laugh falls from my lips. *Somehow, that's so on-brand for me.*

5

PIPPA

"Pippa? We're ready for you in the conference room," Shelly says through my desk phone.

"I'll be right there. Thank you."

The line disconnects.

My stomach churns as I gather extra documentation to support my proposal, just in case I need it.

I didn't sleep well last night, and this morning was rough. My mind flipped back and forth from seeing Jess to Bridgit's impending decision. It was a roller coaster, going from thoughts of a man who makes me feel giddy to a situation I have no control over that will affect my career's foreseeable future.

"You've prepared," I whisper. "You've worked your ass off. If she goes with Chuck, there's nothing you can do about it. Stay cool."

I smell his cologne before I hear him at my door.

"What do you want, Chuck?" I ask without looking up.

He laughs, the sound resembling a hyena if it ate a chipmunk with a mouth full of acorns. "Are you ready for the big reveal?"

"Absolutely."

"You know, I can't believe no one knew you'd been married before yesterday."

The hair on the back of my neck stands on end, and I look up. He's leaning against the doorframe. The man who hasn't worn a tie in two years decided today was the day to break that streak.

He grins, taunting me.

Stay calm. "Do you know what I find odd? That you care."

"I *don't care*, Pippa. Don't be confused. I'm just tired of working with a generation that thinks they deserve jobs they're unqualified for and opportunities they have no business accepting because they're *special*. That's what I care about."

I lift a brow. "Since we're sharing, I'm tired of working with a crass man who thinks I'll back down when he puffs up his chest and tries to look and sound bigger and more important than he really is. That's what I care about."

His hyena laughter goes right through me.

"I'll see you in the conference room, *Chuck*," I say before closing the door in his face.

My fists ball at my hips, and I shake with irritation. He's trying to rattle me. I know this. I know this is a part of his game. But fucking hell, do I want to scream.

I give myself a few moments to cool off and slowly gather my things. Then I straighten my knee-length black skirt, adjust the white bow on my blouse that hangs off the side, and open the door.

"You okay?" Shelly asks, walking toward me. "I saw Chuck in your doorway and couldn't miss the dickish look he wore when walking away."

I paint on a practiced smile as we approach the conference room.

"Does he drive you as nuts as he does me?" she whispers. "He walks around here like he's God's gift to matchmaking when, if I were guessing, he hasn't had a reason to use his cock since the eighties."

I snort so hard that it scratches the back of my throat.

She gives me a megawatt smile and holds the door open for me.

The management staff, all eight of them, sit around the long granite table. Travel mugs full of coffee form lines down each side. Bridgit sits at the head on the other side of the room, looking as regal as ever.

My heart pounds as the weight of the moment comes over me. All the work I've done for the past couple of weeks comes to a head now.

I glance down the table, my gaze landing on Chuck. His smirk is deep and smarmy as if he has this in the bag. I wink at him, then redirect my attention to Bridgit.

"Good morning, team," she says. A chorus of muddled greetings ring through the air. "While we wait on Todd to return with my coffee, I wanted to go over a few things—the first being acknowledging all the time and energy you all put into Bloom Match's expansion. It truly means a lot to me. It's my hope that we can eventually get to each of your ideas and bring them to fruition."

The door creaks open, and Todd walks in. He hands Bridgit a mug of coffee, then takes a seat next to Chuck.

Each second that passes may as well be a month. My palms sweat, and there's a spattering of perspiration around the band of my bra. I can't adjust it without making a scene, so I squirm as discreetly as I can in hopes to get things in a more comfortable position.

I want to be selected more than I've wanted anything in a very long time.

I love what I do—helping people who want to be committed and in love find and keep that. It feels like I'm doing something productive, *something good* in the world. And after having parents belittle you, guilting you that if you don't use your abilities and connections to become a surgeon—like you were born and bred to do—you're wasting your life. You're pathetic.

You're a disappointment.

This selection would be a validation that I'm contributing, I'm growing—that I'm making a difference in the world. That my work matters, even if it's not repairing children's hearts or helping women with their reproductive systems.

I take a long, deep breath and blow it out slowly.

"Our decision today holds a lot of weight," Bridgit says. "The direction we choose to move into, *to grow into*, will affect Bloom Match for years to come. It's going to be a lot of work—require endless attention—and I'm going to need help."

She looks at Chuck, then at me.

I hold my breath, silently pleading with her to spill it. *Tell us who you choose.*

"The person whose proposal we accept today," she says, pausing for dramatic flair, "will be promoted to the head of the expansion team. Once the project is off the ground, they will take over as the department lead."

Oh. My. Gosh.

I ignore the not-so-subtle attempt at stealing my attention as the room breaks out into chatter. No one expected this—least of all me.

My brain scrambles, trying to wrap itself around the implications of Bridgit's words. *Head of the expansion team. Department lead.*

One of us, Chuck or me, will get a big freaking promotion that doesn't happen often at Bloom Match. It's like the Supreme Court, in a way—once you're in, you never want to leave.

And to have that type of job security and perks—*and pay*—would be phenomenal.

Chuck holds up his hand. "Ms. French," he says to Bridgit. "I'd like to say something, if I may."

I roll my eyes, earning a giggle from Shelly.

He stands, smoothing his green and brown tie down his belly like he's some kind of power player.

"I just want to take a moment and thank you, Ms. French, for the chance to work for such a fantastic company," he says.

I can't help it. All I hear is hyena now.

"My proposal, for couples workshops, is based on a need I see in every neighborhood in Florida," he continues.

"*What's he doing*?" Shelly mouths.

I shrug.

He clears his throat. "I know this idea seems rather basic on the surface. But statistics prove that when couples attend workshops together, they walk away happier and more equipped to tackle their issues. Further, happy clients are the best form of marketing. All of this is not to mention that the cost Bloom Match would undergo to get this process on its feet is extremely minimal compared to other proposals."

Oh, please.

Chuck looks around the room, his smile wavering, before he sits again.

My coworkers glance around at one another. *Are we supposed to clap? Say thanks? Give counterpoints?*

Bridgit smiles, clearly confused at Chuck's impromptu lobby for the job. "Um, thank you, Chuck. I suppose I should offer you a moment to speak, if you'd like, Pippa?"

Fuck.

"Yes, of course," I say, standing because Chuck did.

What the hell am I supposed to say? I can't pass up the chance to speak since Chuck did. Ugh.

Bridgit's decision has already been made, and I know damn good and well that my coworkers don't want to sit and listen to us debate like we're running for office.

No one likes politicians.

Chuck smirks at me. I lift my chin and do the only helpful thing my parents ever taught me—put on a face and then put on a show.

"I will keep this short because we all have jobs we need to get back to," I say, fortified by the nods and mumbles of agreement from my tablemates. "Thank you, Ms. French, for the opportunity to play a part in Bloom Match's growth."

"You're welcome," Bridgit says.

"I believe in my proposal," I say, clearly and confidently. "From a purely business perspective, couples retreats can easily be expanded across the country—across the world, if we choose. The vertical growth is endless. Further, retreats are customizable for each couple and will be designed to enhance communication, strengthen problem-solving skills, and afford them an opportunity to have a few days of fun, laughter, and deep conversation in a neutral setting." I pause and give everyone a moment to absorb my words. "It would be an absolute honor to be trusted to bring my vision not only to Bloom and our community, but also to the infinite number of couples out there that we can touch."

I smooth down my skirt and take my seat.

My heart pounds a mile a minute. A bead of sweat trickles down my spine. I force a swallow down my throat and steady my breathing.

"May I make a point?" Chuck asks.

Keep your emotions in check.

"Um, sure, Chuck. Go ahead," Bridgit says, her brows pulled together.

He looks at *me*. "You can't realistically expect to send two people off into the wild and expect it to make them fall in love."

What the fuck?

"Actually, *you can*. Sometimes, getting away from the rigors of life —dirty dishes, kids' schedules, the neighbors who squeak in your ear about this or that—can be enough to remind you of who you fell in love with in the first place."

"Statistically speaking, eighty-five percent of couples that participate in workshops save their marriages," he says.

"It's funny you bring up statistics because I did a little digging," I say, proud of myself for taking the time last night to research instead of scrolling Social. "Thirty percent of couples that participated only in workshops felt their marriages were worse two years later." I glance at Bridgit. "I'll concede that workshops may be a better solution for relationships with a specific pain point or issue. But Bloom Match already offers couples counseling. With couples retreats, we're able to offer couples with no specific problem—couples that may be looking for an opportunity to grow closer with one another—a solution. We can't do that now."

It's as if a mic dropped. And Chuck hears it louder than everyone.

He stands. "Hiking isn't going to fix a marriage, and it isn't going to make Bloom any money either. *My proposal will.*"

"That's true. Workshops make money. We know that. *We already offer it.*"

I hold his gaze, refusing to back down.

His jaw locks in place. "The numbers show I'm right. Numbers are facts. They're hard data. You can't deny them."

"Chuck, with all due respect, the very last thing that will bring in new customers is offering them a math lesson."

Todd snickers, trying to cover it with a cough. Bridgit fires him a look.

"If you will please sit down, Chuck ..." Bridgit says, waiting for him to follow her request. Once he's seated, she folds her hands on the table. "Thank you. Now, after a thorough investigation into your proposals, I've decided to go with ... Pippa."

I blow out a breath as an overwhelming sense of relief washes over me. It's shoved out of the way with elation. *I did it. Oh my gosh, I did it.*

It's a struggle not to dance in my seat, and I suppress a squeal that would be utterly unprofessional. Instead, I scream on the inside and make plans to get celebratory drinks with Kerissa tonight.

My joy is short-lived.

"How confident are you in your plan, Pippa?" Chuck asks, his voice a notch too high for business conversation.

"Extremely." I try to sound confident, but my tone has a slight wariness. Even I hear it.

"Then may I ask why you didn't try it with your *ex-husband*?"

His beady chipmunk eyes drill into mine. If looks could kill, I'd be dead.

I glance at Bridgit, hoping she'll call him off. But she leans back in her chair as if she's willing to wait for my response.

"We were young," I say, irritated. "It was a short-lived marriage." For some reason, Jess pops into my mind. "We realized we wanted different things for our futures, things we didn't discuss before we got married."

"But you said that the two of you still see one another—that he's obsessed with you."

I force a swallow. "I didn't say he was *obsessed with me*, Chuck, and I'm not sure how you think any of this is your business. Or that my private life is fodder for business meetings."

"She's right." Bridgit leans forward. "That's enough, Chuck."

His cheeks are fire-engine red. I take a bit of satisfaction from that. *Fucker.*

I squeeze my fists together under the table, meeting Chuck's glare with one of my own.

"I was thinking, however," Bridgit says. I sit up straighter, zeroing in on her tone.

The almost melodic way the words fall from her mouth makes my stomach twist. What is coming? A challenge? I press my hand on my stomach, praying that it calms while I wait on the edge of my seat for whatever Bridgit is thinking. I don't know where this is going, but there's a plan in place and my anxiety has my heart fluttering in my chest as I wait.

"I would like someone, *a couple*, to take a retreat—maybe the one you proposed, Pippa, and see what kinks there might be to work out. Not go as an employee, per se. I don't want someone going through the motions and not experiencing it. I want feedback from a potential customer."

"I'm happy to put feelers out for candidates," I say.

"No, no," she says, waving her hand in the air. "I think someone on our team needs to have firsthand experience." She looks around the table. "Has anyone gone on a couples retreat before?"

My mouth is hot. Adrenaline fires through me. I sense where this is going, and I want to throttle Chuck.

"I think we're all in committed relationships or marriages," Chuck says, a death stare aimed at me. "Except Pippa. How convenient."

"Pippa, do you think you and your ex-husband would be interested in testing out your proposal?" She glances down at the binder I turned in with my data. She takes off her glasses and looks at me. "You did say the two of you are on great terms, didn't you?"

Oh fuck.

Oh fuck, oh fuck, oh fuck.

I think I nod. I'm pretty sure I must say yes because Bridgit's eyes light up, and she looks very pleased.

I want to say things like, "*But a couples retreat is best attended with a couple who are committed or considering a relationship with each other." Because that is the purpose of them, Bridgit.* But, of course, I'm not brave enough.

I think I'm still in shock.

"Fantastic," she says as everyone stands. "Pippa, if you could get that scheduled and confirm with me on Monday that it's a go, I'll get the plans in place to open Bloom Match Retreats." Her heels click on the floor as she stops in front of me. "I am thrilled to be working with you in this new way. You are intelligent and trustworthy. Welcome aboard."

Chuck storms to the exit.

"Thank you," I say, wanting to melt into the floor, never to be seen again.

"Talk soon." She heads for the door. "Todd, can you get me the file from the ..."

The door closes.

I'm left alone with two new titles—Director of Bloom Match Retreats and ex-wife.

Now to find an ex-husband.

6

JESS

"You have to be shitting me." I rip a sticker with Banks's face off the inside of the dryer. "I swear these things are like Gremlins—they replicate at night."

I toss the round paper with my brother's best Playgirl smolder in the trash. Even though it's annoying as hell, I can't help but grin.

"How do you manage to be a pain in my ass even when you're not here?"

I grab the laundry basket, enjoying the lavender scent from the little crystal things I sprinkled in. A woman used them to break the ice in the middle of the soap aisle in the grocery store the other day. She was borderline hot, so I humored her and took a container as she suggested. Unfortunately for her, I did *not* take her number. Rings on left hands are a big red flag. If they'll cheat on their guy now, they'd cheat on me too.

I've lived and learned.

The hard way.

I carry the clean, warm towels through the house.

The last rays of sunlight filter through the window, casting an amber-hued glow across the living room. I plop the basket down and take a seat on the couch.

A couple is on the television, announcing which house they'll purchase out of the three options given to them. I settle against the cushions as the announcer goes through each location one final time.

"Two," I say to the female half of the duo on the show. "Go with two. House one has too many rooflines that'll cause you trouble down the road. Three needs way too many updates for that price—and your guy hates it. Read the room."

"We're going with ... house three," she says, squealing with delight.

I grab a towel. "You're paying half a million dollars, and you probably test crayons for a living. You're gonna have *at least* another quarter-mil in renovations and won't be able to move in for probably a year. Great choice."

People are fools.

I glance through the window at Mom's house. The kitchen light is on, and I find myself smiling.

This time of day is my favorite. Everything is quiet and calm—everyone is in their place. It reminds me of the few hours after whatever practice was in season and before dinner growing up. Mom would be in the kitchen cooking, and Foxx would be at the table overachieving on his homework or overcomplicating a science project because he could. Moss would have a ball of some sort in one hand and Banks on his heels. It was loud and chaotic. There was something really comforting about that.

"Hey, Jess! You home?" Moss's voice calls out.

"Yeah. In the living room."

The door snaps closed, and Moss's steps fall against the wooden floors. I lower the volume on the television as my brother comes in and flops in the recliner on the other side of the room.

He looks at me with a wary yet amused look on his face. I know this look. *I know Moss.* My stomach knots.

"What's going on?" I ask, making quick work of a purple towel.

"How long have you been home?"

"A couple of hours. Why?"

He strokes his bottom lip with his finger.

"*Why*?" I ask again, picking up another towel. "Why are you looking at me like that?"

"What have you been doing the past couple of hours?"

I give him a pointed look. "Typical Friday night shit when you're our age. Laundry. Ran on the treadmill for a while. Showered. What's it to you?"

He smirks. "You haven't looked outside in a while, huh?"

I toss the towel into the basket, the knot twisting harder in my stomach.

Whatever my brother is about to say will be a headache. Hell, my head already hurts. I don't even know what's going on.

Work today was long and hot. The city sent an inspector to check the legality of a storage unit we're using to hold our tools after hours because, apparently, a neighbor has complained every single day since we began construction.

So that was fun.

But I bet whatever Moss is here to tell me will be an even bigger ball of joy.

I narrow my eyes. "No. I haven't looked outside in a while."

"You might want to do that."

I narrow my eyes. "Do I, though?"

Moss snickers.

"What did that fucker do?" I ask, my voice rising.

Moss's snicker turns into a fit of laughter. "I love that you automatically think of Banks."

"What other option is there?"

Banks has left me alone all day; I haven't heard a thing from him. It was like the good old days when he had Maddox to pester.

It was too easy. I should've suspected something.

"Jess, you have a giant cock in your yard," Moss says.

"*A what*?" The basket slides across the room as my foot makes contact. I side-eye a hysterical Moss as I make my way to the window, hobbling because my foot was still sore from the block, and part the blinds. "What. *The fuck*. Is that?"

Moss laughs louder.

"I'm gonna kill him," I say, storming out the front door. "The boy has bit off more than he can chew this time."

The evening heat blasts me in the face as I peer through the golden hour. Standing in the middle of my yard with its face toward Moss's house is an oversized, multicolored metal rooster. It's probably ten feet tall.

I glance at Banks's house as I make my way down the walkway. "Where did he even get this thing?"

"I have no idea. I just got home, and he was driving away with a shit-eating grin, towing a trailer."

Shaking my head, I knock against the thing with my knuckle. The metal pings. I rap against it again.

"What are you doing?" Moss asks.

"Making sure this isn't some type of trojan horse. For all I know, it could be filled with something that's set to explode in the middle of the night."

Moss looks around. "I'd be quiet in case he's listening. He probably didn't think that far ahead. You don't want to give him any ideas."

No shit.

"How am I going to get this out of here?" I ask, taking a step back.

Moss stands beside me. "No clue."

"Was Maddox in on this?"

"Surprisingly, I don't think so. I don't think he's been home from work yet. I mean, did he know? That's another question."

The streetlights flicker on. The light reflects off the colorful metal, nearly blinding me. I shield my eyes and step to the side.

Banks's truck roars as he comes up the road. You can almost feel his glee in the rumble of the engine. He pulls into his driveway and gets out of the vehicle. He does not come toward us.

"What the fuck is this?" I shout.

"Don't you love it?"

"I'm going to love beating your ass over it."

Even from this distance, I can tell that Banks is grinning. "I had a really nice wolf picked out, but you shot down the wolf pack."

"Wolf pack?" Moss asks.

"Don't," I warn Moss.

He snorts.

"Since you were a no to the wolves, the only thing I could think of was getting you a giant dick—you know, something I know you could relate to. But Mom refused to let me put a giant dick in your yard because your house is too close to hers. So I did a little work-around and found a huge cock instead."

I rub a hand down my face. *I hate him. I really do.*

"Don't worry," Banks says. "I didn't tear up your lawn, old man."

I drop my hand. "If this thing isn't off my lawn by morning, I'm going to throw it through your fucking window."

Banks walks into the road. "You're just mad that you got shot down yesterday. Don't take it out on me."

Here we go.

A wash of warmth floods my veins at the memory of Pippa. *What an interesting, gorgeous woman.*

"Banks, shut the hell up."

"You know," he says. "You might be able to land her if you had a better attitude."

Moss holds out his hands. "Can someone tell me what's going on?"

"And you could walk without a limp if you would've had more common sense," I tell Banks.

"I can walk just fine."

"You won't be saying that tomorrow if you don't get this thing gone."

He stops in the middle of the road, halfway between Moss's house and mine. "Or what?"

Is he serious right now? "You wanna challenge me, Sparkles?"

He narrows his eyes.

Banks is the best fighter out of all of us. He's scared of no one ... except me. I'm not absolutely sure I could take him if we were really fighting, but I'll never tell him that.

Maddox races up the road and pulls into his driveway. He's out of the Jeep before the engine shuts off.

"What the hell is that?" he shouts, laughing.

"Banks's ticket to hell," I say.

Maddox points at me. "I want you to know I had nothing to do with this. Not a damn thing."

Banks gasps. "Why are you throwing me under the bus like that?"

"Because I have a reason to live now."

"It's like you got married, and now I'm nothing to you," Banks says. "I thought we were closer than that. What happened to bros before …"

Maddox fires him a warning look.

"… before throws," Banks says, improvising.

"Good life choice," Maddox says.

I cross my arms over my chest. "No. You don't get to set boundaries with him now, Mad. I've already called dibs on that. He's yours. Forever."

Maddox rolls his eyes. Before he can say anything else, another car comes up the road. Mom and Dad stop next to the curb.

"Interesting lawn decor, Jess," Mom says, giggling.

"Like it? Banks can bring it to your house."

Dad slings his arm out the window and grins cheekily. "Your mom has all the cock she needs at home."

Moss and I chuckle as Banks loses his mind like he does every time Dad makes a joke about having sex with Mom.

As entertaining as it is to watch Banks act like a child, it's also fun to watch Mom ruffle Dad's hair like they're teenagers as he riles up their youngest son.

Their relationship has always been goals for me. They've been married almost forty years and act like they started dating six months ago. Together, they raised six kids, ran a business, and bought all the houses on the road for their children. Sure, they'd fight every now and then, but they'd make sure we saw them fix their problems too.

That's probably why I've never been engaged. I've never met someone who I could see myself going to all that trouble with for forty damn years. The only girl I've ever even considered going the distance with doesn't see herself going the distance with me.

Because that's how life works.

You never get what you want.

"You don't understand art," Banks shouts over his shoulder as he starts back to his house.

"Get it out of here by dawn," I shout back.

He flips me off.

"Good luck with this," Dad says, chuckling as he pulls away from the curb.

I storm back into my house, Moss following closely.

"Our parents have one fatal flaw," I say.

"What's that?" Moss asks, shutting the door behind him.

"They didn't know when to stop having kids." I stop at my shoe rack and grab my sneakers. "Think about it. What if the boys stopped with Maddox, and then they got Paige?"

"We'd be bored."

I consider that and shrug. "Why are you still here, anyway? Where's Brooke?"

"She took her grandma dinner. Honey was supposed to come over tonight but had an upset stomach, so Brooke took a plate over to her."

I head into the kitchen. "Did you already eat then? I'm going to La Pachanga to give Banks time to get that fucking thing out of here."

"Yeah. I got off early tonight, so I came home and made dinner for Brooke."

I roll my eyes.

"What? Why should she have to come home and make dinner every night?" he asks.

I shrug. "She shouldn't. It's just funny seeing you so owned by her."

"Trust me, it's worth it. *It's so damn worth it.*" He hops onto the counter. "So what's this *you getting shut down* stuff Banks was talking about?"

I look at my phone and scroll through my text messages so Moss doesn't see my smile.

"Nothing," I say. "We ran into Pippa Plum yesterday at Shade House."

He whistles through his teeth.

You have no idea. I slide my phone in my pocket. "Go with me to grab dinner. I'll buy you a drink."

"And tell me about Pippa?"

I turn toward the door. "Sure. Why not?"

I might as well talk about her. I sure as hell can't stop thinking about her.

7

PIPPA

"This is perfect," I tell the hostess. "Thank you."

Beachfront Boulevard is below us in its full Friday night glory as Kerissa and I take our seats. La Pachanga's rooftop patio is *the* place to be in Kismet Beach on the weekends. It's tucked in an older building with poor outside lighting. That might seem sketchy. But tourists never seem to find the hidden gem, which makes the locals flock to it in droves.

"What can I get you two?" Jenny asks. "We're slammed tonight, obviously. If I'm a little slow, forgive me. *Please*."

I laugh. "Coming from a person who used to wait tables and flirted with entirely too many nervous breakdowns in the storage room, I already forgive you."

"Yeah, we have nowhere to be," Kerissa says. "If you need to pass us to take care of someone else, we're good."

Jenny's shoulders fall. "You're a godsend. What can I get you guys to drink?"

"I'll have a coconut lime margarita," I say immediately, having already made this decision on the way home from work.

Kerissa's eyes go wide. "Well, on that note, I'm having water."

"Water? *Come on*. We're drinking. I've had a hell of a day, and I need you to drink with me. Solidarity tequila. You know how it works."

"The last time we had *solidarity tequila*, I woke up with a tattoo, your belly button was pierced, and the only way we know who did it was because there was a receipt in your pocket," Kerissa says.

Jenny giggles.

"Oh, okay," I say. "We're just going to forget about you accidentally going live on Social while having a conversation with the bartender about which alcohol makes you the horniest?"

She gasps. "Hey, he went home with me that night and tested my theory that whiskey makes me frisky. I regret nothing. Not a damn thing."

I snort.

"So a marg and a water?" Jenny asks.

"No, two margs," I say.

Kerissa lifts a brow. "I'm just having iced water."

"Can I add an extra shot of tequila in my margarita?" I ask, laughing. "That sounds like a country song. Could be a Kenny Chesney hit, I think."

"Will you stop it?" Kerissa says, laughing too. "I don't think you need an extra shot tonight. Good grief."

"One of us is going to enjoy this Friday night, and that someone is *me*."

Kerissa rubs her forehead as if she's the one who's going to wake up sick tomorrow. At least if I'm throwing up, I won't be thinking about my plethora of external problems. It's the cheap way out, and I know it. But a girl can only take so much shit in one day.

"I'll be back," Jenny says before scooting off through the tables.

The breeze is hot despite the fans in each corner of the patio. The tarp covering the ceiling rattles in the wind, creating an interesting backdrop to the mariachi music playing overhead.

Kerissa takes out her phone and starts swiping around the screen. I side-eye my device sitting on the table, but the idea of picking it up and opening apps requires more energy than I currently have to give it. Instead, I breathe in the wonderful aroma of spices from the kitchen below us and watch a family across the patio celebrate a little girl's birthday.

I smile as I watch them, enjoying the glee on their faces despite my mood.

Kerissa watches me with a puzzled expression.

"What?" I ask.

"I'm not sure ..." She narrows her eyes. "You asked me to meet you here in a very shouty, aggressive-ish text, so I assumed you had news about work. But then you order a margarita with an extra shot of tequila and are talking about country songs."

"So?"

"*So* that sets off my best friend spidey-senses. That combo usually means you're trying to forget whatever happened in the twelve hours prior."

I point at her. "You would be correct. Damn, you're good."

She sighs. "I should've ordered that margarita."

"Well, I tried to insert *my* best friend logic into this situation, but you overrode me. Now you're going to have to endure the pain of dealing with my drama without the buffer of an adult beverage. It's your own fault."

"Sometimes I wonder how we function together."

"Easy," I say. "Only one of us can be dramatic at a time. Right now, I call dibs."

"And what if I have a little drama to share?"

I make a face. "*Excuse me*? You have drama and didn't start this conversation with that? Do tell."

"I thought you called dibs."

My hand flicks through the air. "I did. But my drama is painful drama. Yours is usually hot, sometimes kinky drama, and I wholeheartedly live vicariously through you and your sordid life. You get *whiskey frisky,* and I get ... rum ... numb."

Kerissa furrows her brows, chuckling. "What does that even mean? You don't drink rum."

"Nothing rhymes with tequila. You get whiskey frisky, and I get, what—tequila Argentina?"

"You know what? This is a perfect example of how you misalign your manifestations. You give me whiskey *frisky*. Frisky is a playful, sexy kind of word." She cocks her head to the side. "You gave yourself *numb*."

"What was I supposed to say? *Rum bum*?"

"Would've been better than numb. Or *rum cum*."

I make a face. "Ew. No. That just ..." I shiver. "No."

"Just something to consider."

"Or not." I pull a napkin out of the dispenser in anticipation of my drink arriving. "I don't know whether to laugh, dance, or cry about my day, so let's start with yours."

"Fine. But can I have a quick rundown so I can prepare for the conversation in advance? The way tonight is already going, I'll need a minute to get myself ready."

I lean my head back and sigh.

My body aches. The toll from the day—the roller coaster of emotions leading up to it and following Bridgit's decision—settles in my bones. I considered tucking myself into a hot bath with a pint of ice cream, but Kerissa has a way of taking my mind off things while also solving them—or at least making them seem less overwhelming. *And I could use a little of that tonight.*

I level my chin. "Okay. Quick rundown goes like this—we had a meeting. Chuck made an impromptu last-minute filibuster of sorts, so I got put on the spot to say my state of the union or whatever."

"What's with all the political shit?"

I lean forward. "Because that's what it felt like, okay? Like I was running for some sort of office and my opponent is smiling for the cameras and lying through his teeth." I pause as reality hits me over the head. "In a huge bout of irony, I was the one smiling and lying. But let's not focus on that."

Kerissa struggles not to laugh.

"*Anyway*," I say. "Bridgit picked me."

"Yay!"

"And Chuck semi-lost his cool."

"Also, yay!"

"And then …" I tap my hands against the table in a pathetic attempt at a drumroll. "I got finagled—*how*? I'm still not sure—into taking the trip that I used in my proposal with my nonexistent ex-husband."

The smile melts from Kerissa's face.

"Yeah. *That part*," I say, taking my drink from Jenny. "Thank you."

"Do you guys want food?" Jenny asks.

Kerissa forces a smile and turns to her, still processing my revelation. *Take your time. I haven't fully processed it either, and I've had all day.*

I should be on top of the world tonight. I should've gone home, set up this dinner with Kerissa, and then called my mother—and left a message because it's not like she'd actually answer—letting her know that I'm the new department head at work. She'd dismiss it and act like I was promoted to head pudding taster or something equally pointless, but at least I would know that she knew.

I should be reveling in my success and taking a moment to appreciate it. To start preparing for my new adventure. To celebrate the huge step I made toward purchasing my own home someday—a goal I've had since my parents walked out of my college apartment and told me they would not be supporting my life if I bailed on med school. I would be on my own.

But I'm not doing either of those. I'm not partying in delight. I'm fretting over a situation that I have to control, yet I feel like I have no control over it at all.

"She's going to have to eat something if she's drinking," Kerissa says, pointing at me. "But we need a minute to get her life in order, okay? She'll be two sheets to the wind in about fifteen minutes because she's a lightweight, and in the meantime, I have to figure out how to get her married and divorced by next week."

Jenny laughs. "If you pull that off, I have some shit I could use some help with by Monday."

"I'm here to assist," Kerissa says, shrugging. "But I don't dig holes, and I can't afford your bail. Just keep that in mind."

I take a sip, choking on the tequila. "Damn, that's strong."

"You ordered an extra shot," Jenny says as she walks away.

"If only ordering an ex-husband was that easy," I say, sighing. "I don't know what I'm going to do, Kerissa. My promotion basically hinges on this. Bridgit wants me to try the retreat—*experience it*—before we go balls-to-the-wall implementing a whole department around the concept. That makes sense, but *I can't go*. I understand the assignment, I just can't complete it."

Kerissa breathes in and out, motioning for me to follow along.

But I don't. I don't have time for that.

"*I can't lose this job*. I love it," I say. "To be the director of this whole division? That's huge."

And it'll be a real—in your face—to my parents.

"But I also have mounting guilt about lying in the first place, and my conscience is nagging at me that this will come back and bite me in the ass because that's what happens to liars."

If Kerissa gets quiet, a problem exists.

And Kerissa is silent.

A ping-pong ball volleys in my brain. The ball slams into one side of my head and then the other *repeatedly*.

I don't know what to do. I have no clue how to effectively extricate myself from this situation and keep my new job. And not give Chuck the Schmuck an opportunity to steal it out from under me.

I almost hate that I was chosen. It's a big-level setup for disappointment, and if this falls through, *I* will be at fault. There will be no one to blame but myself.

Thank God I got the extra shot. I take another long drink and feel the heat of the tequila pool in my stomach.

"Here are chips and salsa," Jenny says, sliding the containers onto our table. "I'll be back. I haven't forgotten you."

I press my forehead with my fingertips in a futile attempt at relieving the pressure in my skull.

"Tell me about your day. Give me the gossip from the mayor's office," I say to Kerissa. "Distract me from my woes."

She scoops salsa onto a chip. "Well, Mayor Chamberlain campaigned and got elected with a promise to bring more businesses into Kismet Beach. Jovie Rey from the tourism board—do you know her?"

"I know *of her*."

"She's been helping us try to recruit potential employers to the area and found this super cute boutique that's opening shops along the East Coast. Halcyon. Have you heard of that?"

"Yeah," I say, nodding. "I've bought a couple of their things from ads online. It's an upscale Always Thirty-One, if you know what I mean. For those of us who can't quite wear teenager clothes anymore."

She snorts. "Yes. *That*. Well, Jovie and I have been collaborating on ways to lure them down here. I had lunch with her this afternoon, and we plotted. It was fun."

"I'm glad someone had fun today," I say, downing half the drink.

"That's a smooth transition into the gossip part of my day." Her eyes twinkle. "The mayor had a lot of *fun at work* today too."

I furrow my brow. It takes me a second to sort through the rising fog in my brain to read between the lines. My jaw drops. "With whom?"

The sparkle in her eyes gets brighter.

I'm not sure if the tequila is hitting me especially hard and fast, or if I'm just reading too much into things. But Kerissa does love a good splash and screwing her boss would certainly be one way to do that.

No pun intended.

"Let's just say for legal purposes, I'm being transferred next week to the tourism board," she says. "Since I'm doing such an *amazing job* and all."

"An amazing job doing what, exactly?"

She smirks.

I gasp. "*Kerissa*."

"What?"

"*Are you fucking the mayor*?"

She swats me, knocking over the basket of chips. "Don't broadcast it to the whole place, please."

I giggle as she picks up the chips.

"He's cute," I say, steadying myself as the tequila swirls in my head.

"*He's packing*. Like, the man is seriously endowed." She brushes the salt off her hands. "And at this point in my life, that's all I'm really looking for. Humor me. Wine and dine me. Give me an experience to remember."

I take a chip and point the end at her. "Good for you for knowing what you want and going after it."

She parts her lips to reply, but nothing comes out. Instead, she grins as her eyes follow something behind me.

"What are you looking at?" I ask, afraid to turn around.

"Guess who just walked in."

My hand drops to the table. The vibe she's putting off makes one thing clear—whoever just entered the patio is interesting. And when I consider Kerissa's definition of interesting, that also makes me nervous.

It could be my parents—that would equate the mischief on her face. Kerissa loves making snide little comments wrapped in sugary sweetness to Dr. and Dr. Plum. Or it could be Mayor Chamberlain making his way toward us. *Am I supposed to know about their dalliance*? Hell, it could be Banks, and Kerissa feels feisty enough to take him on.

"I'm afraid to look," I say.

She drops her gaze to mine. "I didn't tell you to look. I told you to guess."

"No."

"Why?"

"Because when it rains, it fucking pours, Kerissa, and I don't have an umbrella. I'm also on the precipice of pneumonia from all the storms today, I think, and I can't take anymore."

She shakes her head as if she doesn't know what to do with me.

"I—"

"Well, hello, *Pippa*."

My blood turns from a tequila-spiked heat to a bone-chilling cold.

I stare at Kerissa like if I don't look to my left, Chuck won't be standing there.

But it's him. *I can smell him*—the nasty cologne I now associate with an acorn-eating hyena.

"That's not where I thought you were going with this," I tell my friend.

"Because that's not where I was going with it. This is a wrong turn down a path I would've warned you about."

I blow out a breath and wonder if I've pissed off God somehow.

My stomach churns, turning to an acid that wants to come up. The physical reaction to Chuck is nearly impossible to hide, and I wonder if I'd be better off just to vomit on his shoes. *Would that deter him from bothering me anymore*? Probably not.

"What brought you all the way to Kismet Beach tonight, *Chuck*?" I ask, my sarcasm thinly, if at all, veiled.

"My wife wanted to go to the beach, and we thought we'd stop here for dinner." He points at a lady entirely too sweet-looking to be married to him. "That's Debra."

I hum. "She looks nice."

"Who is this?" he asks, motioning to Kerissa.

"Her best friend," she says, giving him an icy glare. "I'm not as nice as she is, for what it's worth."

"Did your best friend tell you that she got a huge promotion today?" he asks, his eyes getting beadier by the second.

Annnnd lift off ...

Kerissa looks over my head before snapping her gaze back to Chuck. "She did. We're celebrating. Would you like to join us?"

I kick her under the table. *What are you doing*?

Chuck rests his hand next to the salsa. It's an attempt at being casual, but it comes across far more predatorily than I think he realizes. *Or maybe he does realize it, and that's the effect he's after.*

"No, I don't want to bother the two of you," he says. "I was hoping, though, that I could meet the ex-husband. This isn't one of the nights you have dinner with him, is it?"

I scoot away from the table, needing air that's not scented with asshole.

"You know what, Chuck? We aren't in the office right now, so my threshold for putting up with your bullshit is down quite a few notches."

He chuckles angrily. I return the vibes right back at him.

"Let me give you a lesson in boundaries," I say, getting to my feet.

Kerissa, unsure what's happening, stands too.

"We work together, *Chuck*," I say, squaring my shoulders with him. "Actually, we don't even work together now since *I'll* be heading a whole new department."

I lean back just in case the steam coming out of his head blows off his toupee.

"Let's get one thing clear," I say, my frustration from the past couple of weeks coming to a head. "My life has absolutely nothing to do with you. And if you continue to make me feel uncomfortable, I will file a report where necessary."

"Oh, *please*," he says, his eyes narrowing. "You and I both know the real reason you're so defensive. *It's because you're lying*. And as soon as Bridgit finds out that you're a liar—and she will because I'll make sure of it—I'll have your job. The job I've been working toward for the past *six fucking years*."

"Fuck you, Chuck. Disrespectfully, of course."

He laughs, the sound filled with hatred from his cold, black heart. "I'm not letting this go. I'm not going to stop pushing until I prove that there's no ex-husband—"

An arm slides around my middle from behind me.

"Hey, Dream Girl. Sorry I'm late."

8

PIPPA

Heat radiates from my face, and the room begins to spin. Vaguely, I notice Kerissa's amusement, but I don't have the wherewithal to register it.

Even if he hadn't spoken, I would've known who was touching me. And the way he cinches his forearm around my waist—almost as if he's creating a barrier between me and Chuck, makes my knees weak.

My body sags against Jess's. He makes no effort to back away or to step to the side. His chest is hard against my back as his fingertips press lightly into the bend just above my hip.

Get it together, Pippa.

My head spins as I try to put together the pieces of the moment. I'm not sure what Jess is doing or if he knows my current predicament. *How could he know? Did he hear my conversation with Kerissa the other day in Shade House? Did he hear what I was saying now?*

Chuck flinches, making note of every move between Jess and me.

Game on.

Please play along, Jess.

"Jess," I say, smacking his forearm. "You signed the divorce papers. You know you can't call me *Dream Girl* anymore."

My stomach flutters at the sweet and slightly silly term of endearment.

"We might be divorced," he says, lowering his lips to my ear. There's a slight apprehension in his tone that I pick up. Hopefully, Chuck doesn't. "But that doesn't mean you're not my dream girl."

Kerissa's jaw drops, and hearts fill her eyes like she's in a *Looney Tunes* cartoon.

The heat of his breath skirting across my neck makes me gasp. I buckle against him, my body moving against his just enough that he can't miss it.

"You look beautiful tonight," he whispers just loud enough for me to hear.

I exhale, the air shaky and filled with the swell of desire triggered by his mouth's closeness to my body. *Did he say that to me—for me? Or is this a part of the role he's playing?*

I'm not sure I care. I eat it up all the same.

This is precisely why Jess has always been kept at arm's length. My physical reaction to him with slight brushings of our arms or bumping into each other in a crowd is bad enough. *But to have him touch me? Hold me? Whisper sweet nothings into my ear?*

I may never recover from this. *Ever.*

As much as I don't want to—as much as it's the last damn thing I want to do—I lift Jess's arm off my stomach and step away from him. Despite the heat of the Florida night, my body chills without his against mine. The pull I fight to reattach to him is maddening.

So I grab my margarita and take another swallow.

Chuck runs a finger along his bottom lip.

Right. Chuck's here.

I clear my throat. Fire from the tequila fills my mouth. Images of me blowing a blast of flames at Chuck's head makes me giggle. I realize I didn't need that last drink. Kerissa must realize that, too, because she discreetly slides the glass toward her and out of my reach.

"Chuck," I say, smiling broadly. "This is my ex-husband, Jess. Jess, this is Chuck. We work together."

Jess extends a hand, side-eyeing me with amusement. Chuck shakes it with a heavy dose of suspicion.

"You two get along very well," Chuck says, baiting Jess to say something he can latch on to. To prove his theory.

"Not every marriage has to end badly," I say. "Sometimes, instead of having problems for years on end, couples decide to go their separate ways so they can have a peaceful life."

He knows what I'm getting at—that his marriage could be a talking point if he doesn't stop.

Jess slides a hand into his front pocket and smirks down at me. "I have loved this woman my entire life. I'm not about to stop now."

Kill. Me. Now.

Jess Carmichael has never *not* been hot. I've seen him in a wrestling singlet, covered in drywall dust, with bedhead, and morning hair. Not from my bed in the morning, unfortunately, but bedhead, nonetheless.

And in every single instance, *he's delicious.*

But in this casually confident pose, with his hat on backward and professing his fake love for me in front of my asshole nemesis—the man has never looked this good.

He licks his lips, watching me for a reaction. I can't react the way I want to because that will get me arrested. Indecent exposure is a real thing.

"Our two years of marriage are something I'll always remember," I say, looking up at him and batting my lashes.

He grins. "They were the best two years of my life."

"Well, I was a pretty great wife."

He chuckles. The sound licks at my libido, stroking it higher and hotter.

"And you were a good husband too," I say, my heart pounding. I should stop. I shouldn't make this worse for myself. But I can't because having this banter with Jess is too easy and too much fun. "We had so many *amazing* times together. You always made sure I was happy."

"You better fucking believe I did. I made sure you were *happy and satisfied* every night."

I gulp.

My face is red. Heat ripples from my cheeks as I absorb the heat in his gaze. If I ever wondered if Jess would be a great lover, I don't now. Only a man who has absolute confidence in his skills would be this overt about them.

Oh, the things I wish I knew for certain.

His grin turns mischievous, and his gaze hoods. A shiver snakes up my spine, leaving a trail of goose bumps on my skin. He glances at my arms and then back at me.

"Looks like I still have an effect on you," he says, his tone cocky.

I make a point of looking him and up and down, letting my gaze drag across his long, lean body. "Your mouth has always turned me on."

His jaw clenches, and he takes a step toward me.

I have no idea what I'm doing, and something in the recesses of my brain is trying to throw out roadblocks to stop me from crossing the line that I'm toeing. But logic is no match to a perfect specimen looking at me like he wants to use his mouth in ways I can only imagine. *In ways I do imagine*. In ways *I will imagine* as soon as I get home.

"Remind me why we got divorced again?" Jess asks, his voice rough.

"Yes, I'm curious too," Chuck says.

And, just like that, I snap back to reality. Chuck's intrusion into this surprising conversation is like a bucket of cold water.

"What happened between you?" Chuck asks.

I look up at Jess, trying not to panic.

I don't know what happened between us. This is the first time I've been afforded the opportunity to make my situation even worse. I'm not prepared. Luckily for me, Jess takes my hand like he does it every day and laces his fingers through mine.

His palm scratches my skin. The size of his hand easily encompasses mine. He holds it firmly, yet sweetly—in a way that's protective yet careful. This is yet another thing I'll remember after this moment is over.

"That's private," Jess says. "You need to mind your own business."

"Chuck, isn't your wife over there?" Kerissa asks, jamming her thumb toward the lady in the corner.

He glances over his shoulder. "Yes. She is. I suppose I should get back to her."

Jess moves me so that I'm closer to him. For the performance, *mostly*, I rest my head on his arm. *Might as well play it up while I can.*

"Hey, Chuck, before you go," Jess says, giving my hand a gentle squeeze. "I want to make one thing clear."

Chuck's gaze flips to mine before resting on Jess again. "Sure. What's that?"

"Pippa and I might be divorced, but she's still my girl. Now that you know that, I'm going to take it as a personal insult if you ever approach her again like you were when I walked up here tonight. Got it?"

A bead of sweat dots Chuck's forehead.

"Good. You can go now," Jess says, effectively dismissing my antagonist.

Chuck sucks in a hasty breath and then scurries off toward his wife.

I don't realize I'm not breathing until Chuck is across the patio.

Jess pulls out my chair and holds it as I sit. To my surprise, he sits next to me.

"Can I ask what the hell that was all about?" he asks. "Not that I mind that we were married, Dream Girl."

I give him a look that makes him chuckle.

"You two are entirely adorable," Kerissa says, her arms crossed over her chest. "And if I didn't know better, I'd think there was something going on between you."

My cheeks heat.

"I'm getting closer," Jess says, bumping my shoulder with his. "I've asked her out a million times. Somehow, we jumped over dating and marriage and went right to divorce, but I can work my way back."

I laugh, relief washing through me. It's as if a bomb has been defused, and it's just my friends and me again.

"Thank you for jumping in like that," I tell Jess. "How did you know what was going on?"

He folds his hands on the table. His fingers are thick, his wrists wide. The veins in his forearms are roped, and if you could sell pictures of forearm porn, his would be worth a fortune.

"Your back was to me, but Kerissa caught my eye," he says, nodding a *thank you* to her. "I really didn't like the way he was looking at you, so I came to ... you know, say hello."

My heart skips a beat.

"I heard him call you a liar and say something about there being no ex-husband ..." Jess shrugs. "I just made it clear that he better back the fuck off and then took your lead."

"You had perfect timing because it was about to turn ugly."

He grins. "For the record, I didn't come to your rescue. I'm sure you could've handled it like the boss you are. But I couldn't stand by and watch someone bother my ex-wife like that. What kind of ex-husband would I be?"

I burst out laughing, the sound releasing whatever tension remains in my body.

Kerissa pushes away from the table. "I'm going to let you two chat and go mingle with the people."

"If you see Moss, will you let him know I'm up here?" Jess asks.

Kerissa grins. "Will do."

Jess watches her leave. Once she disappears down the stairs, he faces me again.

My lord, those eyes.

"I kind of just grabbed hold of you around the waist, and I apologize if that was not cool," he says. "I should've probably—"

"Hey, it was fine. Honest. I'm ... glad that you did it."

He grins. "Okay. Good. It was instinct, I guess, but that doesn't make it right."

"Look, that conversation was heading in a bad direction. There's a chance that I would've leaped into your arms and kissed you to prove a point if you hadn't wrapped your arm around me."

His eyes go wide.

"So thank you for saving me from apologizing to you."

"Is there any way I can ask for a redo?"

I laugh again. This time, he laughs too.

"What was that all about?" he asks. "Why the weird need for an ex-husband? I'm confused."

"It's a long story."

"I have time."

When people say that, they're usually being polite. They've already gotten themselves into a conversation and don't want to look like a jerk and say—*Oh, cool. Thanks for saving me the explanation because I don't care*. But Jess doesn't move or flinch, nor does he seem to notice or be distracted by the people buzzing around the patio.

He's focused on me. Like he really does have time. *Like he really wants to know.*

"So I got a promotion today at work," I say, smiling.

"Hey, congratulations. That's great."

"Thanks." I smile. "But in the middle of the chaos of it, I might've told my coworkers that I've been married before, and Chuck might not believe me. Chuck might also want my head on a stick and is hell-bent on outing my little white lie to our boss."

Jess balks, not expecting that explanation. "Well, that took a turn."

"I just blurted it out because I let him get to me and now, I'm stuck in this story that I can't get out of." I frown. "Thanks for playing along. It helped buy me some time to think about how to fix this."

"Oh yeah. *That was terrible*. You *should* thank me after the trauma of having to hold you and pretend we've done all these nasty things to one another. *The horror*."

I try not to grin.

"You know how you could *really* thank me?" he asks.

"*How*?"

"We could recreate some of the best times of our marriage —*ouch*!" he says, chuckling as I smack his arm. "I'm just saying it would be nice to have a memory of my first wedding night."

I shake my head and grab my glass. The margarita is nearly gone, and I wonder where it went. *Did I drink all of that?*

"Jess, you couldn't handle me, buddy," I say, fueled by the tequila and a shot of adrenaline.

"I assure you, Miss Plum, that I would give you all you want and then some."

Now that it's just the two of us and my fight-or-flight response has eased, the weight in my lower stomach is obvious. The heat in my core. *The pulse between my legs.*

I should nip this in the bud. I should laugh it off and change the subject to something less flirty, a topic that's more neutral. But my mind is blank when I search for things to bring up that don't lead to some type of sexual innuendo, so I give in.

Screw it. The day has gone to hell in a handbasket anyway.

"I believe you seriously underestimate me," I breathe, leaning toward him.

"Any time you want to test your theory, I'm game," he says, running his lips around his mouth.

My insides quiver at his proximity mixed with his words.

"Why do you always turn me down?" He leans toward me lazily, as if he's deciding whether to move in for a kiss. "What is it about me that you don't like?"

Slowly, I lift my eyes from his lips to his beautiful green irises. It's as if he was waiting to capture my gaze, prepared to lock me in place until I give him an answer.

"Don't give me it's because we're friends or some shit like that," he says. "We're not in high school anymore."

"It has nothing to do with us being friends."

"Then what is it?"

I consider how to answer him—how honest to be.

Do I tell him that I think about him often? That it's his face, his hands, those lips that I imagine when I'm in bed alone in the middle of the night? That I had a vibrator a few years ago that I dubbed Jess *because that's who I imagined more often than not was making me come?*

"I've told you this before," I say, searching his eyes. "You're a

Carmichael. You're born to have six kids and a gorgeous wife who travels to wrestling tournaments on Saturday mornings and goes to your parents' for Sunday dinners."

"So?"

My heart drops. *Exactly*. "So ... we're not the same."

"How do you mean?" he asks, his brows pulling together. "The crux of that setup is me having a gorgeous wife. And while I'm not proposing marriage, you're fucking gorgeous. You're more than fucking gorgeous, but let's keep it simple." His grin turns shy. "You're my dream girl, Dream Girl."

I blush. My God, this man is dangerously sweet and sexy. *Has he really been serious all these years? Has he really always wanted a shot?*

How could I be his dream girl?

"I'm not pressuring you," he says. "I'm not that kind of guy. Just know that I think the world of you, and if you ever need anything or change your mind ..."

His shoulders fall forward, his lips turning toward the floor. *It's the face of a man being turned down.*

I want to explain that anything between us would end in disappointment. He would be upset that I led him on when I'm already absolutely certain that none of the things he admits he wants are what I want. I'd be hurt when I see him silently judging me for my choices—just like the men before him—and the pain I'd endure when I lost him would wreck me.

There's no doubt.

How would you survive having your heart broken by Jess Carmichael?

But explaining all of that to a guy who's just asking me on a date would assume that he would want something more. Maybe he would, or maybe he wouldn't. But that really wouldn't matter because *I would want more.*

How could I not?

And that's why I must save us ... from me.

My adrenaline drops, and I'm suddenly so damn tired that sitting up straight requires more effort than I have energy for.

"I've had a day," I say. "Right now, I want to go home and get some rest before morning comes and I have to make some hard decisions." *Like how am I going to get out of this retreat and save my job at the same time?*

His jaw sets, but he nods. "Do you need a ride home?"

I glance over my shoulder, and sure enough, Chuck is watching. *At least this will fortify the ex-husband story.*

"Kerissa will take me," I say, turning around. "I took a ride share over here, but she never lets me ride in them alone after dark."

"Good."

"Did you say my name?" Kerissa stands beside her chair. "What's up?"

I look up at her. "Will you take me home?"

"Sure. Let me find Jenny and pay for our drinks."

I stand too. "I'll pay for mine. You had water."

"Don't worry about it," Jess says. "I got it."

"No," I say, smiling at him. *He's so fucking nice.* "You aren't getting my drink. I've wrapped you up in enough shit for one night. I should be buying your dinner."

"That'll never happen." He searches my eyes before sighing and turning to Kerissa. "Get her home. I'll take care of the bill."

"Got ya," Kerissa says.

I look up at him and take in the handsomeness in his face—the kindness and goodness and sexiness wrapped up in one package.

He's going to make someone a lucky woman someday.

"Thank you for the drink and for helping me out tonight," I tell him.

"Thank you for marrying me."

I burst out laughing. "Thank you for divorcing me."

"Nah, you had to be the one that filed. I wouldn't have been able to walk away from you." He grins, tossing me a wink. "I'll see you around."

"See ya," I say, tucking my chin and following Kerissa out of the restaurant.

9

PIPPA

"And this is why I don't cook often," I mutter as I wipe tomato spatter off the counter.

The kitchen is bright, filled with midday sunlight. I'll need to close the blinds soon to keep the heat out, but for now, I need the mood boost the rays give me.

I hum along to Post Malone playing from my phone and bop around the kitchen like I'm not a jumble of pent-up nerves.

My eyes ache, reminding me that I'll need a nap at some point today. Sleep was not kind to me last night. The sturdiness of Jess's arms around my waist haunted me. The warmth of his breath on my cheek. The way his smile filled my soul with brightness and made me crave more of it. All of that kept me up. And when I wasn't thinking about Jess, I bounced between excitement over my new position and desperation to keep it.

Maybe I should just tell Bridgit the truth and end my suffering.

I teetered on the edge of shooting her an email last night, explaining how my mouth overloaded my ass. How I became caught up in the moment of Chuck needling me, and I blurted out a bit of false information. The only thing that stopped me from coming clean was that even if she understood—even if she blew it off—I would still be starting my new job with a halo of soot over my head.

My reputation would already be dirty. *Do I want to dirty it up over something as stupid as this?*

I pull one bowl of the cold tomato soup and another smaller bowl of tarragon crème fraîche from the refrigerator. I nestle them both in a box on a cute kitchen hand towel that I bought at the Dollar Tree recently, along with a pretty bowl and spoon.

Heat blasts my face, threatening to burn off my eyelids, as I exit my apartment. I cut across the rock yard separating my unit from Honey's.

She spots me through the window before I get the chance to knock.

"Get in here, you little thing," she shouts from inside.

I open the door and stick my head around the corner. Honey is sitting in her recliner with a patchwork blanket covering her lap.

"Did I wake you?" I ask.

"No, I've just been sitting here catching up on my shows. I had a stomachache yesterday, and my granddaughter brought me supper." She sighs, motioning for me to join her in the living room. "I love my Brooke so much, and I appreciate that girl more than she'll ever know. But if she could come when my game shows aren't on ... there are twenty-four hours in the day. She could pick one that's not in a two-hour span."

I set the box on the stand beside her chair. "I didn't know if you had anything for lunch, and I knew you weren't feeling well, so I brought you some soup."

Her eyes light up. "You are the sweetest." She points at the couch. "Sit down. Talk to me while I eat—unless you have somewhere to go, of course."

My heart warms as I sink into her sofa.

"What kind of soup is this, sweetheart?" she asks.

"Cold tomato soup with tarragon crème fraîche. It's my favorite when it's hot out. Kind of a pain to make, and my kitchen is tinted red now, but it's delicious."

She chuckles, pulling the top off the container. "I'll have my grandson-in-law come over and redo your apartment like he did mine." A dollop of the crème fraîche goes onto the soup. "He's a good worker, that boy. I'm thrilled my little Bee found him."

Honey samples my concoction. Her eyes roll to the back of her head as she moans in delight. I laugh at her antics but am secretly relieved and proud that she likes it.

"Where did you learn to cook?" she asks. "This tastes like an old recipe—one of those tried-and-true ones. Was it your mother's?"

I snort. "I'm not sure if my mother has ever made a homecooked meal in her life."

She raises her drawn-on eyebrow.

I sort through my memories, trying to come up with a single instance of my mom standing over a stove. Not one moment comes to mind. I never even realized that cooking was a part of normal life until I became friends with Kerissa in elementary school. The first night I slept at her house, her mom asked what I wanted for dinner. She was shocked I rattled off a few meals from local eateries; I was dumbstruck that she was going to make it herself.

"Tell me about your parents," Honey says.

"You don't have all day."

"Give me the short version."

I sigh. "Well, they're both surgeons. They're brilliant and talented and save lives every day."

"I didn't ask you to tell me about who they are to everyone else. I asked who they are *as your parents*."

Wow.

Honey holds my gaze, a tenderness embedded in her round face that tugs at my heart. I've never thought about my parents, or anyone, like that. It reframes so many things.

"As my parents, they were ..." I try to find kind words. They are my parents, after all. But each adjective that I come across that fits that narrative doesn't truly capture the people I grew up with. "Missing, a lot. Tepid. Generous with everything but their affection."

She puts her spoon in the bowl and sets it on the tray.

"Please don't pity me," I say, smiling. "I have a very privileged life, and I'm doing just fine. You can't have it all, you know?"

She nods. "I'd love for you to meet my granddaughter, Brooke, some day. I think you have a lot in common."

"Really?"

"Sadly. My daughter has many of the qualities you just described, and my granddaughter can probably relate to you."

"I'm sorry to hear that she's experienced what I have."

"Sweetheart, we all experience something. How we come out of the experience makes all the difference."

Her words echo inside my brain, committing them to memory.

I've often wondered what my parents went through growing up to make them the way they are. I didn't know any of my grandparents since I wasn't born until my mom and dad were in their forties. Their parents had passed away. *What happened to my mother and father to make them so cold*?

I pick at a piece of lint on my yoga pants and reflect on my experiences. The biggest effect they had on me is evident in my decision-making processes.

"You're right," I say. "The way I was raised had a huge impact on my relationships now."

"In what way?"

"Well ..." I force a swallow as my anxiety begins to shuffle its way into my psyche. "I'm confident and outspoken, but secretly, I'm always afraid."

Honey picks up the remote and turns the television off.

"I'm kind of terrified to have a serious relationship with anyone," I say, opening to Honey in a way I've never opened to anyone before. "It always feels like *I'm* the deal breaker."

She shakes her head but says nothing. Emboldened by her encouragement—and by the way she truly wants to listen—I let the words flow.

"I've never admitted this out loud, but there's always something in the back of my brain that worries that I'm going to disappoint someone, and that's probably my biggest fear in the world. Of having to look into someone's soul and see their disappointment in me as a human being."

My chest tightens as Honey pulls the lever on the side of her chair and sits up.

"You have every damn right to disappoint people, Pippa."

Huh? My heart beats quicker.

She steels her gaze to mine. "Disappointing people has such a negative connotation to it. But when you really think about it, sweetheart, disappointing someone probably means you stood up for yourself."

Wow. My brain tries to understand—to rationalize—what she's saying.

"If you never disappointed someone, then you've probably never made yourself happy either," she says. "When I look back at my life at this age, the very few things that disappoint me are the things I did that pleased others and not myself."

It makes sense ... sort of. But it doesn't take away the pain associated with losing someone—a boyfriend, my brother, *my parents*—because I didn't meet their expectations.

We sit in comfortable silence. I use the quiet to think back through the years at all the things I've done to avoid feeling like my inadequacies stem from who I am as a person.

I joined the track team in high school because my mother was a track star. I went pre-med in college. I've dated men who fit their standards but lacked in mine.

My fear of failure—not on a success level, but on a personal one—has gotten me into more messes than anything in my life.

"Can I ask you a question, Honey?"

"Absolutely."

I scoot to the edge of the cushion. "I have to make a decision, and I don't know what to do."

"I cook when I need to think, too."

My lips twist into a smile.

"Go on, sweetheart. Tell me what's going on."

"I lied at work and said I had an ex-husband. Then I got a promotion. But the promotion kind of hinges on me and my ex taking a trip together, and now I don't know whether to admit the truth or ... fake an illness or say he refuses to go."

My breath stalls in my chest as I wait for her opinion. *Please don't think I'm a bad person.*

"Why did you lie?" she asks.

"Because this fool tried to get under my skin, and I let him. He commented that I was unqualified to help build relationships because I'd never been in one—and I lost my cool."

She grins. "Oh, he hit on that fear of failure on a personal level you were just talking about. I see."

Damn.

Honey watches the realization of her point soak into my head.

I'd never put two and two together before, but it makes sense. That's why Chuck bothers me so much. He knows what to say to trigger my fear of being a disappointment.

"You want my advice?" she asks.

I nod.

"I'd find me a hunk of a man to pretend to be my ex-husband, and I'd go off and have my little vacation, get the promotion, and tell Chuck to shove it where the sun don't shine," she says.

My hand covers my mouth.

"Your ability to do your job has nothing to do with whether you've been married or not," she says. "And that's none of anyone's business anyway."

"Right. But I feel guilty about it."

She laughs. "Why? I mean, yes, sure, white lies are bad. Yada, yada, yada. But you didn't say it to get the promotion, did you?"

"No."

"So whose business is it?" She shifts around in her chair. "Look, if you go making this into a big deal, it'll look like a big deal. Right now, you responded to someone's out-of-line comment. You are under absolutely zero requirements to give them your life history. You haven't cheated or been underhanded—so you let it go. You've not done anything wrong."

Although I'm not quite sure I believe her, I want to. Because she does make sense.

"Once you hit my age, you realize how much emphasis you put on things that don't matter," she says. "How many times have you left the grocery store or the post office and get back in your car and replay an entire conversation you had with someone just to pick it apart?"

I laugh. "Oh, every one I've ever had."

"That's what I'm talking about. None of that matters. The person you were talking to probably did the same thing, and they were worried about what they said, not what you said." She shrugs. "You're going to keep the promotion. You earned it. And you're going to stop sweating the fact that you told him ... whatever you told him."

"But, Honey, I have to take him on this trip with me. My boss will want to talk to him after to get his input on the program. What do I do about that?"

She grins. "Do you know an eligible bachelor?"

I laugh. "That's what my best friend said to do."

"She's right. Have some fun with this, Pippa. Live. Be young. Do silly things. You'll never get this time back."

I gaze off into the distance. A bubble of excitement forms in my core.

"You're my dream girl, Dream Girl. Just know that I think the world of you, and if you ever need anything or change your mind ..."

Could I, though? Could I ask Jess to go with me?

My muscles clench as my heart rate doubles. Energy bursts through my veins.

He would go. I know he would. I'm pretty sure he would, anyway.

Oh shit. Could I handle that?

I grin. *I could handle that.*

No, you can't. I frown. *That would make this web I've woven even more tangled.*

I snort. *Tangled like our sheets.*

The sound of the recliner lying back snaps me out of my head.

"That soup is delicious," Honey says. "My stomach is a little wobbly, but I'll sip on it this afternoon. Thank you for thinking of me."

I stand and help her organize her blanket across her body. "You are very welcome. I'm going to go, but you call me if you need me. Do you still have my number?"

She nods. "And Pippa?"

"Yes?"

"Call whoever you were thinking about. That smile said it all."

I blush, returning her grin, and head for the door. Once I'm outside, my feet fall faster. It's as though I've made up my mind without my mind knowing it.

How do I ask him? Do I call? Text? Meet him face-to-face?

None of those options feel right. A call is awkward. A text too casual. Seeing him face-to-face makes me want to die, so that's out.

But what's left?

I rush into my apartment and dig around my room until I find the bag I had at Shade House. The notebook is there.

"I'll propose this as a favor—a business transaction," I say, taking the notebook to the table. "I'll play it cool enough to sound like no big deal but formal enough so he doesn't get the wrong idea."

With a few clicks, I find the Laguna Homes website and Jess's email address.

Blood soars past my ears, blocking out all other sounds. My fingers tremble as they open my email app and type in the information.

To: Jess Carmichael
From: Pippa Plum

Re: SEEKING AN EX-HUSBAND

I need a *fake ex-husband.*

Let me explain ...

I may have let it slip to my new coworkers that I have an ex-husband. Now they're fascinated with the details, specifically with him.

Why wouldn't they be? He's gorgeous, has exceptional skills in the bedroom, and is determined to win me back.

But there's a problem. *He doesn't exist*.

The bigger problem? I have to produce him to save my job.

This is where you come in.

I'm seeking someone to play a smitten ex-husband for two weeks. You'll need to remember our love story—details matter when it comes to romance! I need you to be prepared to travel in-state at a moment's notice. We may be in close proximity; sharing a bed may be required.

One more thing—kisses are essential for optics as necessary.

If this sounds interesting or, at the very least, entertaining, let me know.

Signed,

Your Future Ex-Wife

I hit send.

10

JESS

"Are you still here?" Dad's voice makes me jump.

"*Fucking hell.* You scared the shit out of me."

Dad chuckles as he moseys through the house that I've been working on all day.

The three-bedroom, three-bathroom home is one of my parents' best finds. It's barely outside of the city limits and is surrounded by vegetation, so you can't see it from the road. But once you turn onto the driveway and pull through the row of bushes and trees, the lawn opens, and the neatest little house sits in the middle of half an acre.

Moss and I each run a team of construction workers and a designer that completely transforms properties for Laguna Homes. Mom and Dad buy them, we fix them up, and then our parents work with Maddox to sell for a profit.

It's a nice thing we have going. And through the years, Moss and I have never argued over who gets to work on a project. But I would've fought him over this one.

I grab a broom and sweep up the dust and debris from today's work on the floor.

"Yeah, I'm about done," I say. "I didn't have anything else to do, so

I thought I'd get a jump start on this. At least get some of the kitchen gutted so we can see what we're working with on Monday."

Dad stops next to the window and takes in the open space. "There's a lot of potential here."

"I know. I'm really excited to see what we can do with this." I brush the dust into a pan and then dump it in a trash bag I stretched over an empty box. "Now that I've spent a little time in here, I think we consider taking the laundry room out of the hallway and using that for storage. And I don't think it would be that expensive or difficult to build out a butler's pantry thing here leading into the dining room."

"Where are you going to put the laundry?"

"Garage. We can fashion a mudroom out there. There's plenty of space in the back because the bays are so deep."

Dad mulls it over.

"What are you doing today, anyway?" I ask him.

"The truth?"

I grin.

"Staying the hell away from your mom and Banks," he says.

I'm amused. "Banks is fun and games until he's at *your house*, huh?"

"For fuck's sake, Jess. The boy is relentless. I don't know what time he got there this morning, but I come out of the bathroom with a towel on. It's supposed to just be your mom and me there at eight o'clock, so I didn't bother to really hide my junk behind the fabric, you know? And I round the corner into the kitchen and he's sitting at the counter eating a bowl of cereal."

I don't even try to hide my laughter.

"It's not funny," Dad says, chuckling. "Dammit. What did I do wrong with that one?"

"You weren't hard enough on him. Foxx and Moss and I had rules. Curfews. You had expectations of us. Maddox and Banks drank straight from the milk jugs."

Dad grimaces.

I lean against a drawer-less cabinet. "What's Mom up to today?"

He puts a foot on a low rung of a ladder and sighs. "Honestly? Nothing. She hasn't done a damn thing to get on my nerves. But sometimes in marriage you just need space. You gotta get the hell away from the other person for a while."

"Fair."

"You'll find out someday. Just remember that you're not as great as you probably think you are, and your wife will get sick of you just like you're sick of her. Space is your friend."

"I hope you're telling this to Maddox. He's your married son."

Dad shakes his head, but I see the pride in his eyes.

All Dad wanted out of us kids was for us to grow up and be good people. Your word meant something around our house. Making the right decisions didn't mean choosing the easiest route. We didn't have to do anything perfectly, nor were we expected to be angels—which is a good thing or most of us would've failed big time—but we must be respectful and polite, or we'd come to regret it.

They wanted us all to grow up and live a good life and be happy. And, so far, we all are. But I know that when Dad looks at Maddox and Moss and sees them settling down with women who are good and kind, that makes him proud. It's validation, I imagine.

I just hope one day I can join my brothers in that camp.

"What about you?" Dad asks. "You seeing anyone?"

"Well, I was a pretty great wife."

I smile. "Nah. I'm not seeing anyone these days."

"You aren't getting any younger, you know that?"

"Fuck you too."

Dad laughs. "You know what I mean."

Yeah, I do.

I walk around the kitchen and pick up empty water bottles and broken nails.

The more I see of my brothers and their lives now, the more something snips at the back of my brain, telling me that would be nice.

The truth is that I can imagine myself coming home and having dinner with someone. Spending my Saturdays at the farmers' markets or rearranging furniture for the thousandth time. Taking my family to church early on Sunday morning and sitting beside my brothers and their families.

There was a time in my life when I didn't want that. I was sure I'd never have a wife or even want one.

But I see it now. I get it—*if I had the right person*.

I force a swallow. "I hear ya. I'm just waiting on the right girl."

Five-three. Brown hair that looks reddish in the sunlight. A laughter that gets higher the longer it goes.

Not afraid to tease me. A brilliant mind. A woman who won't back down when she's right.

"Who knows if I'll ever find her," I say.

"Well, if you don't, you can always take care of Banks."

"Ha." I stare at Dad out of the corner of my eye. "Give him to someone else. Oh, wait—you know what would be funny?"

Dad grins. "What's that?"

"Give him to Foxx. We'd have entertainment for *days*."

Dad laughs, coming to me to help pull a cabinet away from the wall.

"What are you doing after this?" Dad asks.

"I don't know. I've been here since eight this morning, so I'm pretty beat."

After some tugging and cursing, the cabinet breaks free. It only takes a small amount of drywall with it.

He dusts his hands off. "I'm going to get out of here and run by the store. Mom's making meatloaf tonight, so come over if you want some."

"Cool. Thanks for letting me know."

"Always. Thanks for busting your ass out here today. You have this place ready to roll."

His praise makes me stand taller. "Thanks, Dad."

"I'll see you later, kid."

"Bye."

He steps over a shop vac tube and exits through the side door.

I start to gather my tools when my phone buzzes. It takes me a few seconds to find it beneath a piece of wood I yanked off a windowsill.

Unknown: Octopuses have blue blood.

"What the hell?" I laugh, my fingers flying over the keys.

Me: Seriously, who is this?

I wait. And wait. And wait.

No reply.

I begin to slide my phone in my pocket when it rings. Banks's name is on the screen, and while I really don't want to answer it, I do. Just in case.

"What?" I say.

"What happened to hello?"

"It's called *cutting to the chase*. What's up?"

"Where are you? You haven't been home all day."

I unscrew the cap off my soda. "Work. Did you get the rooster out of my yard?"

"Working on it. What project are you working on?"

"The new one out on Whistler Street. It's just outside of city limits across from that big blue house with the million windchimes hanging off the tree in the front yard."

I pause, waiting for him to respond. But after almost a minute, I get impatient.

"Are you there?" I ask.

"Hey. Yeah. I'm here. Hang on."

"What are you doing?"

He sighs. "I was returning a text."

"You call me and then text someone else?"

"Settle down. You can have all my attention now."

I roll my eyes. "You're missing the point."

My tools are scattered throughout the room, so I work on gathering them and returning them to my toolbox.

The long day of work begins to wear on me, and I'm reminded, once again today, that I'm not a twenty-something anymore. My back aches. My left arm feels like I might've torn my bicep. And my foot still hurts from that fucking block a couple of days ago.

"How long are you going to be there?" Banks asks.

I shrug. "I don't know. I'm getting my stuff together to leave now."

"How much stuff do you have to gather?"

"What's it to you?"

"Why are you so hateful?"

I sigh. "I'm not hateful. I'm just not sure why you're asking me a million questions."

"One more. Want to hang out tonight?"

"No."

He groans. "I need a friend, Jess. Give me a chance."

"You work with people all day. Pick one of them."

"But I like you best."

"Sparkles—"

"Stop calling me that."

"Or what?" I ask, tossing my toolbelt into my toolbox. "What are you gonna do about it?"

"I can't tell you, or that would take the fun out of it."

I really want to be mad because whatever he's alluding to will probably inconvenience me for days—weeks, even. But as much as he frustrates the piss out of me, what would I do if he wasn't around?

Not have to lock my doors . . .

"I'll see you when I get home," I say.

"Later."

"Bye."

I end the call.

It takes just a few minutes to get everything put away. I do one final check for anything that needs to go home with me and then turn toward the door. But as soon as I pivot, I spy a car pulling up in the driveway.

"Who is that?" I mumble.

It comes to an abrupt stop next to my truck ... and then Pippa climbs out.

Her legs are long and tanned, capped with a pair of light-colored shorts. A black tank top stretches across her chest and highlights her curves.

All of them.

She raps against the door. I clear my throat so I don't sound as thirsty as I am.

"Come in," I say.

She pushes the door open and steps inside. Her gaze finds mine moments before her eyes narrow.

"Whoa," I say, laughing. "What's that look for?"

"I can't take it anymore."

Huh? I hold out my hands. "Can't take what?"

"Jess, if you're fucking with me, *stop*. I'm ready to have a breakdown over this because my email stopped allowing me to unsend messages, and I don't know what to do now. I'm in limbo while I wait for you to respond, and you're not responding, and it's been all day. Okay?"

I set my toolbox on the floor. "First of all, breathe."

She inhales a lungful of air.

"Good. Now what the fuck are you talking about?"

She exhales as her cheeks turn pink.

Holy fuck, she's beautiful.

She's naturally pretty, yet not perfect. There's a scar on the side of her neck from a run-in with a fence when she was a teenager. One of her eyebrows was cut at some point in the past, and her hair refuses to grow in the crevice. A slight cowlick lifts her hair just off-center on the right side of her head and all of it somehow works to make her even more attractive.

She's perfect for me.

Her chin lifts. Her eyes are wild. They blaze with a fieriness that makes my cock hard.

"Do you check your email?" she asks.

"Yeah."

"Have you checked it today?"

"Uh, no. I've been working all day."

She clears her throat, shifting her weight from one foot to the other. "May I ask you to let me see your emails, please?"

Excuse me?

I press my lips together, curiosity getting the best of me, and pull my phone out of my pocket.

"Jess?"

"No, you may not see my emails."

Her hands go to her hips. "Please?"

"What are you up to, Pip?"

She reaches for my phone in a quick, bold move. Unfortunately for her, I'm quicker. I hold it up in the air and effectively out of her reach.

"*Please, don't look at them.* At least not with me standing here," she says, hopping a whole foot off the ground to try to reach the device.

I chuckle. "What did you do?"

"Give it to me." She hops again. "Now."

"Not a chance." I swipe the screen and find my email app as she tries to tug my arm down. "Will you stop it?"

"*Jess,*" she says, fake crying. She stops hopping. "Wait."

I laugh at her little pout. "You are so fucking cute."

"I hate you."

"You do not."

The app opens, and I scan my inbox. It's the third message from the top that catches my attention.

Plum, Pippa
Re: SEEKING AN EX-HUSBAND

My body stills—everything except my heart. That organ thumps so hard that I wonder if Pippa can hear it.

She looks up at me through her thick lashes like she's not sure whether to run, cry, or laugh.

Sweet, silly girl.

But I won't let you off the hook that easy.

"What's this?" I ask, teasing her.

"Don't be a dick."

I chuckle. "I sense you're flustered. Why don't you go have a seat somewhere while I read my emails?"

"Keep it up, and I'll send that email to Banks."

I dip my head and lift my brows. "I would *highly* suggest you don't do that."

She grins, biting her bottom lip. *You better watch it ...*

"Why not?" she asks like an innocent little thing she's not.

I could play this back and forth with her all night. And on any normal day, I'd love to. But on a normal day, I wouldn't have received an email from her that looks like a wanted ad.

Nah, Pip. We're not getting sidetracked this time.

"Do you want me to read this thing, or do you want to tell me what it's about?" I ask. "Because I won't open it if you want to talk about it instead."

She sighs and backs away. "What I didn't want to do is deal with it face-to-face."

"Then why are you here?"

She winces. "Because apparently I'm not good under pressure, and as I'm learning is my modus operandi, I'm rather impulsive when stressed."

"Good to know."

She hangs her head.

I touch her chin with the tip of my finger and lift her face to mine. Only after our eyes connect do I pull my hand away.

"What is this about?" I ask, all levity gone. "Joking aside, what has you so stressed that you sent me an email and then ..." *Aha*! "And then called Banks to find out where I was so you could come find me."

She takes a steadying breath, resigned to reality.

I almost tell her that it's fine—that I'll delete the message, and we can pretend it didn't happen. And I would do that if I wasn't certain that something was wrong and she needed my help. She just doesn't want to ask for it.

In a show of camaraderie, I set my phone on the ladder. She eyes it—considers grabbing it and making a run to her car, I think—but doesn't. Instead, her shoulders soften.

"I was talking to my neighbor today," she says. "I've decided that I'm going to go on the couples retreat and get my promotion and not say a word about Chuck eliciting a confession from me that wasn't really a confession."

What's she saying? "Okay."

"And ..." Hesitation fills her eyes. "I was thinking that maybe you would be available and willing to pretend to be my ex-husband and go with me next weekend to Silver Springs."

My eyes widen. *Abso-fucking-lutely I will.*

"I don't have the final itinerary yet," she says. "But we'd probably leave Friday during the day and come back Monday. It would all be paid for by Bloom Match—so you wouldn't be out anything at all. And I would just need you to go on some excursions with me as photographic documentation for my report. You may need to talk to my boss when we get back and give her some feedback on how it went." She grins. "You know, tell her it was great, and you think this will absolutely help relationships. Make me look good."

Like you need my help with that.

I take a step away from her and give myself a second to absorb her offer. It sounds too good to be true. *Pippa Plum wants me to spend a weekend away with her?*

Must be the universe's repayment for dealing with Banks.

"Let me get this straight. You're asking me to spend the weekend with you in Silver Springs?"

"As my ex-husband."

"*As your ex-husband*," I say, nodding. *How is this real?*

"Yes. And the purpose of this trip *officially* is that we're trying to see if it rekindles our marriage or relationship. Which activities do we think will help that goal? What enhances our communication? Do we like having prescribed things to do, or would a self-guided thing work better? Things like that."

I run a hand down my face. *There's no way this is real. Surely, someone is punking me.* I must take a moment too long to respond because she sighs.

"If you don't want to do this, we can pretend I didn't send that, and you can delete it and—"

"Will you stop?" I laugh. "Breathe. Stop talking in one giant sentence because it gets hard to follow along."

She squints at me, looking adorable. "Don't make fun of me."

"I'm not."

"If you don't want to go, or if this is totally unfeasible because I know it's last minute and totally inconvenient ..."

I squint back at her, making her giggle. "You know I'll go with you."

She sighs, her body sagging. "Really?"

"Really. It will be a total hardship, but I'm pretty sure I can go away with you and share a bedroom for a few nights. Poor me."

She picks up a gum wrapper and throws it at me.

"I'll pay you for your time if you want. Well, not me, but Bloom. I can get it approved," she says. "You'll have to miss a day or two of work, maybe. Is that okay?"

"I know the boss. It'll be fine."

"But really, I don't want you to feel like you're not getting anything out of this. I'm happy to ... bake you a cake? I don't know. Something. But I'm broke so don't ask for anything expensive. But now that we're at this part of the conversation, I feel a little guilty asking you to do this." She bites her lip. "Let me do something nice for you."

Here's my opening.

I scramble to think of the best way to utilize this opportunity. Pippa isn't going to feel good about this unless I let her feel like she's paying me back somehow. *What can I do*?

"Okay," I say, nodding. "I have something you can do for me."

"All right ..."

"We'll be gone how many nights?" I ask.

"Three? Maybe four?"

"Great. Then you have to spend three, maybe four days with me outside of the trip."

She stares at me.

"Take it or leave it," I say, knowing she doesn't have a choice—but also knowing I won't make her go through with it if she objects.

I start to think she might actually do that—object—when the severity on her face melts. The tension in her body falls away. There's a brightness to her eyes, a coy smile on her lips, and the woman looking back at me isn't the frantic one who walked through the door.

This Pippa is kittenish—playful and intentionally coy.

She crosses her arms over her chest like she's negotiating a multimillion-dollar deal. "You'll try to take me to dinner."

"You don't know that."

Her arms fall to her sides. Surprise is written across her face. "Then what will you want to do?"

Fuck your brains out. "Day one is spend tomorrow with me. Sunday dinner at my parents' house."

She balks. "I'm not going to their house for dinner."

"Why not?" I ask. "You know them. You know my entire family. It's not like I'm asking you to meet a bunch of strangers."

"You don't think that's weird? What are you going to tell them? They won't think it's odd that you bring this random chick to dinner?"

I smirk. "No. I do it all the time."

A streak of surprise mixed with horror ghosts her features.

"I'm kidding," I say, chuckling. "I'll tell them that their boy got a fake wife for a few days."

She's not amused.

"Come on, Pippa. Spending a few days together will help you relax and not worry about the trip for the next week—because you know you're going to. I'm doing this as much for you as I am for me." *I'm such a liar.*

Her fight wanes.

"Come over tomorrow around eleven?" I ask. "My house is the one with the giant ten-foot-tall rooster in the yard."

She bursts out laughing. "*What?*"

"Long story. We can talk about it tomorrow."

She sighs. "Fine. But I'm only coming to see the rooster."

"That's fine," I say, grinning. "I'll tell Banks you're coming to see my cock. It'll drive him crazy."

She tries not to smile—not to appear as amused as she is, but a grin peeks through anyway. "Thank you for helping me."

"I told you I'd do anything for you." *And to you. If you're willing. God, I hope you're willing.*

She holds my gaze for a long moment and then takes a step back. A long, lingering grin that holds way more than a goodwill gesture plays along her lips.

My body tenses as reality hits. *How am I going to be around her for an entire weekend and not break down*?

But just as the thought crosses my mind, something shifts. As she backs away toward the door, her grin deepens. A twinkle flashes through her eyes. Mischief creeps across her features.

Despite the added distance between us, the room is smaller. The air thicker. The humidity hot and pregnant with so much tension that it threatens to explode.

I lift a brow, inviting her to act on it. *Give me a reason to break this spell you have over me, Pip.*

"I need to get home and scrape the rest of the tomatoes off my countertop," she says, seeming humored by the transition. "I should've done it this afternoon, but I paced instead while I waited for you to email me back because that was a good use of my time."

"Yeah," I say, chuckling. "I'll see you tomorrow."

"*Tomorrow.*"

She leaves me with a flirty smile and walks out the door.

11

PIPPA

I whistle softly, squinting into the late morning sun as I turn my car onto the street. The weather is perfect and beautiful. It's not too ungodly hot, and there's not a cloud in the sky.

My stomach twists and bubbles. Instead of pulling so tight that I wince, which is the stress reaction I'm used to, it reminds me of being young. Excited. *Happy*.

I painted my nails at midnight as opposed to my normal staring at the ceiling and fretting about life. My laundry was freshly folded by two o'clock. By five, I was at the kitchen table, researching things to do in Silver Springs—looking for things to add to the itinerary that Jess may enjoy.

Jess. We've spent more time together in the past week than we have since we were teenagers. And although our dynamic is fun like it always has been, it's different too.

My insides flutter again.

The more time I spend with him, the more I find myself leaning into it. I feel good when I'm with Jess Carmichael. I like the person I am when he's around. When we're together, I'm confident and self-assured—and no one could convince me that I'm not pretty, thanks to his constant reminders. And that's a whole new feeling because I've never been told that before.

But even more, *I like him*.

He's always been the smoking-hot guy who I can pluck out of a crowd with very little effort. But he's so much more than a great set of shoulders and a smile that melts me from the inside out.

Jess is kind. He's funny and sweet. The way he came to my aid with Chuck, whether I needed it or not, spoke volumes. So many people are content to stay in their own world until they can get something out of it. I've turned Jess down more times than I can count, yet he was there for me—just like I know he'd be for anyone he liked. *Even Banks*.

I laugh as my phone buzzes through the speakers. My spirits are so high that I don't even look to see who it is. "Hello?"

Mistake.

"Hello, Philippa. I only have a few minutes, so we must make this quick, darling," Mom says.

I roll my eyes. *Darling? Okay. Who is standing next to her that she's trying to impress?*

"Yeah, sure," I say. "I'm just driving. What's up?"

"I'm with Madeline Morgan. She's the head of a nonprofit at St. Vincent's Hospital."

Ah, that explains it.

"They are looking for someone to oversee their fundraising activities. It might be a perfect fit with your humanities background."

It takes everything I have not to laugh. Not only do I not need—or want—a new job, but my parents removed themselves from my professional life when I told them I didn't want to attend med school. This call makes no sense whatsoever.

"Well, Mother, that sounds like a wonderful opportunity and I'm grateful that you thought of me. But I just secured a promotion at my current place of employment. I'm quite looking forward to taking on this new challenge."

The fact that I manage to say all of that without snickering deserves a cookie.

I would give anything to see Mom's face right now. She does an impeccable job at covering her frustration, however. Her tone is a little over-the-top sweet, but I doubt Madeline Morgan notices.

"Oh, darling, that's wonderful. I'll let Madeline know you'll forward your résumé to her this week," Mom says.

"That's wonderful, Mother. You can tell her whatever makes you happy, and I'll do what makes me happy. Enjoy your day."

"Yes, I must run. We'll chat later."

"*Awesome*."

The line goes dead.

What the hell was that? She's so deluded.

I turn onto Honeysuckle Lane and forget all about my mother. *I've entered Carmichael Land.*

The street is paved with a neat gravel border along the sides. On my right are two midsized houses and then an empty lot. Two houses are in front of me at the back of the cul-de-sac. I recognize Damaris sweeping the front porch. There are two houses on my left. The second one has a massive rooster statue in the front yard.

"Oh, my gosh," I say, laughing. "You weren't joking when you said there was a giant rooster here, were you?"

I pull into the driveway next to Jess's truck. From my periphery, I notice Damaris has stopped sweeping.

A shot of nerves hits me hard, and I fumble around for my phone. I find it and type out a quick text.

Me: I'm here.

I barely hit send when Jess appears in front of my car.

Oh wow.

His hair is wet, styled like he jumped out of the shower and ran his fingers through it. A blue-and-green button-up hangs casually off his tall frame. Chino shorts give him a more polished look than the usual jeans or dirty work pants that I'm familiar with, and I can't decide which look I like more.

He flashes me a warm smile and comes to my door.

"Hey," I say as he pulls it open.

"Right on time."

I climb out of the car and smooth down my long ruby-colored split maxi dress. After forty minutes in front of the mirror, I decided this was the best mix of relaxed yet looking like I tried. It also makes my chest look fuller and my butt rounder—so I'll take it.

He shuts the door behind me. "Damn. You didn't have to dress up for this, but I'm not complaining. You look great."

"Well," I say, spinning in a circle, "this dress was a whole twenty-five bucks online. I'm not sure it counts as dressing up."

"Are you going to do this version of not dressing up next weekend? Because, if so, I need to make arrangements."

"What for ... *Oh*." I laugh as he wiggles his eyebrows. "Speaking of roosters, is this a permanent piece of decor? Because I didn't really see you as a lawn ornament kind of guy, but it makes sense somehow."

"It was supposed to be out of here two days ago, yet here it sits. I think the fact that I haven't lost my cool too much about it fucks with Banks more than if I got truly pissed. It's reverse psychology at its best."

"Is there ever a dull time in your life?"

"Never." He holds a finger between us and then turns his head. "Hi, Mom."

Oh, yeah. Damaris. I spin around. "Hi, Mrs. Carmichael."

"Stop that," she says, beaming. "How have you been, Pippa? I haven't seen you in a long time."

"I'm great. How about you?"

She slides her gaze to Jess and grins. "I'm doing exceptionally well today. Very excited to have you for dinner, honey."

Jess rolls his eyes, and I can't help but chuckle.

"I'm happy to be here too," I say.

She nods toward her house. "I'll let you two ... you know, settle in or what have you. I'm going to go in and finish dinner. Give me forty-five minutes or so?"

"Thanks, Mom," Jess says, humoring her.

She laughs and disappears through the entryway.

"You'll have to pardon my mama," he says, leading me toward the sidewalk to his porch. "I gave her a heads-up that you were coming, and she's ... let's say she's reading into things a little too much."

He pushes the door open and lets me walk in first.

The two-story foyer is airy and bright with a staircase on the right side next to the wall. An oversized chandelier hangs from the ceiling, and I bet it's beautiful at night when the light reflects off all the windows.

A small living area with a fireplace and black leather furniture completes the space, and the openings on either side of the rock chimney open in what appears to be a kitchen.

"I'm still working on it," he says, sliding his hands into his pockets. "But she's coming along."

"This is beautiful. How much of this did you do yourself?"

"About all of it." He walks toward the back part of the house. I follow. "Mom and Dad bought these houses—and the lot between Foxx and Banks, which was supposed to be for Paige—for us. But the catch was that they needed remodeling and updating. They needed a lot of work. As each of us moved out of Mom's and into our own house, we all kind of pitched in and helped get it cleaned up and livable."

"I love how you guys help one another."

He stops next to a white stone-topped island. "That's what family is for, right?"

"Yes, I must run. We'll chat later." Mom's words echo through my head. "I don't know personally, but I think that's probably what nature intended."

His brows pull together as he moves through the kitchen. "What is your family up to these days? Where's Greg? I haven't seen him since we graduated from high school."

"My parents are out saving the world one life at a time. Greg is, too, I guess. He got married a few years ago and has a baby. Their kid will look at pictures someday and ask, 'Who is that lady and why is she in your baby pictures, Dad?'"

Jess offers me a drink. I turn it down.

"So you don't see him?" he asks.

"I haven't seen him since his wedding. He's in Atlanta now, working some medical wizardry with spleens or something. I don't know. It is what it is."

He leans across the counter from me, his hands folded in front of him. His forehead is wrinkled as he takes me in.

I generally hate talking about my family because people don't understand. While I don't care what people think, it gets awkward trying to explain our familial interactions—or lack thereof. I always find myself in defense mode, shrugging off pity.

There are no vibes like that here. Just a genuine curiosity and concern that's relieving.

"What?" I ask.

"Nothing. You're just so ... nonchalant about it."

"About what?"

He looks at me like I've lost my marbles. "*You haven't seen your only brother in years.*"

I shrug and sit on one of the stools.

"Do you see your parents?" he asks.

"Oh, I just talked to my mom on the way over here. She was so excited to tell me that she found me a new job."

Jess flinches. "A new job?"

"Don't worry. We're still going on our trip. Because, despite what my mother thinks, I love my job and think it's more than a glorified hobby and have zero intentions of quitting."

"Your mom thinks your job is a hobby?"

"We all aren't from families like yours, pal," I say, winking at him. "In our family, once you're eighteen, you either follow the path laid out for you or figure out things independently. I didn't choose their way, so I could become the richest woman on the planet, and it wouldn't be good enough."

"I don't know what to say to that."

"There's nothing *to say*, Jess. It's life. It's just my life. And, honestly, I chose this. I knew what would happen if I bailed on being a doctor. It was never a secret." I sigh. "Did I hope that my mom and dad would have a change of heart? Sure. Did it sting for a while? Of course. But I'm almost thirty. Their presence in my life would come with a venom that there's no antidote for, so I accept it for what it is and am grateful that I'm in such a good place."

Because that wasn't always the case.

He moves around the counter and holds out a hand. I don't hesitate to lay my palm in his. His skin is warm, his fist solid as he wraps his fingers around mine. Gently, he helps me off the stool.

"I'm happy to let you know that I'm sure my mother will be thrilled to be your stand-in fake ex-mother-in-law for the next week," he says, grinning. "So prepare yourself for that."

I gasp. "Did you already tell them what's going on?"

He laughs. "Look, it was either me tell them what's happening or bring you over today and have Mom make a lot of *very serious* assumptions."

I laugh too.

"For the record," he says, squeezing my hand, "they think this is funny."

"They don't think it's ... odd?"

"Pippa, *they have six kids*. Five sons who are a bit of a handful from time to time, and a daughter who hooked up with her boss and is now helping raise his son. My parents are prepared for anything, I assure you. Nothing shocks them anymore."

I look into his eyes as warmth floods my veins. I'm not self-conscious after talking about my background and, surprisingly, I'm not nervous about meeting his family for dinner.

Why? I don't trust easily ... thank you, Mom and Dad. *But why am I so calm right now?*

Because this is Jess. Because I trust Jess.

He presses his lips together. "You know, about that email ..."

"What about that email?"

"There was a line in it about kisses being *essential.*"

The heat in his gaze is impossible to ignore.

My breath shakes as I exhale, clenching my core to try to ease the buildup of desire pooling between my legs.

I want to kiss him. I want to kiss him so bad that it's painful. But if I do, we'll miss dinner because I'm not sure one kiss would suffice—for either of us.

There's also the stickiness of needing to make sure that giving in to my lust for Jess is the right move. Do I expect it'll happen while we're away together? Yes. Do I want it to happen? Absolutely.

But do I also worry that I'll struggle to separate sex from ... more?

Every minute of the day.

"In my defense," I say with more confidence than I really feel, "I wrote that before I knew I was sending it to you."

"Oh, *nice.*"

The irritation in his features makes me laugh. "I would've omitted it altogether if I'd have known."

He cocks his head to the side, peering down at me as if he's unsure what to say. He's trying to walk a fine line, and it's adorable, if not downright sexy.

Who am I kidding? We're not getting out of this without having sex. He knows it or hopes it, and I know it without a doubt.

I don't know how I'll keep it separated in my head because there's no future between the two of us beyond our fake divorce. I wouldn't try to take his time knowing our dreams don't align.

But maybe they can align for a few days ...

My blood grows hot as my body responds to giving myself permission to go after what I want—*him.*

"If I would've known I was sending it to you," I say, playing with one of the buttons on his shirt. "I would've said *other things* were essential."

"Really? Like what?"

He widens his stance so his feet are on either side of mine. His arms slide around my waist before he tugs me closer to him.

I lean my head back, the ends of my hair dusting his interlocked hands at the small of my back, and I stare up at him.

"Are you telling me you want fucked, Miss Plum?"

My knees falter. *My lord.*

I drape my hands over his shoulders, pressing my body into his. I can feel his cock against me—hard as a rock—as he holds me close. *I want him. I've always wanted him.*

Be bold, Pippa.

"I've wanted you to fuck me for a long time, Mr. Carmichael," I say, toying with the back of his neck. "Do you think you can live up to my expectations?"

"You have no idea what I'm capable of."

I grin. "Well, I hope to get a lesson in what you're capable of because I have about a week to fuck you out of my system."

He growls, the rumble causing the fire between my legs to erupt.

I'm tugged against him so close that nothing but the fabric of our clothes is between us. I pant as I stare into his eyes, his head bending toward mine.

Unchecked desire, almost animalistic, flashes through his eyes, and I brace myself for what's to come.

His lips hover over mine.

I palm the back of his head, urging it to lower faster.

Just as his mouth brushes against mine, Banks yells from the foyer.

"Hey, Jess! Did I leave my keys over here?"

I sag against his body, unable to contain my laughter. The letdown is a crash of adrenaline. Jess rests his forehead against mine and chuckles too—I think so he doesn't kill his brother.

"Go the fuck away, Sparkles," Jess shouts.

"Here they are! I found them!" The door slams shut.

Jess blows out a breath and pulls away from me. He runs a hand over his head and grumbles. "Have I ever told you how much I hate him?"

My laughter gets louder.

He shakes his head and sighs. "Well, we might as well go to Mom's before she starts calling or knocking because my family clearly has issues with boundaries."

My jaw drops. "*No.*"

"What?"

"You can't just ... *walk away after that.*"

"What do you want me to do?" he asks with a shit-eating grin. "Do you want me to give you a play-by-play? Because I can. I will."

Before I know what's happening, he reaches for me and yanks me into him again. I melt into his arms, my heart pounding so hard I might faint.

"Let me tell you something, Dream Girl," he says, his eyes blazing. "I've thought about what I would do to you so many fucking times that my cock is about to explode with you in my arms."

I slip my hand between us and palm him through his pants. He flexes against me, his nostrils flaring.

"But I'm not fucking you right now," he says, his features resolute.

"*And why not*?"

He lowers his face to mine. "Because when I fuck you, you'll beg me for it, just like I've begged you for years."

Oh. My. Fucking. Hell.

"You're going to sit through dinner, surrounded by my family, with soaked panties while you think of my cock splitting you in two."

I gulp, barely able to breathe. *He's right. I'm already absolutely soaked, and all I can think about is his cock.*

"After dinner, *if you behave*, I'll bring you back here and give you everything you want."

I force a swallow. My lips part, and I suck in a deep breath. His cologne fills my senses, and the room gets hazy.

"You've made me wait. It won't kill you to wait a couple of hours now," he says, smirking. "Let's go have dinner."

"You're not even going to kiss me?" I ask, bewildered.

He chuckles as he leaves the room. "Nope."

Motherfucker.

12

PIPPA

"What's the matter?" Jess asks, reaching behind him and grabbing my hand. He winks, slowing his pace so I can catch up.

Not that I couldn't catch up if I wanted to. I'm just moping. And reeling. Pouting a little bit too.

"Holding your hand is so lame," I say, rolling my eyes.

He chuckles, clearly amused by my antics. "I'm sorry. Are your panties in a twist?"

"For your information, I'm not wearing any. So fuck off."

He stops in the middle of the road between his house and his parents'. The abruptness leaves me stumbling.

He works his jaw back and forth, studying me to discover whether I'm telling the truth.

"I'm sorry," I say. "Is your dick getting hard again?"

It's my turn to wink.

"You think this is funny, don't you?" he asks.

"About as funny as you did when you told me you weren't even going to kiss me."

"There wasn't time."

"How long does it take to kiss me? I'm starting to think you're full of shit, and you've let your mouth overload your ass—which is something I know a lot about. Hence, the reason I'm here in the first place."

He plucks a lock of hair off my shoulder and tosses it back. His knuckles graze my skin, leaving a trail of goose bumps in their wake.

"If I get *the privilege* of touching you," he says, his voice soft, "I'm not hurrying. I'm not kissing you and ending it so we can leave. *I'm not starting something I can't stop*. I've waited too damn long."

My chest tightens as I peer up into his green eyes. "*If*, huh? Do you think there's a chance it won't happen?"

"I'm trying not to get my hopes up, just in case."

Anxiety flickers through me, and I shift my weight from one foot to the other, trying to process which way to go.

I know what he means about not getting his hopes up; I don't want to set myself up for disappointment, either.

Although I'm all in on sleeping with Jess today—*now, preferably*—I haven't forgotten reality.

"Let's make a deal," I say.

"Shoot."

"All bets are off for the next week. Until we get back from Silver Springs, anything goes."

His eyes light up.

"We both want this, right?" I ask.

"Hell, yeah."

"So let's do it. Take disappointment off the table. Let's get our fill of one another and get back to our regularly scheduled programming."

He gives me a crooked smile. "What if our regularly scheduled programming gets new channels?"

"It won't."

It can't.

He looks at me curiously. "How are you so sure? How do you know with certainty that you won't come back from Silver Springs and want to keep things going? I can be very persuasive."

"Not persuasive enough, or we would've fucked before now."

His gaze nearly burns a hole through me. *This isn't helping.*

"Look, Jess, I've told you before that you'll be a great husband and father someday. That's not my future. *I don't want that.* And what I don't want even more is to get to a spot together where we're having conversations that I can already resolve now. I would rather not do anything at all with you than have to do that."

"But you're willing to give me a week?"

I nod.

"What happens if you fall in love with me in a week?" he asks.

"I won't."

"What if you do?"

"You overestimate yourself, buddy."

He leans down, his breath hot on my lips. I expect him to pull away—to tease me like he's been doing. I start to speak when his tongue swipes lazily across my bottom lip.

Gah! The heat, the wetness, all the things he says without saying them with this one single move have me panting. I want more. I need more. *I need more now.*

I lean toward him to deepen the exchange, but he backs away.

"What was that?" I ask, panting.

He makes a wide circle around me and heads to his mom's house. "That was me double-checking my math."

"Your math for what?"

He doesn't answer me until we're at the base of the steps to the porch. By the time we get there, I'm hot, bothered, irritated—and so turned on that my thighs are sticky beneath my dress.

I don't know if I find him more sexy or more frustrating—if I want to tell him to fuck off or to fuck me.

Maybe both.

"I'm not overestimating shit," he says. The humor drifts away from his face and, in its place, is a seriousness that makes my stomach drop. "But I want to be clear. I will be doing my best to make you fall head-over-fucking-heels in love with me. If you're sure you can walk away when we get home from the trip, then I'm going to get every last moment that I can with you. *I've waited almost my whole life for this*. If you can still walk away after that, then fine."

But what if I can't?

Unfortunately, there's no time to answer because Damaris opens the door.

"There you are," she says. "I was just going to take a look and see if you were on your way yet."

Jess's gaze slides across mine. "We're here. Is everyone else?"

"Yes. We're about ready to eat."

Jess and I climb the stairs, and I enter the house behind Damaris. He doesn't say anything else to me, nor does he touch me or give me some sort of idea what's going through his head.

"I will be doing my best to make you fall head-over-fucking-heels in love with me."

My stomach twists.

"Do you need help with anything, Damaris?" I ask.

"No, just enjoy yourself, sweetheart. We're down a few people today. Foxx is still out of town. Maddox had to show a house to someone, and Ashley went with him. Brooke went to Honey's for dinner because she's still not well."

Honey? Not well? Wait a minute ...

We enter the kitchen to noise and scents and *family*. Banks and Moss sit at the table, looking at something on Banks's phone. Kixx stands behind them, a cup in his hand, dissecting whatever is on the screen. Steam rolls from the pots and pans on the stove, and whatever it is—it smells amazing.

Kixx looks up. "Hey, Pippa! Good to see you. I heard you're a part of the madness for the next week."

My heart pounds. "Yeah. I'm officially your son's fake divorcée."

I hold my breath, not sure what the reaction will be. Jess said he told them, and they were all okay with this scenario. But standing here with them all looking at me is a different thing altogether.

"I bet you divorced him over his attitude," Banks says. "He's a dick."

Everyone except Jess laughs. He glares at his youngest brother instead.

I turn toward the kitchen.

"*Or*," Banks says, "you might've left him because you've been sitting on my face."

I spin around to face him. Moss's head whips to his brother. Jess looks like he's going to throttle Banks.

"*What*?" I ask.

Banks grins. "My face is stuck to your ass." He points at me. "I mean ... really."

I reach around to the back of my dress and feel something sticky. I pull it off and look at it—and burst out laughing. So does everyone else ... except Jess.

"You took that the wrong way, didn't you?" Banks smirks, his question directed at Jess. "I'm disappointed you think I'd be that disloyal to you, my brotherhood buddy. But I'm also proud that you think I could pull her in."

"Change the subject before I stuff you in your rooster and roll you back home," Jess says, sitting at the table.

"I thought you gave him a few hours to get that moved?" Moss asks. "It's been days."

Jess's temple pulses. His posture is stiff. I don't think I've ever seen him so ... bothered. He's normally so easygoing, but he's obviously hit his limit today.

Maybe a part of his frustration is from me.

"If you're sure you can walk away when we get home from the trip, then I'm going to get every last moment that I can with you. I've waited almost my whole life for this."

What does that mean? As if staying away is simply impossible, I walk across the room and stand behind him. My hands rest on his shoulders before I begin working them around, massaging the thick muscles.

It takes no time at all for him to relax into my touch. It takes even less time for me to realize this was a terrible idea in front of people.

My sex clenches, desperate for relief—begging for the attention he's promised it.

"You know what?" I ask. "I like Jess's big cock. I hope he keeps it while I'm around."

Banks throws his hands up in the air.

Moss shakes his head. "Well-freaking-played."

Kixx chuckles. "You know what, Pippa? I like you."

I laugh. "I'm glad."

Jess snakes his hand around the back of the chair and grips my leg. He squeezes it, clasping it tightly as if it's a promise of what's to come.

I pat Jess's shoulder and then step away. Every cell in my body tingles—every nerve ending is frazzled.

"Damaris?" I ask. "May I use your restroom?"

"Oh, sure, honey. It's through that doorway and then down the hall on your right."

"Thanks."

Jess's eyes are on my back as I disappear around the corner.

Pictures of the Carmichael kids are framed on the walls. It's amazing how much they all look alike—except Paige—and I wonder how Kixx and Damaris can tell which boy is which. Maybe that comes with birthing a human. It would make sense.

The bathroom is comfortably classy in shades of eggplant and cream. There are bits of green here and there that give it a bit of flair and dimension.

I turn on the faucet and then pull up my dress. The panties I lied about wearing are pointless. They're soaked and irritating, so I slip them off. Not sure what to do with them, and having left my purse in the car, I tuck the thin material into one of the pockets in my dress. *I'll find an excuse to get something out of my car before dinner.*

After a quick wash of my hands and a slight adjustment to my hair, I open the door.

Oof. Jess is standing on the other side. He embodies the sexual frustration pounding through my veins.

"What's going on?" I ask sweetly.

"You just rubbed your hands all over me in front of my family so I can't do anything back," he says. "That wasn't nice."

I gasp in faux horror. "I was trying to be helpful."

He winks. "I'll remember to be *helpful* later."

Oh shit.

I hold his gaze, hoping to find a crack in his armor. *But there is no crack.* There's only a man who knows what he wants and can taste it.

My stomach roils as I imagine what might be waiting for me *later*. But that's exactly what Jess wants—he wants me to be on the edge and unable to think about anything besides him.

Two can play that game.

I take his hand in mine and hold it up. Then I slip my panties out of my pocket and hook them over his thumb.

His eyes darken. *They hood.* He licks his lips, and I wonder for a split second whether he's going to press me up against the hallway and have his way right now.

I wink and then walk as coolly and confidently as I can back into the kitchen, leaving him standing behind me.

13

JESS

"You survived your first Carmichael family dinner." I close my front door behind Pippa and we remove our shoes. "It wasn't that bad, was it?"

"No. It was great. Interesting, actually."

The words *sound* innocent enough, but there's not a damn thing innocent about the look in her eyes.

My blood runs hot. My instincts plead with me not to waste time —to grab her and hold her and take advantage of this situation before something happens and she changes her mind.

But if she wants to change her mind, I want her to do it before I touch her. For both of our sakes.

"Do you know that Banks has a fudge fork?" she asks.

I deadbolt the door. "A what?"

I guide her into the living room. It's the biggest room in the house and the most comfortable. I took a wall out in the kitchen and opened it up to this space, creating a room where everyone can hang out, watch television, or enter the sliding glass doors to the lanai.

"A fudge fork. That's what he called it," she says, glancing at the pool through the glass. "Your mom asked me to get the forks for dessert. I opened the wrong drawer—one full of paperwork and knickknacks. There was a fork sticking out from under a phonebook, so I pulled it out. Banks snatched it out of my hand and whispered that it was his fudge fork like he was giving me the code to Fort Knox."

"What does one do with a fudge fork? Or do I not want to know?"

She looks at me and smiles. "Apparently, your mom buys this fancy fudge sometimes—he specifically mentioned pistachio—and he keeps that fork there so he doesn't have to keep walking to the other side of the kitchen for one. That way he can just slide it over and take a bite." She laughs. "He demonstrated it. Said it saves him time."

I shake my head. "I'm sorry."

"I was hoping you were going to say that."

Pippa saunters across the room. Her lips press together to hide a smile.

I hum as she grows closer. My heart thumps erratically, and my mind tries to accept that this is really happening.

Having her in my house, looking at me like this, is the culmination of every dream I've ever had. Only, in my dreams, I was unable to fully appreciate how satisfying this moment would be—how wild and unbelievable and confusing and amazing.

And how it all makes sense.

Normally, if a woman was here with me, I'd be getting down to business. My mind would be on fucking her for the sport of it. Enjoying my bachelorhood. Making her come so hard that she screams—just to know I can do it—then getting off, and then getting on with the day.

It's lust, a chemical rush, a physical interaction that doesn't extend any further than the moment I pull out.

Throwing the condom in the trash is the period at the end of that sentence.

Done.

But I'm not quite sure how to process this.

This isn't the same.

With Pippa, I want to savor every moment. Take my time, try

things—discover what she likes. I want to please her, show her how fucking beautiful she is, and then do it again.

I want this to be the bar she uses to measure every sexual experience.

And I want all those experiences to be with me.

I've fallen for her. I fell for her before I could drive a car. I just need to convince her that she should give me a chance—that maybe she could fall for me too.

"Did you think I was saying I'm sorry *to you*?" I ask.

She stops a few feet in front of me. "Yeah. That's what you said."

"What would I be apologizing to you for?"

I roll my tongue around my mouth as a cocky little grin graces those lips that will be wrapped around my cock soon enough.

"I don't know. I just thought maybe you were sorry for leaving me hanging earlier."

Chuckling, I shake my head. "*Nope*."

"*Jess* ..." My name is half desperation and half annoyance.

"I seem to remember somebody running her hands all over me, brushing her chest across the back of my neck—telling my family you like my *big cock* and that you hope I keep it while you're around."

She giggles. "*Come on*. That was a good one."

I lift a brow.

"Your dad even thought it was funny," she says.

"That's a low bar. Trust me."

She holds my gaze as she rests her ass on the armrest of the couch. Her dress sticks to her body thanks to the humidity on our short walk back to my house, revealing the true depth of her curves.

Dammit, *I want her*. My fingers itch to feel her skin. I want to feel her pulse around me, knowing I made her feel good. I'm dying to look into her eyes and watch as she gives up control to me. That she trusts me enough to do that.

That she would do that for me.

She slowly licks her Cupid's bow. "What's your excuse now?"

"Excuse for what?" I ask, even though I know exactly what she's talking about.

"Why are you standing over there? And why do I still have my clothes on?"

Dig deep, Carmichael. Don't give in to her. Not yet.

I lift the bottom of my shirt up and over my head. I toss it at her as I walk to the kitchen.

"Ugh!" She gasps, her bare feet smacking against the floor as she trails me closely. "What are you doing? Where are you going?"

I hide a smile. "I'm thirsty."

"*So am I.*"

I peek at her over my shoulder and catch the almost feral look in her eyes. I can't help it. I laugh.

"This isn't funny, Jess."

I open the fridge, keeping my back to her so she doesn't see the amusement on my face. "You want a drink?"

"No, *I don't want a damn drink.*"

"Oh. I thought you said you were thirsty?"

"*You know what I meant.*"

I take a bottle of water and close the refrigerator. "You don't sound very happy, Pip."

Her gaze blazes a trail from my head all the way down to my groin. She may as well use a hot iron because my flesh tingles in its wake.

My cock throbs, and I don't know how much longer I can do this. I didn't know I had this much restraint to begin with—let alone when it comes to her. Because in my lowest moments, when I've dreamed about being with her, I've had her in every position known to man.

Over the couch, on the kitchen countertop, on the dining table, up against the front door, in the shower … *every-fucking-where.*

Yet here I am teasing her.

I take a long drink, hoping the cold water will cool down my insides.

She blows out a breath. Her exasperation is cute.

I screw on the lid and set the bottle down. Her big doe eyes watch me with anticipation.

"Do you remember that birthday party in the dunes? It was a few years ago, and I can't even remember whose party it was now," I say.

"Yeah."

"Do you remember how it started to storm out of nowhere, and you hopped in my truck?"

She grins. "Yeah."

"And how we sat there for hours—even after everyone else gave up and went home?"

"And how I persuaded you to let me teach you how to dance because you were going to ... an event, I think it was? Or a wedding?"

"My cousin's wedding, yeah."

"You turned your headlights on, and we got out in the rain, and I showed you how to dance."

How could I forget? It's a core memory—a life-defining experience.

It defined the kind of woman I wanted to marry someday.

The woman I *want* to marry someday.

Pippa laughs. "Okay. Do you remember the night we were at Publix at the same time? And that little old man thought we were together even though we were just catching up at the deli counter, and we ended up walking around the store with him?"

"I remember. You convinced him to try vanilla coffee creamer."

"I forgot about that!" Her laughter gets louder. "Oh my gosh. He was so sweet. He tried to give us five dollars each for helping him. Do you remember that?"

Oh, I remember. I remember every time I've ever seen you, heard you, picked up the scent of your perfume in a crowd.

For fuck's sake—I've loved this girl forever.

And I have one week to convince her to love me too—or make enough memories to last me a lifetime.

"We've had some fun together," she says, her eyes following me as I move back into the living room.

"That we have."

I sense her moving behind me. She comes into the lanai as I sit on a barstool at the bar that Moss and I installed a few summers ago.

I struggle to keep my breathing even as I sort through my options.

She stops in front of me. I take her hand and pull her closer to stand between my knees.

"So ..." She's smug. Her nipples are hard under the thin fabric of her dress, and I have to practically sit on my hands so I don't touch them. "What now?"

"What do you want?"

I know the answer. I just want her to say it.

"I want you to fuck me so hard that I forget my name," she says.

Fuck. Me. "That's awfully specific."

"We have a week," she says, looking me in the eye. "I want you to do me so hard that when I see you out with another woman, I know she can't possibly be getting you like I did."

What. The. Actual. Fuck. Is. Happening?

"Is that really what you want?" I ask, giving her one final chance to back out. To modify her request. To change her mind.

She licks her bottom lip. "Take me, Jess."

"Back up," I say.

Mischief plays along her features as she does as she's told. "Yes, sir."

I give her a look. "Take off your dress."

She bends over, giving me a clear shot of her cleavage as she lifts the edge of her dress. Slowly, inch by inch, she moves the fabric up her body.

My mouth goes dry.

It's like watching a present being unwrapped right before your eyes.

Thick thighs that touch just below her shaved pussy.

My God.

I groan, shifting in my seat to keep from coming in my fucking pants.

Her hips are soft and round before dipping in at her waist. Heavy, teardrop-shaped breasts are covered by burgundy lace with straps over her smooth shoulders. The material comes over her head, and then she tosses it at me.

"Damn, Dream Girl," I say, taking her in. "Spin around."

"What?"

"Let me see you. Turn. Let me see what I get to play with."

Her cheeks pink as she makes a slow circle for my enjoyment.

"Do you have any idea how fucking perfect you are?" I ask as she faces me again.

"I'm glad you like it."

I blow out a breath. "Take off your bra."

She holds my gaze, her eyes fiery as she unclasps the back and then lets the lace fall forward.

"Drop it," I say.

It lands unceremoniously on the floor.

I hop off the stool and stalk across the lanai. I grab her jaw and bring it to my face.

"Now you're getting somewhere," she says, challenging me with a look.

I don't know if it *is* the challenge, or that I'm finally touching her, or that my body is coursing with so much testosterone and adrenaline that I can't think anymore, but I capture her mouth with mine.

She moans, threading her fingers through my hair and urging me to kiss her harder. Move my tongue deeper.

I move my other hand to her face and hold her with both hands. Her mouth is hot and wet. It sends a shot of energy straight to my cock. I bite her bottom lip just sharp enough to make her gasp.

Damn.

I pull back as her eyes fly open. She pants, *flushed*, as she tries to gather herself.

But I don't give her time.

I slip her panties out of my pocket and walk to the bar. "Come here."

She joins me as I move the barstools out of the way. Then I turn to her and lift her by the waist, setting her on the bar.

"Give me your hands."

14

PIPPA

I've played it pretty freaking cool, I think—*since we got back to Jess's house, at least.*

It helps that he makes me so comfortable. It's impossible not to be confident when a man like him fawns all over you in the most authentic, genuine way. But it's also impossible not to want to lose your mind when he delays your gratification. I'm currently sporting the female version of blue balls.

My thighs are stuck to the cool white stone countertop, and I know there will be a spot from my ass when I get up—but I can't worry about that right now.

I have more important, hotter matters to contend with.

"Here you go," I say, dangling them in front of him.

I wonder if he can hear my heart pounding. *Does he see the flurry of goose bumps breaking out across my skin as he takes my hands in his*? He gives them a gentle tug, scooting me forward.

His chest is a work of art; his shoulders are crafted by the hands of angels that woke up feeling like doing a favor to women on Earth.

"What are you doing?" I ask him.

He brings my palms together. Then he wraps my underwear

around them, cinching my wrists together a little tighter than necessary, and quickly fashions a knot.

"You better hope I didn't like those," I say.

"You aren't getting them back anyway. Now lie down."

I'm not? "Can I have another kiss first?"

"Nope."

He helps me swing my legs onto the counter and then reclines me until my back is flat against the stone.

"Arms over your head," he says, taking my bound hands and dragging them where he wants them. Until I'm stretched out and displayed just for him.

Oh fuck.

My breath shakes, coming out in raspy waves.

The countertop is hard and cold beneath me—and I am totally exposed.

I gulp, squirming to find a more comfortable—less vulnerable—position. But as I start to move, Jess puts a hand on my belly.

"Stop moving," he says.

I begin to draw my arms down, but he snatches my hands up and moves them back to their original position.

He smirks. "Remember how *helpful* you were at dinner?"

No...

He trails a finger around my stomach, feathering the pad along the ridge of my sex. I shiver at the contact. I lift my hips to encourage more contact, but he grips my leg suspiciously close to my opening and holds me still.

"I'm going to explore every piece of your body," he says slowly, stroking my leg to my calf and back up the inside of my thigh.

"You should try between my legs. It's been a long time since it was explored."

He grins. "I'll get there."

"You should hurry."

"Nah, I think I'll take my time. You seem to like it when I do that."

"It makes me hate you, actually."

He chuckles. "Okay. Whatever you say. Pretty sure you're not in charge here."

He works his way up my hips, stopping to appreciate the curve before making his way to my chest.

His hands cup my breasts, weighing them in his palms. His thumbs roll across the pebbled nipples—and that's what does it. It breaks the calm I've been able to maintain so far.

I moan, earning a smile from him.

"Oh, did I find your switch?" he asks, rolling them between his fingers. "Is this what you like?"

"Yes. *Fuck. Ah.*" I lift my hips off the table again, squeezing my eyes shut. "You win."

"I always win. Remember that."

I suck in a breath as his mouth replaces his fingers on my nipple. He flicks it with his tongue and massages my other breast with his hand. Each lick and nibble against the sensitive bead are like a bolt of electricity.

My knees fall to the side, back arching, head digging against the countertop so hard that it makes me yelp.

There are too many feelings washing over me—my clit throbbing so intently, screaming for attention—that I can barely concentrate.

He kisses across my chest and up the side of my neck. I turn my head, giving him access to do whatever he wants.

The tenderness of his kisses mixed with the bite of the fabric binding my wrists is maddening.

"You're driving me crazy," I groan. "Please—*fuck*!"

A finger slides inside me as he captures my breath in his mouth. I bring my arms down, draping them over his shoulders, kissing him so feverishly that our teeth clash against each other.

He presses against my clit, earning another moan into his mouth.

"You think I drive *you* crazy?" he asks between kisses. "Woman, you have no idea what you do to me."

I'm so wet that I can feel it running down my legs. My ass slips against the counter as I work my hips into his hand—craving more friction.

Jess nips my bottom lip between his teeth and pulls until I yelp.

He adds another finger inside me. "Yeah, I think you're ready for me."

"Wow. You're a genius," I hiss as he strums my pussy. "What's the holdup?"

He chuckles. "I'm trying to decide whether I'm going to make you suck my cock before I let you come all over it."

"As long as you don't stop touching me," I say, gasping as he pumps his fingers against my soaked flesh. "I'll suck you dry."

He hums. The flash of desire in his eyes is telling.

"Do you want to get off in my mouth, Jess? Do you want me to take you all the way to the back of my throat and swallow your cum?"

He pulls his fingers away, then walks to the end of the bar.

"Hey," I say, as panic mixes with irritation in my tone. "Where are you going?"

"Settle down."

My jaw drops. "*Never tell a woman to settle down.*"

He grabs my ankles and slides me down the counter. My ass squeaks against the stone, then balances on the edge as he places my legs over his shoulders. My opening is level with his mouth. The view of him framed between my thighs is nearly enough to make me orgasm.

It's a sight I'll never forget.

"Since you seem to like delayed gratification so much ..."

"I don't," I say, shaking my head back and forth. "Hate it. Despise it. I like instant gratification."

His face buries between my legs before I can compute what's happening. I suck in a breath as he sucks on my clit.

"I can come on your face," I say, barely able to get the words out. "That works—*oh!*"

He shoves two fingers inside me, twisting them before pulling them out. He continues this repeatedly until the rhythm couples with the assault on my clit and has me teetering on the precipice of bliss.

"Just like that," I say, grinding against his face. "Fuck, *Jess!*" His name comes out higher, almost a squeal, as the onslaught peaks—almost painfully so.

And then he stops.

What? I pant, heat boiling through my body.

He stands, my juices coating his face, and grins. My ankles are up in the air, held together with one hand so I don't fall off the table.

"What the fuck was that?" I ask, struggling against the confines of my panties.

"Was that *helpful*?"

I can't sit up without my hands. Still, I scramble for a position that doesn't feel as impotent.

"As much as I like watching you squirm ... here." He helps me to my feet, my body sliding roughly against his chest as I go. He towers over me. "Better?"

"You know what? Not really."

He laughs.

"*This isn't funny*."

"Ah, do you get angry when you're horny?"

I make a face at him and try to free my hands. He rolls his eyes and grabs the knot, giving it a quick yank. The fabric breaks.

"No," I say, glaring at him and rubbing my wrists. "I get angry when I don't get off."

"You are so impatient." He swats my ass as he passes me. "I didn't have you pegged as being so demanding."

"Really?" I ask, lifting a brow. "How can you say that with a straight face?"

He rummages around a drawer next to a deep gray outdoor sofa, seemingly unaffected by my misery. "Get over here."

"Why should I?"

He turns around and, while holding my gaze, drops his shorts and boxer briefs.

Shit.

He grips his cock and pumps it. "*I'm not going to ask you again*."

"Good thing I don't want to wait anymore. I won't make you ask me again."

He hands me a condom. "Here. Put this on me."

"Of course," I say facetiously. "I'd love to. I'd love to stand here dripping all over the fucking floor while I touch you."

"I'd watch your mouth."

I grin. "I *would have* let you watch it wrap around your cock."

He groans as I wrap my hand around the base. But before I roll the protection over his length, I lock my gaze with Jess's. Slowly, I lower my head to the tip. A bead of pre-cum sits on the head, so I swipe my tongue over the top, then suck the head of his cock into my mouth.

He flexes against me, hissing, as I roll my tongue around him.

His hand presses roughly against the top of my head. "Get on your knees."

My sex aches as I kneel before him. I drop the condom and cup his balls instead, stroking his shaft with the other.

"Suck me, Pip," he says, pushing my head against his length.

He digs his fingers into my hair and guides my head up and down, thrusting himself into my mouth.

My spit drips down him, rolling off his balls and down my forearms.

"Deeper," he says, his voice filled with the sexual frustration raging inside me. "That's it. Suck it, Pippa."

My eyes begin to water as I take him up and down my throat, the speed encouraged by his guidance.

"Good girl," he says through clenched teeth.

He begins to swell, his balls tighten, and I brace myself for him to come in my mouth. But just as a saltiness begins to hit my tongue, he yanks my head away.

I suck in a lungful of air, gasping, and wipe my mouth with the back of my hand. My eyes are blurry, but I look up at him anyway, needing to see his face.

Needing to see his satisfaction.

His eyes are dark and wild, a smug smirk gracing his lips.

"Why did you stop me?" I ask, squeezing my thighs together in a failed attempt to stop the intense throb between them.

He takes my hand and helps me to my feet. Before he answers me, he presses a soft, sweet kiss to my lips.

Out of all the things that have happened tonight, it's this kiss that leaves me speechless.

He pulls back, studying me for a few seconds. "Get on your knees on the sofa and bend over the back. I want your ass up in the air."

My heart pumps a mile a minute as I climb onto the sofa. The cushion is surprisingly sturdy, yet the fabric is soft and not scratchy. I look over my shoulder as he stalks toward me, rolling a condom over his cock.

I consider saying something cocky—goading him a little bit—but the fire in his eyes stops me. Whatever is about to happen doesn't need more gasoline on the fire.

And I'm ready. So fucking ready to have him deep inside me.

"Ass up," he says.

I lean over the back. He grips my hips and pulls me back, positioning me so I'm level with him.

"I want you to remember something," he says.

"What's that?"

"You asked for this."

What? I glance over my shoulder as he places the head against my opening. "Jess, I—*fuck*!"

He slams into me *hard*. With the first thrust, he's all the way in, hitting the back, drilling into me with a force that takes my breath away.

I try to yell, but nothing comes out.

"*You. Are. Perfect*," Jess hisses. "*Dammit*!"

He grips my waist, his fingertips digging into my skin so hard it burns. He slams into me once, twice, three times. On the fourth, a flurry of colors clouds my vision.

The combination of the rhythm and force skirts the border of pleasure and pain. It keeps me in a place of uncertainty, and that, in turn, keeps me focused on every move Jess makes.

My head hangs between my arms—but only for a minute. He grabs what's left of my ponytail and yanks my head backward.

My neck stretches, constricting my airway, and I struggle to breathe.

"You wanted fucked," he says, the words gravelly. "Is this what you wanted?"

I hope that's a rhetorical question because I can't answer it. Words are out of my reach—but an orgasm is not.

"Do you like it?" he asks. "Was it worth the wait?"

There's nothing to say, nothing to control. There's no safe or easy ride to the top of this orgasm. But the word "yes" is being shouted within my mind.

Yes. This. Him. All of it.

I'm flailing amid a sea of sensations—sharp, wet, smooth, and *so much pleasure*—that I give up. I grab the back of the sofa, squeeze my eyes closed, and clench my body around him.

"Come for me," he demands, letting go of my hair. "Your pussy wants to explode."

I suck in a hurried breath, barely registering my blazing scalp.

I whimper, letting my head fall. But as Jess rails me from behind, my head smacks off the wicker.

My teeth clench as my body begins to shake. "*Jess* ..." I say, the words as shaky as my legs.

The sound of his palm connecting with my ass cracks through the air. I scream as the contact sets off a series of explosions that wreck me with the most intense, fierce—*exceptional*—orgasm that I've ever experienced.

Ever.

"What the ... *fuck* ...." Jess sucks in a long, hasty breath.

He clamps down on my hips and shoves himself so deep inside me that I'm not sure where I start and he ends. His cock swells as he rolls his hips against my ass.

"*Pippa*," he moans, dragging his palms to my bottom and squeezing my cheeks. "*Fucking hell, that feels good.*"

I rock against him, letting him sink as deep as he can go. Hearing my name in the middle of his orgasm might be the sexiest thing I've ever heard.

Finally, he sags. He rubs my backside gently as he pulls out of me.

I fall forward—my body drained and weak. My eyes flutter closed as the post-haze of my orgasm caresses me.

I sense Jess walking away, then returning. He sits beside me.

"Hey," he says softly. When I don't move, he pulls me over his lap and cradles me. "You okay?"

"Yeah." I force my eyes to open and peer up at him. *My lord, he's handsome.* "You okay?"

He chuckles. "Something like that."

"If you are one of those guys who wants a round two right away, I'm out. I'm tapping."

"You're in luck. I'm not young and full of unbridled testosterone anymore, so it takes me a minute to gear back up."

I grin.

I've never felt like this after sex before. Cherished. Adored. Truly and thoroughly *fucked*. It's akin to whiplash going from being ravaged to being held so tenderly. It's confusing and erotic and so mind-blowingly amazing that I can't imagine ever having anything else now that I know this exists.

He brushes a lock of hair out of my face. "You sure you're good?"

"Yeah. I need a bathroom, though."

His brows pinch together, and he adjusts his hold on me. "How would you feel if we went upstairs and took a bath?"

"What? You don't have to do that. I can go home."

His smile turns shy. "Stay with me. I only get a week, right?"

Either he's playing me like a pro or I'm a sucker. Or there could be a third option.

No. It's way too soon for that. It's ridiculous to consider I could be falling for him.

I can't fall for him. That's not what this is or will be.

"Do you have bubble bath?" I ask, smiling up at him.

"Actually, I do. And I have a giant tub and the fluffiest towels because I'm a laundry master."

"Ooh, you win. I'll stay."

He stands with me in his arms like I don't weigh a thing.

"I can walk," I say, laughing.

"I'm aware."

There's no point in arguing with him. I might be able to win, but I don't really want to.

He presses a kiss to my forehead, his lips lingering a moment longer than necessary before he carries me like his treasure to the stairs.

15

PIPPA

"I should really go home," I say, making no effort to move.

Jess hums. His eyes are closed, his breathing steady.

I smile against his bare chest as he nudges me closer. Instead of getting out of his bed, my leg repositions atop his beneath the sheets.

Jess's bedroom suite takes up one whole half of the upstairs. The other side of the landing hosts two bedrooms with a Jack and Jill bathroom. He said the expansion of his space was yet another project that Moss, and this time Maddox, helped him finish a few years ago. He combined two bedrooms and another shared bathroom into one giant space with a private bathroom and massive closet.

The walls are white with dark wood trim. There is a dresser with a glass bowl and a lamp with a Tiffany-style shade in blues and greens. His bed is unexpected; an old four-post wooden structure facing the windows overlooking the backyard. It sits high and is covered with the softest sheets, marshmallow-like blankets, and fluffy pillows.

He dusts his fingertips down my side, feathering them against my skin.

"How many days did you say we'll be gone?" he asks, his voice husky.

"I actually have some leeway with that. The point is just to test the premise, and I proposed three- and four-day getaways. But we can really do whatever."

"I'm up for whatever works best for you."

Of course, you are. "I was messing around with some ideas last night. Is there anything you particularly like to do?"

"You."

I chuckle. "I'll make sure to schedule that."

"Schedule *lots* of that."

"I'm being serious." I smile. "What do you want to do?"

"What are my choices?"

"Anything, really. I proposed Silver Springs, so I assume that's where we'll go. But, I mean, I can change that if you would rather go someplace else."

He moves to see my face. A playful smirk graces his lips.

"*What*?" I ask.

"You really don't get it, do you?"

I struggle to sit up. He resists me detaching from him and frowns when I finally manage. *You're so freaking cute.*

"What are you talking about?" I ask, pulling the sheet over my chest. "I really don't get what?"

He narrows his eyes. "First of all, you don't get that I don't like you hiding from me."

"I have no idea what you're talking about."

He sits up and reaches for me. I hold my breath as he loops a finger around the top of the sheet and tugs it away from my body. His knuckle slides down my sternum as the cotton drops to my waist.

I give him a look.

Despite my obvious displeasure with having the sheet pooled at my waist and my breasts on full display, he just stares at me unbothered.

"You didn't mind being naked for me earlier," he says.

"That was a slightly different situation."

"How?"

"Well, earlier I had hormones flooding my system because I'd been on edge for hours."

He smirks.

I pretend to glare at him. "But I'm satisfied now and thinking rationally, and it's just ..."

His gaze softens. "Just what, Pip?"

I've never had a man ask me why I might be self-conscious or feel any particular way. *I don't think any of them have cared.* And the mixture of potential embarrassment from explaining myself when it comes to not wanting to sit in front of him naked and the tenderness in his eyes puts me on shaky ground.

"Come on," he says, resting his palm on my sheet-covered thigh. "Talk to me. What's going on?"

"Nothing is going on. You know, it's just that ... I don't have body image issues or anything. I'm aware that the models on the internet are airbrushed, yada, yada, yada. But you're ... *you,* and I'm sitting here with boobs that aren't quite as perky as they used to be. Maybe a couple of extra stretch marks here and there." I tuck a strand of hair behind my ear. "It's a pride thing, I guess."

He grins.

"Don't you even think about laughing at me," I say, smacking his leg.

"You think I'd laugh at you?" He squeezes my thigh. "You don't know me at all."

"But you're smiling."

Now the bastard laughs. "I'm smiling because this is, like, the pinnacle of my life, and you're sitting there thinking I'm mentally sizing up your tits or something."

My cheeks flush.

"If you want to cover up, then do it," he says. "I want you to be comfortable. But, my God, Pippa, if you had any idea how lucky I feel to have you sitting in my bed." He shakes his head as his face flushes. "Okay, how about this? The whole time we've been lying here together, I've been waiting on you to want to go home."

He searches my eyes as if he's desperate for a life raft.

"Why would a girl like you want to stick around with a guy like me?" he asks shyly. "You can have anyone you want, Pip. How on earth would I ever get you to pick me?"

I don't know what to say to that, but I figure I won't have to say anything. Surely, he'll smile or wink or say something arrogant that will break the preciousness of the moment.

Except he doesn't.

I tilt my head, my hair brushing against my shoulders. *Can he actually be serious*?

"I hope you're joking," I say.

"About what part?"

"All of it." I pull my knees up under me so I'm sitting on them. Fully aware that I'm uncovered, I let the sheets lay on my lap. "You aren't serious, are you?"

"Yeah. Why wouldn't I be?"

I study him, trying to determine whether he's screwing with me or playing me ... or telling me the truth.

"How on earth would I ever get you to pick me?"

I've not doubted that Jess is attracted to me. I believe that he thinks I'm pretty and wants to have some sort of physical relationship with me. But all of the times he's said or joked, I thought about truly wanting something deeper together—I thought he was just being sweet. Or playful. Or charming.

But maybe I was wrong. *Is it possible that Jess Carmichael has feelings for me? If so, what in the hell are we doing?*

A shot of panic—a distinct need to protect myself—ripples through me.

"Jess ..." I swallow with more force than necessary. "You don't have to say all of this stuff, you know. I know you like to play around that I'm your dream girl or whatever, but I get it. You don't have to take it this far."

He pulls away, his forehead marred. "You think I'm playing around?"

I still. "You are, aren't you?"

He laughs, but it's anything but amusement. It's almost disbelief as if he can't process the situation.

That makes two of us, buddy.

"Let me get this straight," he says. "You've thought I was joking around for the last *fifteen years*?"

"Well ..." I grin. "You know, yeah. I guess. Mostly."

He scoots up until he's sitting against the headboard.

The lines of his muscles shine in the Golden Hour rays filtering in through the window. He's brilliant and beautiful. Tanned skin, swollen lips, messy hair from the hour-long bath we took together where he washed me, massaged conditioner in my hair, and told me stories about growing up with four brothers.

There's no mask, no veil to hide behind. No joke on the tip of his tongue. He doesn't even try to hide behind his trademark smirk.

Instead, he watches me with an openness that takes my breath away.

He chuckles, shaking his head like he, too, can't believe this is happening. "All right, let me be crystal clear so we're on the same page."

I hold my breath.

"I think you are the most interesting, witty, capable woman I know. I could sit and talk to you for hours—and then replay the conversations in my mind for days. Just being around you makes me walk a little taller when I leave because it feels special to breathe the same air as you."

"Stop it," I say, smiling so hard my cheeks ache.

He snakes his hand beneath the sheet and rests his palm on my hip. "When I call you my dream girl, I'm not fucking joking. God could let me build a chick and put her together exactly how I wanted, and she'd be a poor excuse for you."

"What is happening here?" I say, snuggling up beside him again.

He pulls the blankets over us, forming a cocoon around our bodies.

I giggle against him, riding a high from the compliments. *How can this be real? Why did I not believe this before? Would it have made a difference if I did?*

He strokes my back and presses a kiss to my forehead. And through it all—the words, the touches, the sweet gestures—I realize that this is exactly the life I want. This is the vision I've always hoped exists for me in the world.

My smile falters.

"You're aware that every female you've ever met has a vibrator at home named Jess, aren't you?" I ask.

He bursts out laughing.

"I mean it," I say, laughing too.

"Do you have one?"

"*Maybe*."

I take in the pleased, smug grin on his face. "What's Vibe Jess like?"

I giggle. "Vibe Jess? Well, Vibe Jess gets the job done. Not as well as Real Jess, I'll give you that, but he's given me more orgasms than any other person—real or fake."

"So I have competition?"

"I can't handle this conversation," I say, the giggles turning into laughter. "This is so ridiculous."

"No, what's ridiculous is that you've used a plastic toy *when all you had to do* is call me. You're so goofy. But now I want you to bring Vibe Jess on our trip. I want to outperform that little fucker, and I want him to watch."

I snort. "Stop it."

He pulls back and smirks. "I mean it. Bring it with you, or you're getting spanked."

"*Ooh*," I say, wiggling my brows. "Is that the moment I get to call you daddy?"

His smirk fades. "I'd watch saying that."

"Why?"

"Because I happen to know that you have a knot on the top of your head, a handprint on your ass, and your pussy is going to be sore tomorrow. It would behoove you to give yourself a few days before I do it all again."

He's right—my sex already aches. But that smolder in his eye makes me clench for him anyway.

Jess looks away and focuses on something across the room. "Let's change topics before I fuck you again."

Probably a good idea. At least for now.

I draw small circles on his stomach, laying my leg over his again.

"For the record, since you were so honest with me ..." I press my cheek to his chest. "You make me laugh harder than anyone I've ever known. I forget all about my life's fuckups when you're around, and I've never met a man who consistently—and honestly—shares compliments. Who doesn't play games. No one except you."

He kisses the top of my head.

"You're amazing, Jess. Honestly. There are sixty-nine million reasons any woman on the planet would pick you."

"I don't care about any woman on the planet but you."

He wraps his arms around me and holds me tight. It's as if he thinks I might pull away and never come back.

And, if I was using my head, that's exactly what I'd do.

"I'm sorry," he says, the gravel back to his tone. "I'm completely putting you on the spot here."

"No. Don't ... don't apologize. I appreciate your honesty. I just ..."

I work my bottom lip between my teeth, a surge of fear racing through my veins. *What do I do?*

"Jess, I ..."

My breathing is uneven as I inhale. The exhale is just as shaky. All I can do is be honest with him.

He stays still. He doesn't move—not even a muscle.

How do I verbalize what I feel? What I fear? How do I tell this beautiful man the one thing stopping me from returning his sentiments is that I'm absolutely certain that a time will come when he changes his mind?

If there's one person I don't think I'd cope with seeing disappointment in me, it's him.

"Disappointing people has such a negative connotation to it. But when you really think about it, sweetheart, disappointing someone probably

means you stood up for yourself. If you never disappointed someone, then you've probably never made yourself happy either."

Even if what Honey said about this is right, I don't think it would be standing up for myself that would bring about that disappointment. *It would be ensuring Jess gets what he deserves.* So I have to speak the truth.

"It feels really unfair to return your sentiments when it's a dead-end road," I say softly.

"But do you feel the same way?"

There's a hopefulness embedded in his curiosity that hits me in the heart.

"Does it matter?" I ask him. "I mean, really? Because for me, sharing how I feel with you now that I know *how you feel* would be like winning a ticket to paradise and knowing it's closed."

His chest rumbles with a suppressed chuckle.

"I don't think this is funny," I say.

"Sit up."

Huh? "Why?"

"Sit up," he says, nudging me.

I press off him, pulling the sheet up and tucking it under my arms to hold it up. It's a childish act of defiance. But if he wants to be bossy, I'll keep a little control, *thank you very much.*

He smirks, amused with my antics. "Let me make sure I understand what you're saying."

"Okay."

"You feel the same way about me as I feel about you." I lift a brow. "But for some reason, you think that you can deny all of that because you've conjured up some imaginary reason in your pretty little head that would make *us* impossible long-term?"

"Well," I say, shrugging nonchalantly. "It really sounds simple when you put it like that."

He laughs. "Because it is simple."

"No, *it's not*. You're oversimplifying a complicated topic."

"*Okay*, says the woman who decided she was some kind of a seer who can predict the future."

I smack his leg.

He watches me with a cocky, thoughtful grin. I have no idea where this is going or what he's thinking, but I know that the look on his face makes me want to sit on it.

Not now, Pippa. Focus.

"Once we settle this," he says, pointing at me, "I want to know what thought just crossed your mind."

"*Okay*, says the man who decided he was some kind of a mind reader."

He knows he caught me, but he lets it go. "How about this—you give me this week, since we're together anyway, and let me show you how good things between us can be?"

My stomach knots.

"Let me have a chance," he says, his eyes shining. "At least give me a fair shot at winning you over."

Oh, Jess. You already have.

I want to launch my body on top of his and have him hold me. I need to feel the warmth of his skin and the softness of his touch—the safety I only feel in his arms.

If I do those things, I'm giving in. *But just how bad would giving in truly be?*

My defenses are down. I'm in a state of post-orgasmic vulnerability that I know is dangerous. But when I take in his green eyes that beg me to give him a chance, I realize that orgasm or not—I'm fucked.

Jess is the only man I've ever thought I could be with wholeheartedly. He's the guy who makes my heart skip a beat every time I see him—the one who makes any situation seem manageable.

There's something special between us. I've always known it. And maybe it can't last forever, but maybe I deserve to enjoy the beauty of it for a few days.

Besides, could I be any more in love with him than I already am?

This is going to hurt when it's over.

And it *will be over*. I could never deprive this beautiful, amazing, caring man of having a family. That's what it would be—depriving him. I just couldn't do that.

"I already told you I'd give you a week," I say.

He shakes his head. "No, you agreed to a week *for fun*. I want seven days. But considering the whole couples retreat, *I'm your ex-husband scenario*, I want you to give me seven days where you're playing the part of my girlfriend."

I blink.

"Date me," he says. "Not as a show for other people because I could give a shit what anyone else thinks. But for one week, tell yourself that you and I are a thing. Let me treat you like you're mine. Pretend we're in a real relationship. Give me that."

Oh shit. I gulp, knowing I'm in too far—but also in too far to back out.

"I'm serious," he says. "I want a real chance to make you fall for me."

"What do I get out of this?" I ask, unable to hide the unsteadiness in my tone.

He grins. "Besides the obvious?"

I look at him like I'm unimpressed.

"Fine. You get to walk away at the end of the week without me mentioning this again."

He holds my gaze, silently pleading with me to say yes—to go along with his plan. And even though I know in the bottom of my gut that this is probably akin to emotional suicide, I can't say no.

I can't deny myself the opportunity to be loved by him—even if only for a week.

I lick my lips, watching as his eyes light up. "Fine. But I have one more condition."

"Hurry."

Grinning, I run a hand up his leg. "You have to kickstart this fake—"

"Real."

"—relationship by burying your face between my legs."

The heat in his eyes nearly burns me. "Lie back and spread 'em."

So I do.

16

PIPPA

"You look glowy today." Shelly leans against the doorway to my office with a vase of bright pink roses in her hand. "Have a good weekend?"

If I wanted to pretend I wasn't on cloud nine, I couldn't.

"Something like that," I say, unable to wipe the smile off my face. "How was your weekend?"

"Considerably worse than yours, it seems." She walks in and sets the vase on my desk. "I saw these in the reception area when I walked by, so I grabbed them for you."

Damn you, Jess.

"Do you have a new guy in your life, or are these from the ex-husband?" she asks.

"The ex-husband." I take the envelope out of the blooms. "We had an interesting weekend."

"If you get flowers and a glow like that—tell me where I can get that kind of an interesting weekend. In my world, interesting weekends are when you have a funny smell in the refrigerator and aren't quite sure where it's coming from."

I laugh and open the card.

Pippa,

I hope you have an amazing day.

You're beautiful.

I'm thinking about you.

I can't wait to see you tonight.

Jess

This man.

My heart sings. I could twirl around my office like a character on a silly musical—holding out my arms so little animals can hop on them and harmonize with me on a catchy melody.

"Did things change between you when you asked him to go on the retreat?" she asks.

"Something like that."

"Well, I'm jealous. I haven't had a man in my life for months now." She sighs. "I wonder sometimes if you can go too long without a man. Like, is this the start of turning into an old maid? At what point do I start yelling at people to stay off my lawn?"

I laugh. "I think you have a while to go before you're swatting a broom at the neighborhood kids."

"I don't know. I've been eyeing kittens at the shelter."

"What does that have to do with anything?"

"Cats are always a part of the old maid storyline," she says. "It's long hair, a broom, usually a wart on the nose, but I'd like to forgo that detail, if possible. There's also a small garden with pie plates hanging to scare away the birds and a cat." She furrows her brow. "You know, if there's a cat involved, why do they need the pie plates? Wouldn't the cats keep the birds away?"

I snort. "What's gotten into you?"

"Not your ex, that's for damn sure."

My ex.

Jess made it abundantly clear that he's not to be referred to as my ex-husband anymore. He can be my boyfriend, my man, or my lover. For the next seven days, we are the fakest real item the world has ever seen.

I must admit that it's fun. He's leaned all the way into his new role with a gusto that's been lacking in my life. He gave me a massage, cooked me carbonara for dinner, and watched an episode of my favorite show—well, most of it. I ended up giving him a blow job before the show was over to repay him for the oral he expertly delivered earlier in the night.

And when it was time to go home, he lobbied for me to stay. If we were really dating, he said, I'd already have half of his closet filled with my things. So in all fairness, I should just sleep over.

Except there was more talking, laughing, and kissing than sleep. But who's complaining?

Chuck. I smell his hyena stench well before I see him. I make a face, unable to control my visceral reaction to the odor. Shelly's confused until Chuck stops at the door.

He's returned to his no-tie life, and the bags under his eyes are dark. He focuses his attention on Shelly.

"I just sent you an email with ad copy for the Whistler campaign," he says. "There are a few tweaks since the earlier draft, and marketing needs it by lunch. Could you take a look at it as soon as you can?"

Shelly's brows shoot to the ceiling. "Um, sure, Chuck. I'll look at it as soon as I get back to my desk."

"Thanks."

He glances at me warily before giving me a curt nod and disappearing out of sight.

Shelly checks the hallway before coming all the way into my office and shutting the door. "What the hell was that?"

I grin mischievously.

"I mean, Chuck was almost *nice*," she says, baffled. "And he managed an interaction without saying something shitty *to you*? What the hell? Did he run over someone on the way to work this morning or what?"

My hand flies to my mouth, covering my laughter. "That's not funny."

She throws her hands in the air. "Explain it to me then. *Because that's not Chuck.* That was almost a regular person."

I drop my hand and grin.

The satisfaction of seeing him put in check is better than I even imagined. But knowing it was because Jess went to bat for me without being asked to? I don't think I could've imagined a better scenario. I know I've put Jess in the not going there basket, but have I really had blinders on for so long that I've missed how genuinely nice he is?

Except when he's denying orgasms.

And giving Chuck his walking papers.

"What?" She narrows her eyes. "What happened? What do you know?"

"Nothing."

"Pippa—*don't you lie to me.*"

I twist my lips to keep from smiling, but it's futile. "Fine. I was with my friend, Kerissa, on Friday night, and Chuck and his wife just happened to frequent the same establishment."

She gasps.

"Naturally, Chuck decided to stop by our table to say hello. But he was bringing extra pissiness due to the meeting on Friday, and I was bringing extra sass thanks to La Pachanga's coconut lime margaritas. We were about to square off once and for all when Jess happened to walk in at just the right moment."

She leans back. "Jess?"

"The ex-husband."

You could hear a pin drop in my office as Shelly's eyes bug out. All I can think about is how Jess would promise a smack on the ass if he heard me call him that.

I should remember to address him like that tonight.

"This is like a fairy tale." Shelly shakes her head in disbelief. "Keep going. Tell me there's an alpha moment in this story, dammit."

I laugh, unable to contain myself. "Girl, if you could only see the way Jess came up behind me, wrapped his arm around my waist, and put Chuck the Fuck in his place."

Her eyes twinkle.

"Jess was like—now that you know I exist, if you ever approach Pippa like that again, I'll take it as a personal insult."

Shelly leans dramatically onto my desk as if she's collapsing.

"I know," I say, sighing happily. "And that's really what ... you know, brought us together this weekend."

Admitting out loud that we're together—even if for a week—turns a little nugget of worry in my stomach. Every time I consider how poorly this might end, I shove it out of my mind. I refuse to give it any ground to grow.

Jess promised me that, no matter what, we would always be friends. That if I decide in a week's time that I was right and that this is a terrible idea, he will never walk away from me.

And I want to believe that. My lord, I want to believe that.

I want to believe that he would never change the way he sees me. I hope that I'll never be judged because I want, or don't want, certain things in my life. I pray there's never a day that I see regret in his eyes.

We're one day in, and I already know that would destroy me.

No. I trust him. He's the best man I know.

A knock on the door makes Shelly jump. She stands straight and smoothens out her skirt.

"Come in," I say.

Bridgit opens the door and steps inside. "Am I interrupting anything?"

"No, ma'am," Shelly says. "I was just bringing her flowers that I saw as I walked by the front desk. Chuck stopped about the Whistler campaign, so I'm off to address that."

"Thanks for bringing me the flowers," I say.

She winks. "Talk soon." She shuts the door snugly behind her.

Bridgit drops a few files on my desk before dropping herself into a chair across from me. "You know, when I was younger, I lived for Mondays."

"Really? Because when I was younger, Mondays often came with a hangover."

She laughs. "Well, I came from a family where work came before all else. There were no parties and drinking and fun, really, of any kind. It was work, work, work."

"That sounds like no fun."

"It wasn't. I mean, look where I am now—CEO of Bloom Match. I can't complain. I just look back on my life and wonder if I could've had more fun."

I sit back in my chair and take her in.

Bridgit's hair is perfectly highlighted, blown out, and coiffed. Her nails are manicured with fresh French tips. Her signature navy suit has been tailored to hug her curves and her pumps have red soles which means *expensive*.

She's the walking, talking, flexing woman who so many want to be. *Who knew that she was thinking about having more fun?*

"Has Chuck given you any trouble today?" she asks.

"No, actually. He's been well-behaved."

She looks impressed. "I expected him to have a tantrum. I'm not sure if I'm happy about that or if I'm sad I don't have a reason to fire him."

I snicker.

"I shouldn't be saying that to you," she says. "But I suppose if I can't be honest with my senior staff, then I'm among the wrong group, right?"

Senior staff. I sit a little taller as pride washes over me.

"Do you know what my favorite thing about you is, Pippa?"

"No."

"You don't take any shit. You know what you want and aren't scared to go for it. No one better get in your way."

Really? "Thank you. That's very kind of you to say."

My mind scans through all of the things in my life that haven't felt that way at all.

Choosing to forgo med school. Telling my parents. Telling Greg. Taking a job with a matchmaking company even though I had no background in the field and it didn't pay extremely well.

Moving to Kismet Beach and into a small apartment that needs more work than I can put into it. Putting myself out there with the project proposal at work.

The fear of giving things with Jess a try.

I don't know who Bridgit thinks I am, but I have to disagree.

"Have you confirmed the details for the retreat?" she asks.

"Well, yes and no. I've talked to my ex-husband, and he's willing to give it a try."

She grins.

I turn toward my computer screen. "I've been playing around this morning with different options to see what makes the most sense." I open a spreadsheet and enlarge it. "The leading contenders are Silver Springs, like we talked about, or this little place outside of Miami."

"What are you leaning toward? I personally liked Silver Springs. It's centrally located and there are a lot of different options we can explore."

"I agree. But here's the catch ..." I highlight two columns. "Everything in Silver Springs is booked for a month, more or less, starting this weekend. Carrington, the place by Miami, has options available next weekend."

"*Oh*."

I swivel around to face her. "This won't be a problem once we solidify our packages. I've been in contact with a few proprietors in each area, and they're more than willing to work with us on reserving rooms as needed. But, for right now, this is what we're looking at."

She places her elbow on the armrest and thinks. "I really think Silver Springs is the way to go."

I shrug.

"Are there openings this week?" she asks.

"Yes. All week until the weekend."

"So you could go tomorrow?"

What? "Yeah, I mean, if I'm not coming to work."

"What about your ex-husband? What's his name again?"

"Jess."

"Oh, sexy name."

I laugh.

"Okay, well, is there any way Jess can take off this week?" She groans. "That's so inconsiderate of me to ask. Who can take time off work last minute? Who am I kidding?" She sits up. "I guess we try Carrington next weekend."

I point at her, shaking my finger. "You know what? You're right. It's totally inconvenient and asinine to ask someone to take a few days off work midweek—at the last second, no less. But let me just ask Jess. He probably won't be able to, but you never know."

Her eyes light up. "That would be amazing. If you could talk to him and let me know what happens. If it's a no-go, let's book Carrington. I think our demand for Carrington will be much less based on our demographic, but we have to get some sort of experience with this under our belt."

"I agree. I'll ask him and let you know."

She stands. "If he can go this week, just book the appointment and we'll consider it a paid vacation." She heads to the door. "You've earned it, Pippa."

Wow. "Thanks, Bridgit. I truly appreciate it."

"And I appreciate you." She bends forward and whispers, "And thanks for not getting me into a lawsuit by knocking out Chuck. For heaven's sake, he's a piece of work. We have to find a legal way to get him out of here."

I smile.

She twists the knob. "Oh, one more thing."

"What's that?"

"I know Jess isn't your ex-husband."

My jaw drops to the table. "You do?"

"I knew what you were doing, and I can't blame you. It's also none of my business if you're married or not."

Oh, fuckety fuck!

"Wow. Bridgit, I'm sorry about all of that." I frown, my stomach tightening. "That kind of defeats the point of me going on the trip, don't you think?"

She looks at the flowers and laughs. "Absolutely not. This man sent you flowers. You look like you've had a very *refreshing* weekend." She winks. "I'm curious to see what happens. If this concept of yours can work on people not in a relationship, that makes me even more confident that it can work on people already committed. And, think about it—new marketing angle. Not only is this for couples in trouble, but also people considering a relationship. It's smart."

I don't know what to say to that. Exhaling the stress I've carried on my shoulders for the past two weeks feels like a million bucks.

"Let me know about this week." She smiles and leaves, closing the door behind her.

It takes me a few minutes to get myself together before I find my cell phone. Jess picks up in three rings.

"Hey," he says. "How's my girl?"

"She's looking at a vase full of gorgeous pink roses, actually."

"Wow. Someone must not be able to stop thinking about her to send her flowers in the middle of a workday."

I beam. "They're beautiful. Thank you."

"You are very welcome."

"I have something to ask you."

"Sure. What is it?"

A power tool starts in the distance, and I realize I'm bothering him at work. Suddenly, I feel bad.

"We can talk about this later," I say.

"Or we can talk about it right now."

"Are you sure?"

"Talk."

I grin. "This is last minute and really ridiculous to even do—and I am not going to be upset if you say no and laugh in my face because that's really what I expect. But ... to make a long story short, Bridgit has offered to let me take off work this week to go to Silver Springs. I told her I doubt you can go, but I'd ask."

The line stills.

"Jess, I know you probably can't, and I probably shouldn't have asked."

"Um, yeah, you should've. Let me call Moss and my dad real quick. We're just demoing this week, which the crew can do without me. And I haven't taken a day off in like ... maybe ever."

I smile. "So ... maybe?"

"Maybe. Let me call you back in a few."

"Awesome. Thanks, Jess."

"Anything for you. Talk to you in a bit."

"Bye."

I end the call and go back to researching potential retreat packages, the staff we'll need to move to the new department, and the expected budgets for each trip. When the phone buzzes beside me, I realize a solid hour has gone by.

Jess: Sorry for the delay. Dad was in a meeting.

Me: No worries.

Jess: Dad is going to check on the guys this week. I'll be with you.

I squeal.

Me: Really?

Jess: Really really. But I have to go now to get things in shape to leave. We go tomorrow?

Me: Yes. I'll make all of the plans now.

Jess: Perfect. I'll have to work late to get things squared away, but feel free to hang out at my house if you want.

Me: <laughing emoji> I have an apartment.

Jess: But my house is always open to you. I want you to know that.

Me: <heart-eye emoji> You're sweet. But I need to go home and get packed.

Jess: We'll see. <winking emoji> I'll call you when I'm out of here. Okay?

Me: Okay. Thank you for making this work.

Jess: <heart> Anything for you.

Anything for you. He ... what do you say to that?

"Let me treat you like you're mine. Pretend we're in a real relationship. Give me that. I want a real chance to make you fall for me."

Damn you, Jess.

Damn you, Jess.

17

JESS

I place a pod in the dishwasher and close it. A few quick presses of buttons and the machine starts whirring.

"Done." I grab a kitchen towel and dry off my hands. "Kitchen cleaned. Suitcase packed. Trash out to the road for pickup Wednesday morning. And I think that's it."

I toss the towel on the counter and start toward the living room. But as I move, I catch a glimpse out the window. Banks is walking down the road toward my house.

"Nope. Not tonight."

Racing through the sitting area and to the foyer, I snap the locks on the front door. Then, before he can see me, I make sure the door to the garage is locked and the slider in the backyard too.

I wouldn't put it past him to hop the fence and get in that way. Again.

The knocking begins. "Jess! You home?"

"No, I am not," I say, grabbing my phone and heading into my office. I open my call log and press the top name.

"Hey," Pippa says. "I was just thinking about you."

"Then come over."

She laughs. "I can't. I have too much stuff to do."

I sigh dramatically.

"Stop it. I can't go away with you for three days if I can't get my to-do list done."

"Need help? I'm helpful."

"If you come over, the only help you'll be is helping me find what room I like you fucking me in best."

"That's necessary information. I can be there in fifteen minutes."

The sound of her giggle is music to my ears.

I can't imagine if this life was *my life*. What would it be like to have access to Pippa all the time? To know, for a fact, that I'm going to see her. To be assured that she'll call me at some point in the day. To be able to send her flowers or lunch—to know she expects me to be there if she needs me.

There have been points in my life where all of that sounded like the worst thing that could ever happen to me. Most of my life, that's been the case. The idea that someone thinks they can just call me up and change my plans for the day was annoying. I wanted no part of the pressure of making sure a woman felt special. All those things were more of an irritation than a privilege—until now.

The doorbell rings through the house, and I groan.

"What's wrong?" she asks.

"One guess." I reach over and flip on the surveillance system. It takes it a second to connect. "But I'm pretty sure that you're so right that it's not even a guess anymore."

"What's Banks doing?"

I rest my elbow on my desk and watch him on the front porch. He's looking right up into the camera.

"You can't do this to me, Jess. I know you're in there," he says, pointing at the video recorder.

"Oh, Banksy—I can *and I am*."

"What does he want?" Pippa asks.

"On the surface, he wants to come in. Down deep, he wants to worm his way onto my couch, distract me, and take up all my time tonight. I just don't have the time or energy to screw with him."

He gets closer to the camera. "How do I know you haven't fallen and hit your head, huh? What if you were shaving and you sliced the vein in your throat? I'm out here worrying about you. Just let me know you're okay, man."

Pippa laughs. "Oh, my gosh. He's dramatic."

"This is only the tip of the iceberg."

"Fine. I hope you're not bleeding out in there," Banks shouts, so close to the device that all I can really see are the blurred insides of his nostrils. "Just remember, I was the one concerned. I was the brother who tried to check on you, but you *locked your doors.*"

"He really has boundary issues, doesn't he?"

I tilt my head. "Can you call them boundary issues if he doesn't acknowledge the boundary to begin with?"

"Good question. I don't know."

"Me either."

He turns his back to the camera, pulls out his phone, presses it to his ear, and marches toward Mom's.

I sigh. "It's like he holds me captive in my own house."

"You love him, and you know it."

"Meh."

I peek through the blinds until he disappears into our parents' house.

Does he need a hobby? Therapy? A puppy?

That's it. That's the problem.

He is the puppy.

"Banks is like having a puppy, and it's still potty training. It's so much work and inconvenient. But you look at their little face, and you just hope it's worth it."

Pippa cackles. "That's not nice."

"No, but it's true." I stand and stretch my free arm over my head. "What time do you want me to pick you up in the morning?"

"I don't know. It'll take us two or two and a half hours, I think. Check-in is at four. So we could leave at two and be fine."

"Cool. I'll be there at eight."

"Jess!" she says, laughing.

"What? My internal clock goes off at six. I'm used to sleeping with you now, so I'll probably be up all night anyway."

"*I slept with you one night.*"

I shrug. "So? You're addictive."

"You're full of shit."

"I'd rather you be full of me."

I can hear her smile. It's enough to draw the corners of my lips to the ceiling.

She must turn on the sink because water running fills the background. Dishes clatter, a drawer rolls, and silverware being dropped into a dishwasher basket rings through the line.

"I saw Chuck at work today," she says. "He was very non-Chuck-like. Nodded my way and kept on going."

"Good."

"Oh, also, I booked us a few things to do because I have to for work—that's the point of it to begin with. But I left a lot of downtime for us to do what we want."

"Is that an innuendo?" I ask, peering out the blinds again. Banks leaves Mom's house with a box.

"Maybe."

"Don't forget to pack Vibe Jess."

She laughs.

"I mean it," I say, grinning. "I want to see what Vibe Jess can do."

"He's already in my bag."

My eyes go wide as I nod appreciatively. *Nice.*

I start to nail down a time to pick her up when a car pulls in front of my house. Banks walks up to the side of it and chats with whoever is driving. The camera angle is too low to get a good view of what the car looks like but the hairs on the back of my neck stand up.

"I'll call you back later, Pip."

"What's wrong?"

"I ..." I pause as the door opens and feet hit the asphalt. And then the man and Banks make their way toward my walkway. "Someone is here with Banks."

"He's back?"

I roll my eyes. "He's never really gone."

The men get closer until, finally, I make out who it is with Banks. *Skylar Schultz.*

What the fuck? "I gotta go. I'll call you right back."

"Jess—"

I end the call, grimacing that I accidentally hung up on her but figuring I'll make it up to her tomorrow in oral favors.

They ring the doorbell before I can reach the door. I tug it open to see Banks and his box standing beside Officer Schultz.

"What's going on?" I ask.

Banks gestures toward me. "Ah, man. He's fine."

"What the fuck is going on, Sparkles?"

"Can you not call me that in front of people?"

I glare at him and then look at the cop. "What are you doing here?"

Skylar Schultz went to high school with Maddox. I don't really know him, just know *of him*. And I know that he can be a prick when he wants to be.

As we all can.

"I'm just here doing a well check," Skylar says. "We got a call that you weren't responding and someone needed to make sure you were okay."

My face falls. I whip my gaze to my brother.

Banks holds a finger in the air and takes a step back. "Don't assume it was me."

"Of course, it was you."

"You don't know that."

"*Banks.*" I hold out my hands in frustration. "What in the ever-loving *fuck* are you thinking? You're wasting the police's time because I didn't answer the door?"

He frowns. "So you were ignoring me?"

I jam my finger at him. If a cop weren't standing ten feet away from me, I'd probably knock Banks out. "You crossed a line tonight."

Skylar grips the cords on his chest and rocks back on his heels, watching the show.

"Me?" Banks asks incredulously. "If you were in there dead, you'd be changing your tune."

"I'm not dead. I'm alive. I'm fine. I'm ready to kick your fucking ass." I turn to Skylar. "I'm really sorry. My brother is a fool."

"A fool?" Banks gasps. "You do realize that no one else in this family cared about you tonight, right? Where's Moss? Where's Mad —*off with his little wife*?" He rolls his eyes. "Where's Foxx? They. Aren't. Here. *But I am*."

I don't know what it is about Banks, but somehow, someway— even during his shenanigans—it's hard to be mad at him. *Sometimes.*

"Again, Skylar, I'm sorry about this. I don't know what else to say."

Skylar's face is blank.

Shit.

"What were you doing in there that was so important that you couldn't answer the door?" Banks asks.

"That's none of your damn business."

"Pippa isn't here. So what? I just get written off now? I'm a nobody?"

I sigh. "Banks, I have to get packed. I can't do this with you and that—this—is why I didn't answer the door."

He lifts a brow. "Packing? For what?"

"Pip and I are going out of town in the morning."

"*On a work day*?"

"What are you, my father?"

Skylar tries not to smile.

Banks blows out a breath angrily. "So that's it, then. You're going to leave me too."

"I don't ..." I shake my head. "This doesn't even make any sense."

He adjusts the box in his hands.

"What's in that?" I ask.

He peers inside the container. "My high school wrestling trophies from my bedroom at Mom's."

Huh? "And why do you have them in a box?"

"Because she told me this morning that I can't have the Amazon password. So I called to get it from Paige, and she said Mom said I can't have it, and Paige can't help me jailbreak it." He looks at Skylar and sucks in a breath. "Is that disrespectful to call it jailbreaking in front of you?"

Skylar smirks. "It's fine. Keep going. This is entertaining as hell."

Banks turns back to me. "So if Mom doesn't want to act like a mom and share her passwords, then she doesn't get to keep my trophies."

What? I run a hand down my face. *What is happening here?*

Just a few minutes ago, I was relaxed and ready to go to Silver Springs with Pippa in the morning. And now I'm on the front porch, with Banks and a cop, listening to Banks complain about Mom's Amazon password.

What is this life?

"I can't. I'm done," I say shaking my head. "Skylar, again, I apologize. But at this point, if you want to arrest me, go ahead because at least I won't have to be with Banks in the back of your car."

Skylar turns his head to Banks. Banks slyly looks at Skylar. And together, they laugh.

I recoil, not sure I understand what's going on.

Why are they laughing?

Are they laughing at me?

"What's going on?" I ask, my teeth grinding together.

"Jess, I'm sorry," Skylar says, still laughing. "I told Banks I'd come by tonight and pick up the keys to my wife's car. He did me a favor this week and took a look at it. They couldn't figure it out at Mike's Mechanic in town, so Banks said he'd give it a look."

"So you thought you'd ... *what?* Pretend Banks called in an emergency because I wouldn't answer the door?"

"Well, I was here anyway and it kinda worked out," Skylar says. "We were just playing around."

"Cool." I flip my gaze to my brother. He walks backward, his eyes round as saucers. "I'm going to kick your ass."

"No. Love you. Be safe on your trip tomorrow." He makes his way down the sidewalk toward Skylar's car with Skylar on his heels. "And text me if you know Mom's password."

"Fuck off," I shout.

"Buckle up," he shouts back.

I shake my head and go back inside.

And I lock the door again.

Make it until morning. All things will be okay in the morning.

18

PIPPA

"Naturally, the one day I have off work, you decide to take a vacation with your new boyfriend," Kerissa says.

I put her on speakerphone and set it on the bed. Then I continue shuffling through my drawers for a lime-green bikini I know I own but can't seem to locate.

"We could go out to lunch, do a little shopping ... grab a latte and hit the bookstore," she says.

I laugh. "Lattes and bookstores? Pick me up in twenty. Forget Jess."

She laughs too. "What time are you guys leaving?"

"Soon. We can't check in until four, but he wanted to leave at eight this morning."

"Aw. That's sweet."

I grin. *It is.*

I'm surprised he let me talk him into a delayed departure. I'm even more surprised that I talked him into one. While I did have a lot of things to do before we leave, the hedonist in me threatened to say *screw it* and stay with him last night ... and *screw him*.

Knowing he's alone and wanting to be with me is a hard thing to fight against.

But I busied myself with tasks instead—paying a few bills, sending emails to keep the ball rolling at work while I'm away, and using up the rest of the fresh food in my kitchen that will go bad by the time I get home. I kept reminding myself that I'm happy to play along with his *real chance at making me fall for him*, but I have to keep my head on straight. Enjoy the attention, sure. But I must remember that this is a ticket to paradise with an expiration date.

I can't go all in.

Even though, in a perfect world, I'd dive in headfirst.

"When do you start at the Tourism Board?" I ask.

"Monday. I have today off—well, kind of off. I met Jovie for breakfast to go over a few things for my new position. We were supposed to have a meeting with Halcyon this afternoon, but they canceled. I don't know if I was supposed to go back to work or not, but no one is expecting me there so I'm not going."

"Fair." I glance down at the screen. "Hey, I need to call you later. There's a number calling that I don't recognize, and it could be about work."

"Don't worry about it. Go take care of your stuff. Call me as soon as you get back from your trip with all the sordid details."

I laugh. "I will. Bye."

"Goodbye."

I grab the phone, taking it off the speaker, and say hello.

"Hello, Philippa."

My stomach churns. *Seriously, Universe?*

I spot the string of my bikini under a tote bag—*why the heck is it there*?—and pull it out.

"Hi, Mother," I say with as much sweetness as I can inject without puking. "Two calls in one week? To what do I owe the pleasure?"

"I thought our conversation last week constituted a follow-up."

I toss the swimsuit in my suitcase and sigh. "Did you?"

"Philippa ..." She sighs right back at me. "I will never understand why you refuse to allow your father and me to help you in life."

"Excuse me? What are you talking about?"

My blood pressure soars because I know where this is going.

I rub my forehead, wishing I hadn't picked up. But the irony of her calling on the one day in years that I've woken up with an *almost joy* isn't lost on me.

And I hate that—for me ... and for her.

"You know what I'm talking about," she says, the words snappy. "I haven't interfered in your life in ages, and I'd hoped that maybe you'd grown up. Maybe you had run the defiance that's nearly ruined your life out of your system."

My mouth gapes.

"Can you imagine how it feels to have the head of one of the largest nonprofits in the country ask you about your children? And you have to tell them that, yes, you have a daughter and, yes, she chooses to waste the tools we equipped her with to play matchmaker?"

I stare into the mirror, not sure where to even start.

"Don't worry," she snarks. "I didn't put it to her like that. I wouldn't want to embarrass you."

I laugh sadly. "No, Mom, you didn't want to embarrass *you*."

My breath holds in my chest while I wait for her to correct me. I can't help but hope that she'll backtrack and explain that I've misunderstood. To say I don't embarrass her.

But I know deep in my gut that the clarification won't come. *There is no such thing as emotional nurturing in the Plum household.*

A swell of emotion rises in my chest, and I blink back tears. *I won't cry over her. Not anymore.*

"You know what's funny?" I say, my voice clouded.

"None of this is funny."

"You're right—it's really not." I gaze at the suitcase filled with my things for the trip. "I'm happy, Mom. I'm really, *really* happy."

"*How*? How could you possibly be happy? Look at your life and then look at what it could be and explain to me *how you could possibly be happy*?"

I sit on the edge of my bed and stare at the ceiling. There's really no point in trying to explain anything to this woman—especially happiness. Her definition of the word includes dollar signs, designer brand logos, and auspicious plaques she can hang on the wall in her corner office. My life will never make sense to her.

And *I'm* okay with that.

Still, there's something inside me that wants her to understand. If she'd only listen to what I'm saying, she could get it. She's logical and highly intelligent. This isn't a complicated topic to grasp.

My phone buzzes with a text. I pull it away from my face to read it.

Jess: I'm dying over here. Can I come and get you now?

A SLOW SMILE spreads across my lips as a wash of warmth floods my veins.

"Philippa?" Mom asks.

Me: Please do. Xo

Jess: THANK GOD.

I CHUCKLE AND STAND, pressing the speakerphone button again.

"I'm happy, Mom. I don't know what else to say." I toss the phone on the bed and organize my bathroom essentials into little spill-proof bags. "Every morning, I go to a job that I love, helping people navigate their relationships so they can be happy too. Then I come home to a place that's peaceful. Sometimes my neighbor lady will come by with a piece of pie for me. She'll ask me about my day and then tell me stories from when she was my age. And other times ..."

My hand stills over my bags as I imagine Jess's smile. The thought of him is like getting a hug. It gives me the confidence to keep talking.

"And other times my boyfriend will call me on his way home from work and tell me how lucky he is to get to spend time with me." I laugh. *Jess would love to hear me say that*. "It's a good life."

"But you've done nothing with it, Philippa. You have nothing to show for it. Your father and I were talking with Greg last night, and we want to remind you that there's still time to turn your ship around. Greg said he will—"

"I don't want Greg's help with anything. I'm surprised he even remembers who I am."

She scoffs.

"Look," I say, closing my suitcase. "I don't have a doctorate on the wall, but I have pictures of Kerissa and me singing karaoke in a dive bar in Tampa. I don't have fancy letters at the end of my name, but maybe someday I'll have three in front of it because someone really loves me and wants me to have them. When I die someday, no one is going to talk about the lives I've saved like they will you and Dad and Greg. *You are all incredible*. But if someone stands over my casket and can tell a funny story about us or remember a time when I made them feel seen, or that I was a friend to them when no one else was—I'm better than good with that."

Mom sighs, the tone filled with frustration.

"Thanks for calling." *I think*. "But I made stuffed peppers for my neighbor to eat while I'm gone, and my ride will be here shortly. So I have to go."

"Oh, Philippa ... Fine. I give up, anyway."

"Great. Talk soon."

"Hmmm."

The line clicks, and she's gone. *Not even a goodbye*.

I blow out a breath, anger and frustration licking at old wounds. *No, Mom, you "gave" up many years ago*. Unlike a certain man who says he's waited for me for fifteen years.

Thoughts of my family evaporate and are replaced by thoughts of Jess. *He'll be here soon. I better hurry*.

I tug my suitcase off the bed and wheel it by the front door. Then I hurry to the kitchen and collect the containers I made for Honey before jetting over to her house.

The sun is scalding as I stand on the porch and knock on the door. I peer in the window and spot her waving me in.

"Look at you," I say, stepping inside. "It's nice to see you up and moving around."

"I'm a bit slower than I'd like, but I'm getting there."

I close the door behind me and follow Honey into her kitchen. "I'm going out of town for a few days and was planning on making stuffed peppers this week like we talked about the other day."

She stops at her sink, her eyes lighting up.

"You have family to take care of you," I say, "and you have food."

"And I can use DoorDash," she says, proud of her new skill.

"I know you can use DoorDash." I laugh. "But I won't be here to eat these, so ..."

She reaches for the containers. "I'm not turning down homemade peppers." She takes them from me. "You are such a sweet girl."

The compliment catches me off guard after the conversation I just had with Mom.

"Where are you going?" she asks, putting the food in the fridge.

"Work trip to Silver Springs."

"Ah, fun. I just met a woman, Gloria, at the retirement center. She's been coming in the morning and walking with me. She got us a game of euchre tomorrow with a couple of other ladies. And she arranged for us to have a table that overlooks the pool." She smirks. "We're going to play cards and watch the pool for single men."

I laugh. "Sounds like a good time."

"She's a riot. She's on an arts committee dedicated to bringing art and music back to the schools. Did you know they took it out a few years ago?"

I shake my head.

"Well, apparently, they did, and Gloria isn't having it. She's organized a whole event around this—food, music, a silent auction. A bachelor auction."

"What?" I ask, laughing again.

"I know. She's a wild one."

Honey pulls out a chair and sits, motioning for me to sit too.

"I really have to go," I say. "My ride will be showing up any time."

"Understood. Thank you for the peppers, sweetheart."

"Of course."

I turn to leave. As I face the door, a woman walks in. For a moment, she seems shocked to see me. But she quickly gathers herself.

"Hi," she says, smiling brightly.

"Oh, Bee. You're just in time." Honey gets up and stands beside me. "Brooke, this is my neighbor, Pippa. Pippa, this is my granddaughter, Brooke."

Brooke smiles knowingly. "Okay, I'm going out on a limb here, but are you seeing Jess Carmichael, by any chance? Because there can only be so many Pippas in the world."

"Actually, I am. Well, sort of. We're seeing each other but not really?" I shrug, wishing I had a better explanation.

"Heads-up that Damaris has made you family. She takes Maddox's wife, Ashley, and me out to lunch once a month—and we do a little shopping or whatever. Anyway, we're going later this week and she's already mentioned inviting you."

I gulp. *She did?*

My face grows hot as I try to choose which part of this to focus on. Do I lean into the *oh, my gosh, this is going entirely too fast and is getting out of control*? Or do I ignore that and hear what she just said—"*Damaris has made you family.*"

Brooke giggles. "I've worked for their family for years—well before Moss and I became a thing. So I understand what you're feeling right now because I had the same experience." She shrugs. "Once they mark you as theirs, there's really nothing you can do about it."

"You didn't tell me anything about a boyfriend," Honey says, a hand on her hip. "What am I, chopped liver?"

Brooke and I laugh.

"I know that Jess Carmichael," Honey says. "And he's a ..." She whistles. "Back in my day, we would've called him a hunk."

"Honey ..." Brooke says cackling.

I love this—this feeling of being included. I barely know these people, really, and they're treating me like I'm a part of the group. *Part of the family*. But I don't know what to do with it.

Especially because ... *I'm not*.

"Kixx has decided you're his favorite out of us," Brooke says, grinning.

"Really?"

"Apparently, you have the same sense of humor."

I bite back a smile. "I made a joke about Jess's *big cock*."

"*That's what I'm talking about*," Honey says, nodding her approval.

I can't stop the giggle that pours out of me.

Brooke snorts. "I'll explain later, Honey." She leans back and looks out the window. "Jess is at your house."

My heart leaps in my chest and, suddenly, I forget about everything else but him.

No nasty mothers. No rotting veggies. No lunch invitations that I hope I get but also don't.

I kiss Honey on the cheek. "I'll see you when I get back. Brooke, it was nice to meet you."

"I'm sure I'll see you around." She smiles. "Thanks for looking out for Honey. She's talked about you nonstop since you moved in."

I think it's more like Honey adopted me, not the other way around. Somehow, she just knew I needed a Honey in my life too—and she stepped to the plate. *Well, with a plate—of pork chops, but it's the same thing, really.*

What a wonderful, woman. I want to be like her when I grow up.

"It's not a chore to hang out with her."

Honey pats my arm. "It's kismet, don't you think?"

"What?"

She grins. "Nothing."

"Go," Brooke says, laughing. "You have *a hunk*, as my grandmother likes to say, waiting on your doorstep."

That, I do. "I'll see you two later."

"Be safe, sweetheart," Honey says.

"I'll see you soon, I'm sure," Brooke says with a wink.

I give them both a smile, feeling like my heart is going to explode, and rush out the door.

And there he stands—on my doorstep—in a pair of shorts and a yellow polo shirt that I'm sure makes his eyes even greener. But I don't stop to check.

"Come here," he says, spreading his arms for me.

I don't think about it. I don't make a joke or laugh or tell him that I just met Brooke. Instead, I step into his hug and feel his arms tighten around me.

He kisses the top of my head. "I missed you."

"I missed you."

Because I did. Because I've been thinking about him since yesterday morning. Because my world hasn't quite felt right since I was in this exact spot—in his arms—the last time.

"You ready to go?" he asks.

"Yup."

He pulls away. "Let's get your stuff and hit the road, Dream Girl. I can't wait to have you all to myself."

I stare up into his eyes and see nothing but adoration. And given how I have nothing but absolute joy in my heart right now, I bet he sees the same thing in mine.

19

JESS

"This is *nice*."

Pippa moves through the entryway of our suite and into the living room. "I wasn't sure what the *extended suite* was because I booked last minute, but it said it was for newlyweds, so I went with it."

I set our suitcases down by the door. "Newlyweds, huh?"

"You know, for research purposes."

"I thought we were divorced?" I joke.

She looks at me over her shoulder and smirks. "And I thought you said you'd never divorce me." Slowly, she turns back to the glass.

She stands at the window, taking in the view of the gardens below. I make my way toward her, taking in the view of the woman in front of me.

The drive went entirely too fast despite me going barely over the speed limit. We swapped work stories. She told me about the couple that got married on their first date and went on to name their first baby Bloom. Bridgit gets pictures of the kid every year on their birthday. I told her about the time my ladder fell while I was on a roof. I had to wait an hour for someone to come put the ladder up so I could get down. We discussed our favorite bands, both agreeing that The

Doors were the greatest band of all time, stopped for snacks, and snuck kisses every few miles.

If I had been alone, it would've felt like double that.

I wrap my arms around her stomach from behind and pull her into my chest. She relaxes against me instinctively.

"How long are we here again?" I ask.

She chuckles. "What did you do, just get in the car and figure you'd get the details later?"

"I had all the details I needed to get in the car. The rest are whatever."

"We're here today and tomorrow. We leave on Thursday."

What? "I thought we had like four days or something?"

"There were a few scheduling conflicts. Every hotel and rental is booked from this weekend basically through the end of the month. There are different groups coming in or something. I don't know. It didn't matter to me, so I didn't lodge that information in my head."

I kiss her temple.

"You know what?" she asks.

"Huh?"

"I think I was really onto something with this retreat thing." She sighs with more contentedness than I've ever heard from her before. "Doesn't just being away make you feel different? I mean, I'm happy at home. I don't have marital issues or anything like that, and I still feel like a weight is off my shoulders here."

I rest my chin on the top of her head and smile. "Truthfully, I feel this way at home, too, if you're there with me."

She swats at my leg, making me chuckle. But before she pulls her hand away, she gently presses her fingers against my thigh.

And that's it—that right there. That's the juxtaposition that is Pippa Plum.

That's why I keep falling harder for her.

Pippa is feisty and full of energy. She's quick with a comeback and stands on her own two feet. But beneath all that moxie and strength is a woman with vulnerabilities—a woman who deserves someone to give her what she gives into the world.

And I want to be that guy.

I am that guy.

I just have to convince her to trust me enough to accept it.

She slides away from me and although I hate to, I let her go.

"I have a few things set up for us to do while we're here," she says, heading back to the entryway. "But if there's something you want to do, we can totally change it."

"Nah, I'm just here with you."

She tries to grab her suitcase, but I get it first.

"Excuse me, ma'am," I say, making a face at her.

She laughs. "I'm sorry. I'm not used to having my own private butler." She follows me into the bedroom, checking out the bathroom while I set our things in the closet. "Look at this tub. My gosh."

I glance over her head at an oversized, jetted bathtub.

"That thing is huge," I say. "I wonder how well they had to reinforce the floor to hold that weight."

"What? Is it going to fall through?"

"No." I laugh. "I'm just saying from a builder's perspective, that it's something they'd have to consider."

She looks at me.

"What?" I ask.

"I never would've thought about that." She faces me, smirking. "But you know what I would think about?"

"What's that?"

"You sitting on the edge while I'm kneeling in the water, sucking your cock until you come in my mouth."

I clench my teeth. "Keep it up, and we'll do it now."

"Can't do it now." She grins coyly and breezes beside me. "We have an appointment and then dinner reservations after that."

I hold up my hands, frazzled, as the heaviness in my groin deepens. *Damn her*. I adjust myself as I follow her.

"We're supposed to go paddleboarding in a couple of hours," she says, opening her suitcase. "Well, we can do that, or we can rent a glass-bottomed kayak."

"Can I fuck you in the kayak?"

She grins. "Probably not. I'm pretty sure you'd flip us with your ... enthusiasm."

"You'd definitely scare the wildlife with the way you scream."

Her cheeks flush, and she looks away. *So damn beautiful.*

My pocket buzzes, so I take out my phone. An alert is on the screen that my back door has been breached.

I quickly enter my code, so the police aren't called. And, just as I expect, Banks walks in like he owns the place.

"That little motherfucker," I say, shaking my head. "He didn't even wait."

Pippa looks up, confused. "Who didn't wait for what?"

I lower my phone so she can see what I'm seeing. Banks heads to the fridge and takes out a bottle of orange juice. He forgoes a glass, drinking it straight from the jug while getting comfortable on the couch.

She snorts. "He's saving you dishes."

I roll my eyes.

"Did you really not expect him to do this?" she asks, plucking a green bikini, tank, and shorts from her suitcase.

I smirk. *Yes. I. Did.*

Despite the frustration with my brother over his refusal to stay the fuck out of my house, there's satisfaction that comes along with it. *He shouldn't be so damn predictable.*

I walk into the bedroom, my fingers flying over the phone screen.

"*Jess* ..." Pippa draws my name out like she's concerned. "What are you doing?"

"*Nothing*."

"Jess ..."

I open an app, click a button. Open an email, click another button. Go back to the app and scroll through and exit.

Take that, you little shit.

Pippa stands, holding her garments. "Do I want to know what that was about?"

"You'll find out. Just give it a day or two."

She eyes me suspiciously.

My laugh is full of mischief as I wrap my arm around her and pull her into me. "What do you need? What can I do right now that would make your day better?"

Her head falls back, and she looks up at me with disbelief and confusion.

"*What*?" I ask.

"Let me ask you a question. If you could design the perfect day, what would it entail?"

I shrug. "I don't know, but this one is pretty fucking good."

She shakes her head.

"I'm a simple man, Pip." I pause, waiting for her to respond. But she doesn't. "You don't believe me?"

"I can't figure out if you're ... how serious you are."

"Are *you* serious?" I ask. *She can't be. I tell her the same thing repeatedly.*

"About what?"

I press a kiss against her lips, pulling back before she can deepen it. She's not going to sidetrack me, and I know my breaking point. *Namely, her tongue.* I release her before going into the bathroom and turning on the oversized shower.

"Am I serious about what?" she asks, coming into the bathroom too.

I peel off my shirt.

She stands quietly, watching me undress. It's almost as if she feels cornered, which is not at all what I want. But I do need her to know I mean what I say. I'll be damned if something goes awry because she assumed I wasn't serious.

That's bullshit.

"*Pippa*," I say, her name a whole damn sentence.

"*Jess*."

Her attitude makes me chuckle.

"Fine," she says, tossing the clothes in her hand on the sink. "I hear you say all kinds of things. But there's more to your dreams than me—*even if I am your dream girl*." She rolls her eyes.

I shove my hand under the water and then adjust the temperature.

"What are the other elements of a perfect day?" she asks, peeling off her shirt.

Little minx. I turn my back to her. "Why does this matter?"

"It just does."

I sigh as I drop my shorts onto the floor. "Fine. My perfect day would be sleeping in a little—but not too much because then I get a headache. No line at Muggers *and* they get my coffee right. Come home, maybe we make breakfast. French toast and bacon with real maple syrup, so you don't make me come back and answer that."

I catch her reflection in the mirror. She grins, unsnapping her bra.

Nope. Not yet. I look away. "Clean up the kitchen because Mom's palmetto bug warnings live inside my head rent-free."

She laughs.

"Then ... I don't know, Pippa. What do you want to do? Watch a football game? Work on the house? Go shopping? I don't care. I really don't. I'd take you out to dinner, though, to build the tension so when I get you home, you're all hot and wet for me. Then I can get all the way inside you before we go to bed."

I keep my back to her, waiting for her to fire back another question. But when a full minute goes by and she says nothing, I turn around.

She's naked, her hair piled on top of her head. She's a fucking vision.

My mouth grows dry and I fight myself not to go to her. I don't know what all of this was about, but it's important to her. So we'll do this until she's satisfied.

Then she'll *be satisfied*.

"You could replicate every day for the rest of your life, and you'd be happy?" she asks, her eyes sparkling. "Truly?"

"I mean, I might want some variation because French toast is good, but I also like blueberry muffins."

Her grin spreads until it's splitting her cheeks. "There's nothing else? Even if in ten years—"

"If I have *you* ten years from now and I live in a box on the beach with sand crabs snapping my toes while I sleep, I'll be one happy and lucky motherfucker."

She launches herself into my arms. I catch her, chuckling, and capture her lips just as they land on mine.

My tongue plunges into her mouth, taking ownership of it *and her*.

"We have a little over an hour to get to the paddleboarding place," she says between kisses. "Can I make a request?"

I pull my head back to see naughtiness spelled out on her face. *Fuck*. I roll my hips into her, letting her feel how hard I am.

"Request away," I say.

"Bend me over and fuck me quick and hard. Make me sore."

I flip off the water and snatch her up off the floor. She squeals as I carry her into the bedroom.

My girl asks, my girl receives.

20

PIPPA

"Do you think it's a bad sign that we're the only people out here?" I ask, laughing nervously.

Jess paddles next to me. "Well, it's late in the day on a Tuesday. That probably explains it."

I move my paddle through the water, working to keep my balance on the board. It's both easier and harder than I imagined it would be. The man working the boathouse was shocked that I've lived in Florida my whole life and have never used a paddleboard. *Why do outdoorsy people always assume everyone else likes the outdoors too? So weird.*

"What happens if I fall off here?" I ask.

Jess smiles. "You climb back on."

"That's it?"

His laugh echoes through the forest. "What are your other options, Pip?"

"I don't know." I glance around the water. "I'm just mildly panicking."

"How can you be panicking when you're the one that set this up?"

I glare at him, which only makes him laugh harder. "I didn't think this through, okay? Like announcing I had an ex-husband when, in fact, I didn't. Sometimes I'm impulsive and get in over my head." I peer into the green-blue water again. "I just hope I'm not *in there* over my head."

"I will fight an alligator for you. You'll be fine."

My quick turn toward Jess wobbles the board. My heart leaps and I squeal as I steady myself.

"Stop it," he says, holding out a hand.

I brush my fingertips against his but then pull them back. "I'm fine. This is fine. We're going to be fine."

We float down the river, growing farther away from the boathouse. With every minute that passes, the quieter it gets and the prettier it becomes.

The foliage on either side is thick and green. The water is surprisingly clear and the most beautiful, transparent teal color that looks otherworldly. Fish jump ahead of us. Birds squawk overhead. And beside me is a man who puts it all to shame.

Wearing bright blue board shorts, a white tank that highlights his muscled arms and golden skin, and a pair of aviators, Jess belongs on the cover of a magazine. *Or in a porno.*

"Hey, look at that." He points at the water. "See that?"

I lean forward to get a better look. "Is that a manatee?"

"Yeah." He smiles. "Cool, huh?"

"Yeah. It is."

"There's another one."

We drift across the water, using our paddles to go around the beautiful creatures. It's much less taxing than I feared. The current carries us with little effort.

"You feeling better over there?" Jess asks.

"Yes. The manatees look pretty defenseless, so if they can live in here, surely I can paddle for a couple of hours on top of it."

He grins. "What else have you never done that you've wanted to do?"

"I've never been to the Pacific Northwest."

"That's easily fixable."

"I've never had crème brûlée," I say. "I was watching a food show and they took their spoons and cracked the top—the crack was so satisfying."

Jess laughs. "You are so easily entertained."

"Lucky for you."

"What's that supposed to mean?" He grins as he paddles toward me. "Are you implying that I'm not working hard enough *to entertain you*, Miss Plum?"

His predatory gaze and sexy smirk send a chill racing through my body. It pools in the bottom of my core, making me clench.

The warm air is tempered by the trees overhead blocking the sun. Instead of the intense rays burning my skin, filtered sunlight casts a warm, happy glow over the river.

This definitely needs to go on the retreat menu.

"What's the bar for entertainment?" he asks. "What scale are you using to measure? Am I competing with Vibe Jess?"

"I measure with my heart."

"What the fuck does that mean?"

I try to keep a straight face but fail. I giggle, paddling until my board is floating next to his. "Kiss me." I pucker, leaning far enough over the side to reach him but not too far where I feel like I'll swim with the manatees.

"Oh, you think you can demand kisses now?"

"Well, you sure as hell don't deny me when I ask for other things."

His eyes sparkle as he grins, leaning toward me. "You're damn right I don't."

His lips touch mine. It's brief and sweet but also ... not.

My stomach flutters as Jess pulls away, and I'm left watching him and wondering why that just felt different.

"Hey," he says, dragging his paddle. "Look up there."

"Where?" I follow his gaze into the trees on my right. "What the fuck is that?"

"Monkeys."

"*Monkeys*?" My voice is high, almost chirpy, and the sound causes the monkey to smack its lips. "Why is it doing that?"

"It's just doing monkey things."

My heart thumps as I try to wrap my brain around what I'm seeing. "*There are monkeys in Florida*? How did I not know that?"

Jess shrugs, amused at my reaction.

"There are more of them." I watch as three others join the first monkey on a branch at the edge of the water. "They aren't going to attack us or anything, are they?"

"Probably not."

"*Probably* not?"

The troop begins to make noise, growing louder and louder as we float by.

"They might if you keep acting like you're calling for a fight," he says.

I look over my shoulder. "Can they swim?"

"Very well."

Fuck. "No, they cannot."

"Fine. They can't." He grins. "*But they can*. And they have Herpes B so if they grab you ..." He grimaces. "Not sure I'll fight them for you."

I gasp, making him laugh.

"See? We're by them and they didn't do anything to you," he says.

I paddle more into the middle of the river. "If I'd have known there were monkeys in Florida, I would've picked another adventure."

"There aren't supposed to be, but a boat captain released a few of them on an island out here to help tourism. And, unsurprisingly, they had babies."

"I'm shocked."

He shrugs like I'm the only person in the world that didn't know they were here.

We float without incident for a long time. We spot a couple of turtles and some fish. Jess saw an alligator but smartly didn't tell me until we were well past it.

The sound of the trickling water and the soothing colors of the environment are equivalent to a massage. Stress melts from my body; my mind rests. *Maybe I could be an outdoorswoman after all.*

"What would your perfect day entail?" Jess asks out of nowhere.

"Where did that come from?"

He shrugs. "You asked me earlier, so now I'm asking you."

Fair enough.

Very carefully, just like the instructor at the boathouse showed us, I crouch down and then sit in the middle of the board. I rest the paddle across my knees.

Jess looks at me over his shoulder. "Look at you being fancy."

"I know."

He sits too. "It was really me asking you about your perfect day, wasn't it?"

"Why would that have anything to do with me sitting down?"

"Because you associate a perfect day with being on your back."

I snort.

He drags his paddle, effectively slowing him until he's next to me again. "So answer my question. Your perfect day?"

I raise my face to the sky and breathe in until my lungs strain. Then I blow it out until there's nothing left.

"My perfect day would start with sleeping in—at least until ten," I say.

"That's half the day."

"Hey, this is my perfect day. You had yours."

He holds up his hands in defense.

"Thank you." I clear my throat. "There would be coffee and breakfast waiting for me—probably a chocolate croissant or just a croissant with Nutella on it. Oh, also, a fruit and yogurt parfait. I love those things."

Jess grins.

"Then I'd open all the windows in the house, and it wouldn't be too hot outside," I say. "Then I'd take a bath and do all the things that I never have time to do."

"Like what?"

"Exfoliate. Double wash my hair. Properly condition it. Mani-pedi. Apply one of the twenty lotions in my cabinet all over my body and then kill time with …"

I don't finish the sentence because it scares me.

My perfect day would be spent with him.

"Kill time how?" he asks as if he knows the answer. *As if he hopes he knows the answer.*

I search his handsome face. *Is there any way things could work between us? Any way at all?*

The idea of having this in some way every single day feels like the only answer in my life that makes sense. Going forward, I can't see my life without Jess. I don't want to.

But how is that possible so quickly? Am I just in a crazed state of lust that will diminish over time?

When he gives me his shy smile, the one that's my new favorite, I know how it's possible. *Because he's him.*

That doesn't fix my concerns. It doesn't make me any less terrified to let him down. Imagining him sitting beside me right now and telling me that I either have to change what I want out of life or lose him—like I'm not enough the way I am—causes my chest to ache.

If Jess gave up on me, I'm not sure I'd bounce back.

But I told him I would give him this week to win me over, even though he doesn't need a week because I'm already a goner. I've already bought into his brand of charm.

"If I have you ten years from now and I live in a box on the beach with sand crabs snapping my toes while I sleep, I'll be one happy and lucky motherfucker."

Those words he spoke earlier are burrowing into my heart, making me consider that he *would* be content if we were only an us.

As I search his face and find no shield, no mask—nothing but this man giving me everything he has—I wonder if maybe I should trust the process and give him what I get.

It would be the truth, after all.

I push my paddle into the water and smile at him. "I'd kill time by finding my man and seeing if he could help me rub it in."

His Adam's apple bobs before he slowly—so slowly—splits his cheeks into a grin. "Your man, huh?"

"Yeah. *My man*."

My core twists. My sex pulses as if it has Jess-controlled muscle memory. It correlates that look in Jess's eye with getting his dick shortly thereafter.

"I like the sound of that," he says, his voice rough.

I grin. "I like the sound of it too."

My entire body feels light. Airy. This is how I feel after I go through a cabinet that has needed cleaned out and organized for years and I finally do it. Everything clean and in its place.

All the pieces are where they should be.

He studies me, waiting on me to recant, I think. But I don't.

Out of nowhere, the skies open and rain falls in a heavy downpour.

"Ah!" I say, laughing. I lift my chin to the sky and let the water hit my face.

"Is this some kind of sign?" Jess asks, laughing too.

"*I don't know*." My voice is nearly a shout so he can hear me over the shower. "What sign could rain mean?"

"The last time it rained when we were together, you taught me how to dance."

My heart flutters as I remember that—*and* something Kerissa said after a trip a few months ago. "You know what else it means?"

"What?"

I shove my wet hair out of my face. "When it rains on a wedding day, it means the marriage will last."

Jess's smile couldn't be bigger if he tried. "Look at you, Pip."

"What do you mean?"

"Your couples retreat saved our marriage."

I burst out laughing, the sound mixing with the raindrops bouncing magically on the water.

"I'm definitely giving you five stars when we get home," he says.

"I hope you'll give me five stars way before then."

"How do you feel about skipping our dinner reservation and getting room service instead?" he asks.

"Only if I get to be dessert."

"Let's finish this and get back to the room," he says.

Despite the pouring rain and my shaky legs, I get to my feet. "Say less."

He laughs as I paddle away.

21

JESS

"These things are driving me nuts." I look down at my phone. "What the hell is this?"

"What's going on?" Pippa asks.

"I keep getting these texts about octopuses."

She laughs. "What? Why?"

I shrug. "I have no idea. Moss and Maddox get them too, but about different animals."

Pippa presses the button for the elevator.

Unknown: Octopuses can navigate through mazes, solve problems, and remember solutions. They can take things apart for fun.

I READ it aloud to her. "I can't tell if it's a joke or if someone is marking us for ... death or something."

"Or if it's Banks."

I look at her out of the corner of my eye. *"Or if it's Banks."*

It's the most obvious answer. Occam's razor would draw a line right to Banks's front door. When Moss first mentioned his random penguin texts, I immediately thought *Banks*.

But there's one problem that makes me unsure.

"Except," I say, grimacing. "They are all factoids. I'm sure he could cut and paste them from somewhere online—he doesn't have to know this shit. But, think about it. Would Banks spend his time looking up facts to send to his brothers? It just feels too ... smart."

Pippa snorts. "Be nice."

Me: And to think I've called them octopussies my whole life.

AS EXPECTED, there is no reply.

The elevator rings and the doors open. We step inside and press the button for our floor.

"Speaking of Banks," Pippa says. "What are you doing with that rooster?"

"I have plans for the rooster."

She quirks a brow. "Oh, really?"

"You see, Banks gets off on getting an immediate rise out of you. He likes instant gratification—like some other person I know."

She grins.

"In order to really get to him, you have to drag it out a little. Stay a step ahead. He's incredibly predictable and that's his Achilles heel."

"So ... you knew he'd break into your house when you left?"

"Yup. Granted, I thought he'd at least wait a day—or until dark. That surprised me. But there was no way he wasn't going to sleep on my couch while I was gone."

The elevator buzzes and we step into the hall.

"Why doesn't he just sleep at his house?" she asks.

"Now that, I don't know."

We make our way down the burgundy and gold carpeting.

"So what did you do to stay ahead of him this time?" she asks.

My chest shakes as I chuckle. *I can't wait for this fallout.*

"Are you not going to tell me?" she asks.

I snicker. "I can't risk it. Not that you would tell him," I say. "But I don't want to jinx it. I want to make sure it works before I say a word."

"Ah, I guess that makes sense." She plucks her shirt away from her body. "I can't wait to get these clothes off. I feel dirty and claustrophobic in them."

"No worries. I can't wait to get those clothes off you either."

She wraps her arm through mine, resting her hand on my forearm. Pippa is always playful and fun—but she's not often, or ever, this calm. Peaceful, even.

I'm not sure what happened on the river, but something shifted. I know the exact moment it happened—just before she called me her man. Her entire posture changed. It was like she was giving up a battle inside of herself and chose peace.

Chose me.

I touch the pad with our key, and the lock clicks. The cool air of our room welcomes us with a chilly hello.

"Let's order food before we get sidetracked," I say.

She frowns. "Or we can skip food."

"No." I bop her Cupid's bow as I walk by. "You need to eat."

"Um, I'm not hungry, but thanks."

"You're cute." I slide my shirt over my head and set it on the table. It's dry from the heat, just itchy. "What do you want?"

She sighs. "I don't care."

I find the menu in the drawer under the phone and skim the offerings. "A burger?"

"Great."

"Fries? Or—*what the hell*?" I laugh, swiping her shirt as it falls off my face and toward the floor. "What are you doing?"

I look at her and find her standing in her bikini top. Her fingers toy with the string holding it up.

"What? You're shirtless," she says, cockily. "Me too."

She pulls the end of one of the bright green strings and the fabric slips down her arms.

Her skin is a perfect golden color despite the sunscreen she slathered on before we got out of the car earlier today. Her nipples are already hard. Those big, round tits hang in a perfect teardrop.

My God.

"You were saying ..." She winks.

Fuck if I know. I look down at the menu in my hands. *Right. Food.*

I find the phone and press the speakerphone button, followed by the one labeled *dining* as instructed on the menu.

"Good evening. Room service. This is Taylor. How may I assist you?"

"Hello. I would like to place an order, please."

"Are you in room 707?"

"Yes."

I make the mistake of looking up.

Pippa's shorts are already gone and the strings at her hips are falling to the floor. I give her a warning look but she doesn't care. She gives me a coy smile and walks toward me, cupping her tits in her hands.

My blood heats as she reaches me. Her hands slide between my skin and the hem of my shorts. Maintaining eye contact, she slides my shorts to the floor.

Fuck.

"What would you like?" Taylor asks.

Pippa palms my cock, stroking it slowly up and down.

"Sir?" Taylor asks.

Pippa walks me backward until my legs hit the back of the desk chair. Then with a press of her fingertip against my sternum, sits me down.

I spread my legs as she kneels between my knees and licks the top of my cock.

I hiss, sucking in a hasty breath as her tongue flicks across the head.

"Sir? Are you there?"

"Yeah," I say, exhaling. "Um, I'm sorry. I would like ..." What was I getting? "Two burgers, please. Fries."

I reach between us and cup her breasts. The weight of them in my hands making me even harder.

She stares up at me, batting her lashes, before plunging her mouth over my length.

"Dammit," I whisper as she draws her lips back up again.

She giggles against my skin, sending a bolt of fire through my body.

"Would you like something to drink, sir?" Taylor asks.

"Yes. Two of whatever you have, please."

I give Pippa a look to behave. Naturally, she does no such thing.

She rises on her knees and grabs my balls with one hand. The other moves up and down my shaft. She sucks the head like it's a fucking popsicle before letting her spit drip onto the top and trickle down my cock.

I stand and ball my hands in her hair on either side of her head. Then I guide her mouth where I want it.

She looks up at me with wide eyes as I press myself inside her sweet little mouth.

"Be a good girl," I whisper.

Pippa wraps her lips around me as I slide back out.

"We have ..." Taylor gives me a laundry list of beverages from their quite expansive drink menu while I fuck Pippa's mouth.

Holding her head still, I thrust in and out of her mouth—slowly at first. *So fucking good.* I don't know if it's the warmth or the wetness or her fucking eyes looking up at me like she wants to please me, but it's the best damn thing I've ever felt.

It'll never get better than this.

"Cokes," I say, picking up my pace. "Two Cokes, Taylor."

Pippa cups my balls, lifting them slightly before stroking them downward with a gentle, but firm, tug.

"Just like that," I whisper.

She smiles around my dick.

"Would you like to hear about our dessert menu?" Taylor asks. "We have new offerings this month."

"Sure."

The sound of Pippa's mouth slurping on my cock nearly sends me over the edge. And when she uses her other hand to rub small circles just behind my balls, *I'm on the edge.*

Pippa moans as my cock swells. I scratch my fingernails against her scalp as I hold her head still.

"You want it in your mouth?" I whisper.

She nods as much as she can.

I wink. "Good."

"What would you like, sir?" Taylor asks.

"Surprise me. Thanks, Taylor."

I smack at the phone until the light turns off—just in time.

"Get ready to swallow."

I thrust my cock past her swollen lips and along her tongue repeatedly. Her fingers assault me below. It's too much.

"*Fuck, Pippa,*" I say through clenched teeth.

Every muscle in my body tightens as I tremble with the force of the orgasm. The intensity is so strong that I feel like I'm going to burst out of my skin.

She watches me fall apart, taking every drop of cum I spray into her mouth.

I exhale, the sound shaking as hard as my body. Finally, I open my eyes and slide my cock out of her mouth.

Her eyes are foggy as she wraps a hand around the base and licks up my shaft. Her tongue swirls along the head, causing another head-to-toe shiver to rack my body.

I sigh, collapsing back onto the chair.

"My God, Pip. *What the fuck was that*?"

She wipes her mouth with the back of her hand and gets to her feet. "That was the sexiest thing I've ever witnessed."

I take her hand and pull her until she's straddling me. Her juices cover my cock as she grinds her pussy on my lap.

"Are you ready to come now?" I ask, sliding a finger through her slit.

She cries out. "*Yes.*"

I pull her head to mine and explore her mouth—thanking it for making me feel so good. She continues to grind against me, rocking her hips against my lap, in her desperate attempt for relief.

Finally, I lean back and brush her hair out of her face. Her eyes shine as she looks at me. In the depths of her baby blues—right behind the lust—is a flicker of vulnerability that stabs me in the heart. *What is this about*? I don't know, but I hate it.

"There's not a thing in this world I wouldn't do for you," I whisper.

The flicker grows dimmer.

"As much as I love fucking you, I love hanging out with you and talking with you. And riding in the car with you and texting with you."

A hint of a grin tickles her lips. I run the pad of my thumb over them.

"The fact that you let me have this kind of access to you means everything to me. I'm one lucky bastard," I say, looking her in the eyes. "And I know when you think about that, you start overthinking it—but don't do that, Pip. *Please*. Just let me be your man."

I sound like a desperate fuck, but I don't care. I'll lay myself out there for her if that's what it takes. She needs to know I'm all in. No hesitation. This is what I want—*she's all I want.*

She leans forward and puts her arms around my neck, laying her head on my chest. And I hold her like that, stroking her back and kissing the side of her head, until room service knocks on the door.

22

PIPPA

"Have a good night," Jess says, shutting the door and flipping the latch lock. "Food is here."

The sound of the room service cart jingles as Jess pushes it into the bedroom. I lie in the middle of the mattress—right where he deposited me before getting the door.

My sex throbs and my thighs are heavy. *I need to get off*. But I don't dare touch myself because it won't take much stimulation to throw me into an orgasm. *I'm that close.*

Watching him lose himself from that angle was a sight to behold. The way he groaned with his head back—the veins in his throat surging from the intensity of his climax nearly made me come.

I slide my hand between my legs and then stop.

My jaws are sore. My scalp is tender. But, my God, *that was absolutely divine.*

I've never thought that having someone fuck my mouth would be something I was into. Turns out that I'm *very* into it.

Perhaps a blow job is a trust thing too. *Have I ever given myself willingly before?*

That would be a big, fat no.

"I'm going to give you two choices," he says, rolling the cart to a standstill. He takes off the covers and inspects the food. "You ready?"

"Sure."

He catches the location of my hand and lifts a brow.

I grin.

The lids go back over the food with a *ding*!

"Only one of us gets to eat right now," he says, standing at the edge of the bed.

"I thought you got two burgers?"

He grins. "I did."

Ooh.

"Are you hungry?" he asks me.

"Yes."

"Oh, okay." He bites his bottom lip while he thinks. "I'll get you a burger then."

I prop myself up on my elbows, sticking my chest out for his viewing pleasure. "What's the other option? Maybe I'm not into burgers tonight."

His lips twitch. "Well, that's your only choice. If you eat, you get a burger."

I play along. "Okay. Well, what's the other option then?"

"*I eat.*"

A shiver rips through me at the heat in his eyes.

Wearing only his board shorts from earlier, he walks into the closet. He rustles through things; I can hear zippers and bags moving around. Finally, he comes back into the room with a crooked smile.

My stomach tightens. The hair on the back of my head stands on end. *What's going on*?

"Call it ... who's eating?" he asks.

"What are you up to?"

"Three seconds and I get to decide."

"Jess ..."

"Three. Two. On—"

"*You*!" I say before he can get the last number out. "But what are you doing?"

My heart pounds as he climbs onto the bed. The mattress dips with his weight. "We're going to see which Jess is best." He lies beside me. "But we both already know the answer."

"That we do."

"Which is me."

"Maybe."

He looks surprised but also ... not. "Here." He hands me Vibe Jess.

"Where did you get that?" I ask, laughing.

"It was in your suitcase right on top. I didn't have to go through anything to find it."

My cheeks heat. "Okay. Are you going to let Vibe Jess get me off?"

He shrugs. "Show me what he can do."

I force a swallow and try to calm my heart. *This is a night of firsts.*

Jess lies on his side facing me, his elbow supporting him. He rolls one of my nipples between his fingers. "Go on. Show me."

I moan, already so close to the edge.

Sliding the vibrator between my legs, I bend my knees. Wetness coats my thighs and dampens the bed beneath me.

I press the button until I find the speed I prefer and then insert the tip into my hole.

My eyes flutter closed. "I have to be careful, or I'll come from this."

"You liked that earlier, didn't you?" he asks, amused.

"It wasn't bad. *Fuck.*"

The vibrations move through my body as I twist the head around my opening. My hips lift automatically as I plunge it into my pussy.

"Not as good as you," I say, the words hard to get out. "But good anyway."

I pump it in and out, my wetness sloshing through the room.

"I'm usually thinking about you right now," I say, forcing my eyes to open and look at him. His hooded gaze takes me a notch higher. "I imagine your fingers, your cock, sliding into me. I see your face when I close my eyes."

He drops his face to my nipple and flicks it with his tongue.

"Dammit," I say, shoving my chest toward his face.

I move the vibrator up my slit, the movement toying with my already swollen flesh. My knees fall wider apart as I bring it to my clit.

"This is what I like," I say, unable to keep my eyes open.

Jess's hand is on one of my breasts, massaging it as I did him earlier. His mouth covers the other—licking, sucking, and nipping at my peak.

There are too many things happening, too many things to feel.

"Is that what Vibe Jess does?" he asks, licking a trail to the side of my neck.

"Uh-huh."

"Let me ask you a question." He brings his mouth to my ear and nips my lobe. "Do you want to come on that or my face?"

"You," I whisper.

I'm already struggling not to lose it. But when Jess slides down the bed, gets between my legs, and slides a finger all the way inside me, I moan so loud that he shushes me, chuckling.

"I can't help it," I cry out.

He snatches Vibe Jess away from me. Before I know what's happening, I'm flipped over onto my belly.

"What's going on?" I ask, looking over my shoulder.

He runs an arm beneath me and lifts up my stomach. "Lift your ass in the air."

I get to my knees.

"Put your head down. Grab a pillow if you need one."

I press my chest toward the mattress and squeeze my eyes shut. I pant, anxiously anticipating him connecting with my soaked pussy.

"You let me come in your mouth," he says. "Now you can come in mine."

Fuck. Me.

He smacks my ass cheek, making me yelp again. *I fucking love that so much*.

I wad the blankets up in my fists as he buries his face in my pussy.

"*Jess!*" I scream, earning myself another swat to my backside.

My skin stings in the most delicious way from the contact. And when he places his palm over the spot and rubs it, I think I might pass out from how good it feels.

He turns on Vibe Jess and slides it inside me at the same moment he sucks my clit into his mouth.

And. That. Does. It.

"*Fuck*!" I yell out, grinding my ass against his face.

I can hear him sucking and licking ... and that only adds to the height of the climax.

I press myself as hard as I can against him, swirling my hips to get the most friction I can. The ferocity of the orgasm is so sharp that it makes me cry out.

I try to pull away, the intensity too much, but he grips the front of my thigh and holds me there.

"Don't stop," he says, his breath breezing against my swollen flesh. "Give me all of it."

He presses a kiss to my clit and then runs his tongue slowly, firmly, down the length of my pussy.

The vibrator slows and then stops. It falls away from my body. Jess's tongue swirls against my clit until the last shudder of pleasure has passed.

He helps me fall to the mattress, completely spent.

Jess curls up behind me and pulls me into him. "You, my girl, are the dream."

"What are you doing to me?" I whisper. Every piece of my body is too heavy to move.

He chuckles against the top of my head. "Do you like it? Tell me if you don't."

"I'll put it to you like this—let me take a nap and then we can do it again."

His body rumbles as he laughs quietly, pulling me tighter. "We have to get you cleaned up."

"Not really."

"No, we do."

I yawn. "Meh."

He scoots away from me and off the bed. Vaguely, I sense him moving across the room and hear the tap turn on in the bathroom. Just as I'm about to doze off, he's sliding beside me again.

"Spread your legs," he says.

When I don't cooperate, he does it for me.

The washcloth is warm and his touch is gentle, as he carefully cleans me up.

"I think you should get up and go to the bathroom," he says. "I don't know a lot about the woman's part of things, but I'm pretty sure that's standard behavior."

"I will." *Later*.

My head is so fuzzy, and my bliss so complete, that I'm not about to ruin this moment. Not even the vague memory of dinner sitting idly somewhere is enough to make me wake up.

He pulls the blankets over my naked body and kisses my cheek. "Sweet dreams, Pip."

"Night."

I drift off to sleep thinking about standing in Jess's kitchen with the windows open, making French toast.

23

JESS

"My name is Bobby, and I'm a chef at Chutney here inside the Waterfront Hotel. I'm excited to hang out with the two of you this afternoon."

A storm rages on the other side of the windows behind Bobby. Rain pelts the glass, creating a soothing backdrop to the colorful kitchen. Pippa leans against my side as if she needs to touch me as much as I need to touch her.

We lay in bed all morning and listened to the rain. It was nice not having anywhere to go or anything to do. In our assessment of the retreat, we decided to suggest that couples have a choice to include free days. While paddleboarding was fun and let us experience something new together, our lazy day today shifted our relationship from great to incredible.

Pippa grips my bicep and gives it a gentle squeeze.

"I'm Jess, and this is Pippa. Thank you for your willingness to share your time and skills with us," I say.

"Hey, no problem. I love food and the community aspect behind it. Anytime I can talk about food, I'm in." He laughs. "I heard it through the grapevine that you're thinking about creating a couples retreat package at the hotel?"

Pippa perks up. "Yes, actually, I am. My company will be offering packages in the coming months. Silver Springs is centrally located, and there are so many fun experiences that can be incorporated. I thought a cooking class might be a fun option."

"I love it. Nothing brings people together like food." He looks between us. "Are you two just testing this out, or are you on a couples retreat yourselves or ..."

Pippa smirks. "This is my ex-husband, Jess—"

"Excuse me," I say. "*I'm not her ex-husband.*"

Bobby furrows his brow.

"I'm her boyfriend—her man since we aren't in high school." I grin, challenging Pippa. "She tries to resist me sometimes, but it doesn't change the fact that she owns my heart."

Pippa grins, resting her forehead on my arm. I reach behind her and grab her waist, pulling her closer.

"May I ask who does the majority of the cooking in your relationship?" Bobby asks. "Does one of you do the heavy lifting, or do you both enjoy it equally?"

"I do most of it," Pippa says.

"Awesome. What's your favorite thing to make?" Bobby asks.

"I'm in a cold soup season," she says, laughing. "I just made a tomato with tarragon concoction with a dollop of crème fraiche on top. So good."

Bobby looks impressed. I *am* impressed.

She can cook, too? How does she just get better?

"The tarragon is a nice touch," Bobby says, moving around the oversized island. "So many people are afraid of using fresh herbs, but I couldn't cook without them."

"Me either. The freshness really brings a dish together."

"Have you ever used fenugreek leaves?" he asks.

"No."

"We're going to make a chicken tikka masala today, and the fenugreek leaves at the end do just what you're saying. It gives the dish a maple-y flavor that makes you go, '*Hmm, what am I tasting*?'"

Pippa smiles brightly, taking an apron from Bobby. "I can't wait."

"Thanks," I say, taking an apron too.

We fasten them around our middles, then give our hands a good scrub. While we prepare, Bobby gives us the history of Chutney. As fascinating as it is to hear about the fire that destroyed the kitchen fifty years ago, I'm more interested in Pippa.

I've never seen this side of her before.

She soaks in the information, engaged in the learning process. Her brows pull together, and she nods eagerly. I don't even know what *masala* means. She's speaking a language I don't understand with Bobby ... and it makes me smile.

I take a step back and observe.

Pippa asks questions about spices and cutting techniques, surprising Bobby with a knowledge base I didn't know she had either. She stands a little taller when he asks her if she's thought about working with food professionally.

What else is there to know about her?

"Jess, if you could join us over here," Bobby says, waving me to the island. "We're going to start our chicken prep. I prefer chicken thighs for this dish because they're a juicier and more forgiving cut of meat than, say, breast. But you can absolutely use something else if you'd like."

"I prefer breast," I say, taking an elbow to the ribs from Pippa.

Bobby laughs. "Me too, man. Me too."

"I'm a shoulder girl myself," Pippa says, making us all laugh.

"We're going to pierce the thighs with a fork so the marinade we make can soak all through the meat. Pippa, would you like to do the honors?"

"I'd love to."

She takes a fork off the counter and pokes it all over the thighs lying inside a foil-lined tray.

"While you do that, I'm going to grab the fenugreek," Bobby says. "I leave it out during a lot of these classes, but I think you'll enjoy it."

"Yes, I'd love to try it," Pippa says.

"I'll be right back." Bobby exits the room, leaving us alone.

Finally.

"Can I tell you a secret?" I ask. "I don't have a fucking clue what we're making, and nothing you guys talk about makes any sense to me."

She grins. "I watch a lot of cooking television. When I moved out of my parents' house, I got tired quickly of eating ramen and microwavable macaroni and cheese. So I taught myself how to cook."

"That's one of my favorite qualities about you."

"What is?"

I smirk. "You're a quick learner."

Her eyes find mine, and the fire inside them is exactly what I hoped to see.

"I'm in a very adept mood today," she says, smirking back at me. "Is there anything you think you could teach me when we finish here?"

Fucking hell.

Before I can answer her, my phone chirps. *Family group text.*

And then it chirps again.

And again.

I snicker, drawing it out of my pocket.

"What's that little smile about?" Pippa asks. "You've already washed your hands. You're not supposed to touch your phone."

"Trust me. *This will be worth it.*"

I shove my tongue in my cheek and unlock the screen.

Boom.

Paige: OMG JESS.

Moss: This. Is. Gold.

Maddox: <laughing emoji> <crying emoji>
<knuckle bump emoji>

My fingers slide over the keys.

Me: Did something happen? <smirking emoji>

Paige: I just had to come to Nate's office because tears were streaming down my face. Your brother is going to <knife emoji> you.

Me: Oh, no. Banks is YOUR brother. I've never claimed him.

Maddox: I can't breathe I'm laughing so hard.

Moss: I'm borderline pissed I didn't think of this. This is genius-level shit.

"Okay." Pippa drops the fork and comes around the island. "What's happening? Tell me."

"Banks has had an *interesting* morning."

Her eyes widen. "What did you do?"

Chirp!

Foxx: Someone better be dead.

Maddox: Not yet.

Moss: Jess is on his deathbed. <skull emoji>

Paige: Foxx isn't going to bail Banks out of jail this time, so who's going to do it?

Foxx: He's in jail AGAIN?

Moss: Not yet. <laughing emoji>

A SCREENSHOT LOADS onto the screen, and I burst out laughing. *It's so much better than I dreamed.*

Pippa gasps and tugs the phone to get a better look. Her hand clamps over her mouth.

Golden Years Dating App: For women 65-80 looking for love and companionship.

Name: Sparkles
Age: 25
Stats: 5 ft 7 in, 185 lbs, Brown hair, hazel eyes
Bio: I'm looking for a sugar grandma willing to give me all her attention, and in return, I'll give her all of mine. I have lots of energy and a big cock I'd love to bring to your house.
Might be a match if: You need constant companionship and have no regard for personal space.
Fact that surprises people: I'm a good driver. Need a chauffeur for your errands? I got you.
Together we could: Make each other feel wanted.
Other: Not opposed to a roommate situation.
Contact preferences: Call or text me at 555-555-5555

"Did you do this?" she asks, trying to hold in her laughter. She points at the picture on the profile—the one Banks stuck to every damn thing in my house.

"Look, the little motherfucker needs attention so bad that he broke into my house while I was gone. I have a giant rooster in my front yard, thanks to him, and he made me think he called emergency services the other day. I've had it with him and his shit."

Foxx: He had that coming.

Foxx has silenced notifications.

"When did you do this?" Pippa asks, giggling.

"The night before we left. I couldn't sleep *because someone wasn't in bed with me,*" I say. "And I lay there thinking about how Banks would break in while I was gone and do God knows what. I had some time on my hands and thought—you know, he needs someone with time on *their* hands. Someone who understands adolescents, *who has a house.*" I shrug. "It worked out."

Me: How did you find out?

Maddox: He called me screaming.

Moss: Mad sent me a screenshot.

Paige: Ashley called me.

Maddox: His phone started going off this morning around five o'clock. Then the texts started coming through.

Me: How did he realize what it was?

Moss: GLORIA. <laughing emoji>

Paige: A woman named Gloria.

Maddox: Gloria. She's apparently Honey's friend. She recognized him—so she had to have matched with him, right?

Me: Pip fell asleep early last night, so I did Banksy a favor and matched him with some lovely ladies. All they had to do was match with him back. <smirking emoji>

Maddox: Well, Gloria matched with him, I guess, and then called the number. It went downhill from there.

Moss: Or uphill, depending on which side of this you're on.

Banks: I AM NOT FIVE SEVEN.

I BURST OUT LAUGHING.

Pippa washes her hands while trying to dry her eyes on the sleeves of her shirt from laughing so hard.

Moss: THAT is what you're pissed about?

Me: <laughing emoji>

Banks: I can't even text because MY PHONE WON'T STOP GOING OFF.

Me: Aw, Sparkles. Look at all the attention you're getting. They all want you. This is the pinnacle of your dreams, isn't it?

Banks: I hate you. Also, I AM FIVE-ELEVEN.

Paige: I have to get back to work. Can someone make sure there's no bloodshed?

Moss: Big nope.

Me: Want me to deactivate your account?

Banks: It would be nice.

Me: Will the rooster be gone when I get back?

Moss: SO WELL PLAYED. <clapping emoji>

Maddox: It really is impressive.

Banks: The rooster will not be there.

Me: I come home tomorrow.

Banks: I said it won't be there.

Me: Deal. But I'm just deactivating it—not deleting it. Don't fuck with me.

Banks: <face with steam from nose emoji>

I SWIPE OPEN the app and, as promised, deactivate Sparkles's account.

Pippa sighs. "I wish I had siblings like yours."

"You want Banks? I'll let you have him."

She laughs. "I can't imagine what it's like having that bond. Greg and I never had it. He was the golden boy, and I was the kid sister who couldn't shine bright enough. I was the diamond in the rough who didn't come out of the rough. I just got in the way."

Nope. I pull her into my chest and look down at her.

"But it's fine," she says, smiling sweetly at me. "They're my family but not my people."

"So you wish you had a big family growing up, but you don't want one now. Right?"

She starts to frown but catches herself. "Exactly."

I search her eyes, wondering how much I will have to dig through to get to the truth. The diamond in the rough. Because maybe she's right. Maybe she's been pushed down for so long—maybe even hiding—so she doesn't shine too bright and attract all the goodness that's coming to her.

I'll help you, Pippa. You just gotta trust me.

"Wanna blow this joint and go back to our room?" I ask, wiggling my brows.

She laughs. "No, I don't. Bloom Match paid for this. We need to experience it because I have to be prepared to give Bridgit the details."

I groan, rolling my eyes.

"I'll tell you what," she says, playing with the collar of my shirt. "I'll make you a deal."

"What's that?"

"If you can make it through this cooking lesson, I'll let you pick what we do for the rest of the night."

My brows lift to the ceiling. "Really?"

"Really."

"And you have to do it."

She gulps.

"Deal," I say before she can change her mind.

She's going to squirm for the next hour and a half. I'm going to try not to be too bored with chicken tikka masala. But when this is over, I know what we're going to do.

And it's not what she expects.

I grin. "Here comes Bobby. Let's hurry this up and get out of here."

Then I go to the sink to wash up again, trying not to laugh again at Banks's reaction to his successful foray into app dating. *The fool.*

24

PIPPA

"This is what you wanted to do?" I ask, laughing.

"Don't laugh. It makes me self-conscious."

"*Right.*"

I'm sitting at the bistro-esque table on the balcony of our room. Thunderclaps sound off in the distance before bolts of lightning strike through the sky.

Jess hands me a glass of wine and then sits across from me.

We had dinner at a small restaurant by the river that Bobby suggested. As promised, it was quiet and slow—and the food was delicious. The owner, Ted, came out to check on us, and he and Jess hit it off. I sat back and watched them chat it up about lumber prices, cars, and the best place to fish in the state.

I sipped my wine and appreciated the moment. They welcomed me into the conversation and listened to my unsupported opinions as if they mattered. But even more impressive was how easy it was for Jess to make friends with Ted.

Making friends has never been super easy for me. Growing up, my parents didn't have people they hung out with on the weekends. Greg was always too busy wrestling or preparing to fulfill his destiny to know other kids' names. Even in the two semi-serious relationships I've had, the guy wasn't overly friendly to other males.

I've never stopped to think about why that has always been a reoccurring theme in my life. But now, after seeing Jess and his interaction with Ted—and thinking about the way Jess interacts with the world, I can honestly link my previous choices back to my parents.

I never felt valued. Never felt as though I was worthy of notice.

I orbited their world, but I was never part of it. *I was always so ... alone.*

In retrospect, it makes perfect sense that I dated egocentric men whose worlds were equally small and whose interest in others was virtually nonexistent.

And that is not Jess Carmichael at all. He treats me as if I am *his world.*

"It was nice of Ted to send us back with a bottle of wine," I say before taking another sip.

"I don't even like wine, and this shit is good. It's from a winery in Georgia. Landry Family Winery or something like that."

"We'll have to see if we can find them at home."

Something I said makes Jess's eyes light up, and he sets his glass down.

"We go back to Kismet Beach in the morning."

I can barely hear his voice over the wind.

"Yeah," I say.

"What happens then?"

A lump settles in my throat. The question I feared—the topic that I've worried about off and on all day—is now in the open.

As much as the thought of hearing it made me want to puke ... I also wanted to hear it. It's confusing. The only way this conversation didn't scare the bejesus out of me was being able to partially control when it happened. I knew if I let Jess pick what we do tonight, he'd pick this. And I've spent all day trying, and failing, to prepare my response.

"What do you want to do?" I ask, turning it around on him.

His eyes shine. "You know what I want to do."

I hum.

He reaches across the table and takes my hands in his.

My chest wobbles as I prepare to be the most vulnerable that I've ever been with another person.

Why?

Because he deserves it.

Because I think I love him.

"When I'm with you, life makes sense," I say simply. "When I wake up in the morning, I don't feel so ... small."

He wants to say something. He bites the inside of his cheek, and I know him well enough now to know that means he's holding back.

"Until recently, my life felt like an island floating around in the middle of the world. Other people lived on continents and in island chains, but I was on this rock all by myself. And it was fine," I add as his brow furrows. "It was just the way it was. But then you come along and muscle your way in, and for the first time in my life, I felt like I wasn't alone."

I promised myself I wouldn't cry. No matter how embarrassing or sad or terribly wrong this conversation went, I wouldn't cry.

So I blink back tears as they start to form in the corners of my eyes.

He rubs my knuckles with his thumbs, waiting on me to continue.

"Jess, you won me over before we got here," I say, my voice cracking. "And it scares the crap out of me to say this to you, but I know we have to have this conversation, so I'm trying to just be honest and lay it all out there."

"Why does it scare you? I don't understand."

"Because ..." I blow out a breath. "What are your life's dreams? What do you hope for?"

"Happiness."

"More specifically."

I know his answer—he wants a family. Of course, he does. But I need him to say it, to admit it to me, so I can show him why I'm not sure what I want when we go home.

Or, rather, I know what I want and what I can't have.

He lets go of my hand and sighs. He sits back in his seat, watching me. "Pretty sure happiness is a full sentence."

"You're not getting out of it that easy."

"What do you want me to say? Do you want to go back to the kid thing? Because that's the only argument you've ever proposed about why we could never work that made any sense at all."

I still.

My heart pounds, and blood pressure soars. Panic rises through the bile at the base of my throat.

All I want to do is run.

But I don't.

"Yes," he says. "I've always thought that having kids was in my future. I saw myself doing the same things I did with my dad with my son or daughter. Is that what you want to hear?"

No.

He leans forward, his fingers locked around the base of his wineglass. "Why do you not want kids?"

"I don't like them." I give him my canned answer, but it's the truth. It's been the truth for as long as I can remember. "I've built my whole life around not wanting children, and it's a relief every day when I wake up without a screaming kid. I'm genuinely happy with my life choice. I realize it's not the popular one, but it's how I feel."

"All right." He holds my gaze. "Now what's the real answer."

I push my glass into the center of the table. "I gave you my answer."

"I'm not going to try to change your mind, Pip. I just want to understand you."

Why do you have to be so fucking perfect?

Why do you absolutely terrify me?

I stand, needing to move so I can think. Sitting in one place and looking at him won't help me recall years of trauma.

My heartbeat races, amping up another notch. My palms sweat, and I blame it on the humidity, even though I know that's untrue.

I take a deep breath and blow it into the wind.

This is going to hurt. It's going to be salt into a wound, and it might very well be the moment that I see the disappointment in Jess's eyes. It'll be the moment he realizes I'm not the person he wants forever.

"It took me a very long time to detach emotionally from my parents," I say, my voice hollow. "I had a very ... dark time when I felt this crushing loneliness. But it was that or allow myself to be reminded at every possible moment that there was something I was doing that wasn't good enough." I blink back tears again. "Or, sometimes, that me as a person was somehow flawed. It didn't matter if I dotted all the *i's*. I dotted them, so they were blemished."

I walk to the other side of the balcony and face him.

"I've managed to make a life I love," I say, lifting my chin. "And I worked damn hard for it. I can't imagine having a child with someone and then ..."

Hot tears fill my eyes.

"Then what?" he asks, his tone heavy.

"Then have them change their mind." I wipe my nose with the back of my hand. "Or what if my child doesn't love me? What if I'm a terrible parent and they grow up hating me? What if I'm really my mother and—"

"*Stop.*"

"*But what if?*"

Lightning marks the sky, but it has nothing on the intensity on Jess's face.

I suck in a breath. "I'm not lovable."

"*Fucking stop it, Pippa.*"

"It's true. There's something inside me that's a fatal flaw. I can't fix it. I've tried."

Tears cascade down my cheeks as I say the things aloud that I've never had the courage to say before. Expelling them into the air feels like a dam is breaking, and all of the emotions held hostage by those words come spilling out.

"How? How could you possibly be happy? Look at your life and then look at what it could be and explain to me how you could possibly be

happy? I'd hope that maybe you'd grown up. Maybe you had run the defiance that's nearly ruined your life out of your system."

"You are the biggest disappointment of my life."

"My own parents didn't love me forever, so the chance of some random person choosing to do it for the rest of their life is pretty null."

I wipe my nose with the back of my hand as the tears keep coming. I can't stop now—I have to say it all. I have to tell him my greatest fear so he understands.

"*No one has ever loved me, Jess.*"

His chair scoots back so fast that it falls over, dinging against the sliding glass door. He takes my hand and pulls me into him. His arms wrap so tightly around me, he holds me so close to his chest that I can barely breathe.

My body shakes as I sob against his pink polo shirt that I teased him about all evening. He rubs my back, his chin resting on top of my head, and sways with me back and forth.

The thunder grows closer. In the distance, rain clatters against the tops of buildings and onto the streets. The wind picks up, but Jess holds me like none of that matters.

Finally, he pulls back and wipes my hair out of my face. "I've loved you for fifteen years. Doesn't that count for something?"

I smile sadly. "You're a fluke."

"I'm a fluke that's so in love with you that I can't think straight."

I sniffle.

He grins at me. "I heard every word you said. *All of it*. And you know what?"

"What?"

He holds my face and kisses my forehead. "Even though your parents purport to be highly intelligent, they're clearly not. They're missing out on knowing and loving the most wonderful girl I've ever known. Their loss, Pip. I absolutely, completely, stupidly love you, and nothing will ever change that. Nothing ever has."

My heart swells.

"When I said my dream was for happiness, I meant it for me and you. Because the only way I'm happy is if I have you," he says. "I want to create a life with you that's a little of mine and a little of yours. I want you to help me make my life better, and I want to do the same for you. I want French toast breakfasts and the windows open and bottles of random wines on balconies while we talk about nothing and everything."

I smile.

"This is the woman I love—right here. And I want you just the way you are."

"But what about kids? I won't change my mind, Jess. How can you give that up for me?"

Please be honest. Please don't tell me things you think will keep me with you. That would kill me, Jess.

He sighs. "Because kids were a part of the picture—they were never *the picture*. I come from a large family, Pip. I don't need to replicate that. I really don't." He gently kisses my forehead, my eyes, my cheeks. "I need you to hear me and believe me on this, because it's the absolute truth. For the last half of my life, it's only ever been my dream to have you in my life. For you to be mine. The picture was me and you." He grins shyly. "It's always only been me and you for me."

I bury my head in his chest.

"Do you even know how many kids my brothers are going to have? And Paige? *Fuck*. Our nieces and nephews will run to our house to escape my siblings."

I smile against him. "I could be okay with that."

He groans. "Oh, wait."

"What?"

"There is one more condition."

My heart beats harder. *What now*?

"You're going to have to be okay with raising Banks because I can't get out of it. I've tried," he says.

I laugh, my whole body shaking. The light is back in Jess's face.

Rain begins to fall around us, coming in at an angle and drenching us from head to toe. But we don't move. We don't even flinch. We just stare at each other and smile.

"What about your family?" I ask.

"They love you. My dad thinks you're his long-lost daughter."

I laugh.

We begin to sway back and forth, my arms draped over his shoulders, as thunder fills the sky.

"I love you, Jess."

He lowers his face and kisses me softly. "I've waited for you to say that forever."

"I've waited to say it forever."

"I was starting to think maybe you never would." He grins. "I want to take care of you, Pip. We've given up so many years apart that I don't want to give up anymore."

I take a deep breath. I'm not sure where he's going with this. I'm not sure where I want him to be going with this either. But for the first time in my life, I feel like whatever he says will mean the two of us together.

This must be what it means to be loved. If so, I've never had this before.

It's a feeling of safety—not just physically, but emotionally.

It's being respected enough to be honest.

It's being valued enough to be transparent.

It's not just being seen, but also being heard, and knowing that no matter what you do or say—the other person will still be there. Even if you screw up.

Maybe even because you'll screw up. At least you know you won't have to do it alone.

This is a feeling I'll never forget.

"What are you saying?" I ask.

"I don't want to leave room for misinterpretation."

I grin, my heart so full it might explode. "So interpret."

He chuckles. "It's me and you. We're doing life together now. There's no more fake relationship situations, no more pretending. I'm extending my seven days to get you to fall in love with me until forever. I'll make you fall for me every day for the rest of my life."

My God, this man.

I stand on my tiptoes and kiss him.

He rests his forehead on mine. "So …"

"So …"

He chuckles. "So I need you to please tell me you're in the same way."

I start laughing, wrapping my hands around him.

"I mean it. I need to hear you say it."

"Jess Carmichael …" I wink at him. "I'm. All. The. Way. In."

He kisses me slowly, tenderly, and completely as we dance in the rain.

25

PIPPA

Jess strokes my arm as we lie in bed and listen to the rain.

I think we're both processing our new future together, as well as the fact that we go home in the morning. It's easy to be a couple here—where reality doesn't exist. We're funneled away from work stress, busy schedules, and life stress. Exactly what a couples retreat is supposed to do.

I grin against him and hold him a bit tighter.

There was no way of knowing when I sat down and conceptualized my retreat idea a few weeks ago that it would end like this. I didn't plan on having a fake ex-husband when I blurted out that I had one—and I didn't expect it to be Jess freaking Carmichael.

Or that the retreat would turn out to be exactly what I needed.

Jess kisses the top of my head.

What we needed.

Maybe I was onto something without even knowing it. I was shooting in the dark, having had no real relationship experience to go on. *I hate, hate that Chuck the Fuck was a tiny bit right again.*

There it is—Chuck and right in the same sentence again. It's blasphemy.

Yet by stopping the routine mechanics of life and giving the universe a chance to reframe my relationship with Jess, something truly amazing bloomed.

"What are you thinking about?" he asks.

"About how brilliant I am."

He chuckles.

"Do you think we would've gotten here without Chuck the Schmuck needling me and my reaction?" I ask.

His fingertips leave a trail of goose bumps in their wake. "I'd like to think so."

"I'd like to think so too. But ..." I pause. "Maybe even assholes have their purpose, you know? If it weren't for him getting that reaction out of me, I wouldn't have been at Shade House to vent to Kerissa that day."

"True."

"And if you take it one step farther—if my parents hadn't written me off, I probably would've had more support and would've been able to afford an apartment in Lakely. So their jerkishness in a long, roundabout way, moved me to Kismet Beach."

"Nope. They get absolutely no credit for this."

I laugh. "What are you thinking about?"

He moves my arm and then rolls onto his side to face me. Sleepy, relaxed Jess is my favorite Jess.

His hair is mussed up and his eyes soft. He's thoughtful and pensive, gentle and sweet.

I press a simple kiss against his lips.

"You want to know what I'm thinking?" he asks.

"Yeah."

"I'm thinking about tomorrow."

My stomach twists. "What about it?"

"How am I supposed to go from this—having you to myself, getting to hold you whenever I want—to having to set up an appointment to see you?"

"An appointment? My schedule isn't that full."

"You know what I mean."

I do. I've been wondering that too.

"It's like being given the best treat in the world and then having it taken away, isn't it?" I ask softly.

He grins.

"We'll make it work," I say. "We live in the same town. We both work all day. So we'll just text each other on the way home from the office and see if we can meet up. Or we can put a rule on it—at least four dinners together a week."

His brows pull together. "What about breakfasts?"

"I'm sure we'll be together most weekends."

"What about when we brush our teeth together?"

I laugh.

"What about this—talking about shit in the middle of the night? Or walking by a room and seeing you sitting in there and getting to smile at you just so you know I'm thinking about you?"

I cup his cheek in my hand. "Why are you so thoughtful?"

"Because I don't want to go back to the way it was."

"I ... I don't know what you mean."

But I think I do.

"Look, I've spent the last thirty years without you. And it's been great—I've had a great life. It was fine. But now I know what my life can be. What it should be. And nothing is going to make sense again without you."

My eyes burn with unshed tears. *This man is going to kill me.*

"I get it," he says, his eyes searching mine. "We've done this for a week now. Maybe. But that's not really true, Pippa. Doesn't it feel like we've always done this—we just didn't know it? Like, we were taking the long route to get here?"

I nod, afraid to speak. If I open my mouth, the tears will fall.

"Will you move in with me?" he asks.

"Jess ..."

"I don't want to waste any more time without you. And I'm sure there's shit we haven't thought about, and we'll have arguments because that's what couples do. But I want you to know that there's nothing you could do to make me not love you. Love doesn't start and stop. I think I was born already loving you, and I'll die the same. It's a continuous thread in my life."

I push him onto his back and climb on top of him. I lay my head against his chest as he holds me.

Tears collect against his skin and flow down his shoulder. He places a palm on the back of my head, rubbing it against my hair.

"I'm not pushing you," he whispers. "Unlike my family, I respect boundaries. But I'd rather put the boundary around the two of us. I'd like you to trust me to love you and take care of you like you deserve."

I don't deserve Jess Carmichael. I'm not sure anyone does. And this could be a setup for epic disaster because losing him would be the ruination of me. But it's too late for that.

My head spins as I realize what I'm about to do. But there isn't another choice. When you know, you know.

"I just think a lot of people scramble around and assign the word love to things that probably aren't love at all."

I was righter than I even realized.

"Yes," I whisper against his ear. "I'll move in with you."

A burst of energy—of excitement, anticipation, and joy—fills me. I smile when I look at him. The smile grows as I see the same thing that I'm feeling written on his face.

"Seriously, Pip, if you ever make me sweat something out like that again, I might not make it through."

I laugh and sit up, straddling him. "I'm happy."

"I'm glad."

"But keep in mind that I have a lease to deal with. And utilities. And—"

"And you forget that we're a team now. Those are all things that *we* have to deal with now. Not just you. It's never *just you* anymore."

I lean forward and kiss him. But as soon as our lips touch, it's as if a deal has been reached.

Jess rolls me over onto my back, never breaking contact.

He kisses me intentionally, deliberately—carefully. It's as if he's making promises to me that only my heart can understand.

My legs open, and he moves between them. My hips tilt, and he slides inside me without breaking our kiss.

He moves his lips across my jaw, pressing them softly against my skin. His hips flex into me unhurried. Like he has all night. *Like he has all the time in the world.*

I roll my head to the side as he kisses down my neck. The heat of his mouth and the slow, delicious rhythm of his hips is a new level of intimacy I didn't know existed.

Unlike the other times we've been together, this isn't fucking. This isn't getting each other out of our system. This isn't about the end.

This isn't about the interaction. It's the sum of them.

"I love you," he whispers in my ear before pressing a soft kiss behind it.

"I love you too."

26

PIPPA

Kerissa: I HAVE A STORY FOR YOU.

Me: Tell me.

Kerissa: Are you home yet?

I sit on the edge of my bed and kick off my shoes. *I've never noticed how bright my bedroom is.*

Then again, everything has seemed brighter today.

We stopped for breakfast on the way back to Kismet Beach. We had noticed the diner on the way to Silver Springs—a blue building with rocking chairs on the front porch and bright white trim. The hanging baskets of flowers are what caught my eye initially while I waited for Jess to pump gas. We were thrilled to learn that their French toast and biscuits and gravy were just as lovely as their curb appeal.

He carried my bag into my apartment, continuing the argument that started while we were brushing our teeth that I shouldn't go to my apartment; I should just go straight to his house. I maintained that I needed to go home and get clean clothes. I needed my computer for work. And he had things he needed to do too. He kept talking about checking on the project he left behind. A day apart wouldn't kill us.

I don't think.

"I'll get Banks and Maddox to bring their trucks over this weekend to get your stuff," Jess said. "Start packing, Dream Girl."

Grinning, I tap my fingers on the screen.

Me: I just got here.

Kerissa: How did it go?

Me: I have lots to tell you. But you have A STORY TO TELL ME. You go first.

Kerissa: This one requires being face-to-face and alcohol. Can I come over tonight?

Me: Yes. What time?

Kerissa: Eight sound good? I have a hair appointment at four and it takes her for-ev-er.

Me: Okay, Ham.

Kerissa: Okay, Squints.

Me: That was a great movie.

Surely, Jess has watched The Sandlot. *I'll have to ask.* I smile. *There's so much to learn about him.*

But there's no rush. I have a long time—maybe the rest of my life.

I consider telling Kerissa about my news but wait. I'll surprise her tonight.

Kerissa: See you then. <heart emoji>

Me: Bye. <kissing emoji>

I open my contacts and find Bridgit's number. At worst, I can leave her a message. I want her to know how great the retreat went.

"Bridgit Cooperton speaking," she says.

"Hi, Bridgit. It's Pippa."

"Pippa, hello. How are you? Are you back from Silver Springs?"

I get to my feet and wander aimlessly around the apartment, taking in all the little things I'll have to get ready by the weekend.

"Yes. I got home a few minutes ago. It's already so late in the day, so I didn't plan on coming in the office until tomorrow."

"Take tomorrow off. We're having a staff meeting and that won't really apply to you anyway since you'll be moving jobs. Enjoy a long weekend."

I could start packing now. I grin, thinking about Jess's reaction when he sees that I got started without him. *He'll love that.*

"Wow. Thanks, Bridgit. I appreciate it."

"So tell me about the trip. How did it go? What did we learn?"

"I wish you could see the smile on my face. That would tell you all you need to know."

"*Oh*. Did things go well with your *ex-husband*?" She chuckles. "Chuck got fired yesterday, by the way. But we can get into that next week."

Chuck got fired? My eyes bug out of my head. "I have so many questions."

"Chuck was using his company email for conversations not pertaining to work," she says. "It gets complicated, and there's a murky line between whether what he was doing was illegal or simply against company policy. That's being investigated. But let's not get sidetracked—give me your thoughts from the past few days."

Talk about throwing me a curveball ...

I shake my head and set the Chuck stuff aside. *Focus, Pippa.*

"I'm more sold on this concept now than I was before," I say. "Good things can happen when you just stop being distracted. When you hit pause on life for a moment and have time to think. To feel."

My mind replays Jess on his paddleboard, pointing at turtles and fish—and the monkeys. Watching him make a marinade for the chicken tikka masala. His arm stretched over the back of the wooden booth, his cheeks pink from the wine Ted gave us at dinner and *being still.*

"Having a few days to get to know one another again—doing things we wouldn't have normally done—just changed my life," I say. "It's hard to have conversations when you have to carve time out for them. It's hard to prioritize things when you have work in front of you. But when you're floating down a river with no one around but your significant other or sitting in a new restaurant trying new foods and meeting new people together ... it's making new memories. It's remembering the parts of their personality that you fell in love with."

"I take it you fell in love on this trip?"

I laugh. "I did, actually. Jess and I ... We might've drifted apart —*again*—if we hadn't done this. Or maybe not. Maybe the universe used this path to put us together. But I feel very, very good about what we're offering with this, Bridgit. I have suggestions—lots of them. I'll draft them and send them to you by Monday morning."

"That sounds perfect."

"Great."

"We'll chat on Monday. Talk soon."

"Goodbye."

I slip my phone into my pocket and start emptying my suitcase. I'm not halfway through when my phone buzzes again.

Unknown: Hey, Pippa! It's Brooke, Moss's girlfriend. Honey's granddaughter. We met the other day.

I add her to my contacts list.

Me: Hi!

Brooke: I got your number from Honey. I hope that's okay?

Unknown: Hi!

Brooke: That's Ashley, Maddox's wife.

I add her to my contacts list too.

My smile stretches from ear-to-ear.

Me: Hi, Ashley! Yes, of course, it's okay, Brooke.

Ashley: Things happen in this family every hour. It's best if we're all on the same page. <laughing emoji> <eye-roll emoji> <heart emoji>

Brooke: Like the Sparkles dating app thing? OMG Jess wins that round.

I don't know what I'm doing in this chat or how I got here, but I love it.

Me: Just tell me the rooster is gone. <praying hands emoji>

Ashley: Yes. Maddox made sure of it. I think he was actually afraid of what Jess might do if Banks left it there.

Me: Yeah, me too. LOL

Brooke: Moss and I are going to make some pizzas in my new pizza oven tomorrow night. I'm sure Jess will tell you, but if he's anything like his brother, he'll tell you at the last minute.

Ashley: His other brother does that too. <eye-roll emoji>

Brooke: I hope you're not busy and can come! You don't have to bring anything at all. It's very low-key. We aren't fancy people.

Ashley: Oh! If you hear anything about Damaris getting a new couch—NO, YOU DIDN'T.

I laugh, my heart expanding wider than it's ever been stretched.

How are these people just inviting me over? Assuming I'm going to know about a couch?

Things happen in this family every hour. It's best if we're all on the same page.

I press a hand to my nose to try to prevent myself from crying. It's a trick I learned in elementary school when Dad got mad at me for being "too emotional."

Brooke: Recap—the couch has been an issue since before I came into this family. Damaris has threatened to get a new one and Kixx keeps saying no. But the boys all bought one for her, and Moss and Foxx are picking it up one day this weekend. It's a surprise.

Me: I won't say a word.

Ashley: Final tip of the day—LOCK. YOUR. DOORS. I know I'm all shouty caps today, but I've had a lot of caffeine because Jess has been gone so Banks is back at our house. I'm all shouty capping things BECAUSE BANKS IS AT OUR HOUSE.

Brooke: <laughing emoji> I can't. Every time I think of Banks, I think of that profile.

Ashley: Banks phone went off until Maddox finally made him leave around ten last night. Constant texts. He has one lady that was seventy-eight sexting him things that I didn't know were possible. <horrified emoji>

I burst out laughing.

Me: I'm not sure if I'm looking forward to seeing him or not. How long will he be upset about this.

Brooke: Forever.

Ashley: FOREVER.

Brooke: Jess won that round. But this isn't over.

Ashley: <sighing emoji> It's never over.

Me: I really appreciate the tips. And thanks for reaching out. It really does mean the world to me.

Brooke: Welcome to the family. <heart emoji>

Me: You know we aren't getting married, right? <laughing emoji>

Ashley: You're adorable. <winking emoji>

Brooke: Good luck. <laughing emoji>

I stare at the phone, waiting on their responses, but they never come.

My laughter is a mix of amusement and disbelief. *Surely, they don't really think we're getting married. Right?*

I start to sweat a little.

But as I replay the conversation in my head, like I always do, the sweating eases. It's not out of the question. Heck, at some point, we probably *will* get married. They probably just see the writing on the wall.

Besides, who could be loved this entirely by Jess Carmichael, and not want to marry him?

I grin. *Who could feel this loved by the entire family and not want to be a part of it?*

Before I can think it through, my phone rings again. I don't know the number.

I take a long, deep breath. "Hello?"

"Hi, sweetheart. It's Damaris. Jess said you were home, and I finagled your number from him. I hope you're okay with that?"

I laugh. Might as well. Everyone else seems to have it. "Sure. What's up?"

"Did you have a good time on your trip?"

The way she says it tells me she knows I did. She's already gone over it with Jess.

"I did," I say, coyly. "It was a great time."

"I'm so happy. It does a person so much good to get away. And, on that note, the girls and I—Ashley and Brooke—have a girls' day once a month. It's a break from all the men in our lives. We were going this week, but I got busy in the office. We're thinking maybe next Saturday? Do you think you'll be available? If not, we'll work around it."

What has happened to my life?

I stand in the middle of my bedroom and stare at the wall in utter disbelief.

How are these people this amazing? How do they just open their hearts, and doors, to me like I'm one of them?

Tears trickle down my face.

Well, it doesn't seem like I'll ever be lonely again.

"Next Saturday should work perfectly," I say, fighting the sob in my voice. "Thanks for asking me."

"Sweetheart, of course. I'll warn you now. Foxx says I'm overbearing, and Kixx says I have to get it in control before grandbabies come."

My breath hitches. *Let it go. Trust Jess.*

"But I'm a mom. I've been a mom most of my life. It's what I do. If I overstep or push too far into your business, just let me know. I just want my kids to be happy, and it makes me happy to be with my kids. Okay?"

Tears fall fast and hard.

I wipe a hand down my cheek and sniffle.

"Are you okay?" she asks.

"Yeah, it's just allergies."

"Are you sure?"

"I'm sure."

She doesn't seem convinced. "Call me anytime if you need something, sweetheart. Okay?"

"Yes, Damaris. Thank you."

"See you soon, sweetie."

"Goodbye."

I toss my phone on my bed and go into the bathroom.

My emotions are all over the place. I do an internal check in while I splash cold water on my face to rid it of the stickiness from the tears.

This is just new for me. This isn't new for them. They're excited to have me a part of their lives.

But what do I do with that?

I pat my face dry, noting that my towels aren't nearly as fluffy as Jess's. The thought makes me smile.

As soon as I get back to my room, the phone rings. Again.

"You have got to be kidding me," I say, picking it up. My irritation evaporates when I see Jess's name. "Hey, baby."

"Are you okay?"

I laugh in disbelief. "What?"

"Mom just called me and said I need to check on you."

My laughter grows louder.

"Pip, I'm serious. Are you okay?"

"Yes, I'm okay. For fuck's sake. I told her I have allergies."

He sighs in relief.

I blow out a long, heavy breath. "Your family is a lot. Do you know that?"

"Yup."

I smile.

"Have they already started in?" he asks.

"Ashley and Brooke have texted me, and your mom has called me, and I've not been home an hour yet."

He groans. "I told them to give you a minute."

I laugh again. "I think they gave me one exact minute."

"I'm sorry. They're just ... They mean well. I guess you see where Banks gets it."

"Is the rooster gone?" I ask, needing to change the subject.

"Yes. Surprisingly."

My brows pull together. "Did you think it wouldn't be?"

"It was too easy. Nothing is that easy with Banksy."

"You did just bombard him with grandmas sending him dirty texts."

He snickers. "I know. But he'll retaliate. We gotta keep our eyes open."

We. Our. Us.

"I'm at the jobsite. I came over to check on things," he says. "What time are you coming over?"

Oh, yeah. "Well, Kerissa is coming over tonight. So I'll see you tomorrow."

"I thought you were moving in?"

"This weekend," I say slowly.

He fake cries.

"Jess, it's one night. I need to get things in order here anyway. I have to send my boss an email. I have to figure out what to do about my lease. I know you'll help me, I get it, but I'm capable of doing things too."

He groans. "I'll be there early."

"Don't you work tomorrow?"

"Fuck. Yes. Okay, tomorrow as soon as I get off work. Deal?"

"Deal." I grin. "I love you."

"I love you. Talk to you later."

"Bye."

My world just got big.

I smile and look up where to find moving boxes.

27

JESS

"Hey, Sparkles," I say, smirking as I enter Mom's kitchen. "Anything new happening?"

"Fuck off."

I laugh as I kiss Mom on the cheek. "Hi, Mama."

"What you did to your brother was terrible and horrible ..." She glances at Banks. "And really funny."

"*Mom.*" Banks looks at her in disbelief. "I'm probably going to have to get a new phone number."

"You would've done it to him if you would've thought about it first," she says. "Besides, you put the giant rooster in his yard."

I make a face at Banks. He glares at me.

"Dad home yet?" I ask.

"No. He's with Moss at the hardware store."

"Is Foxx still gone?" I ask.

"Yes. He called me this morning from Atlanta. He should be home in the morning."

Banks rocks back on the chair. "What's he doing in Atlanta?"

"Don't do that to my chair." She lifts a brow until he sets it back on all fours. "He's working."

"Doing what?"

Mom shrugs.

"Does anyone find it strange that none of us really knows what Foxx does?" Banks asks. "Is he in intelligence? Is he a spy? Is he really not our brother at all but a plant from an enemy?"

"That would explain a lot." Maddox walks in and smacks me on the back. "What's up?"

"Foxx likes his privacy," Mom says. "We need to give it to him."

"Oh, *the irony*," I say, making my brothers laugh.

Maddox slides a box on the counter. "Here. This was on the porch."

"Thanks, Mad."

Banks hops up and slides the box to himself. "I believe that's mine."

Mom drops the spoon in her hand against the counter. "Banks Owen Carmichael, if you hacked my Amazon account again ..." She yanks the box away from him and picks up a knife. "If this isn't pods for the coffee maker, you're in trouble, little boy."

Banks backs away, frowning.

She rips the knife across the tap holding the box closed. Maddox and I look at each other, amused.

"*Banks*," Mom says, glaring at him as she pulls out a box of individual packets of potato chips. "Who gave you my password?"

"No one," he snaps back at her. "But I love how you thought you made it the one thing I'd never guess."

"You obviously guessed it."

"And I'm touched."

Mom tries not to smile.

"What was it?" I ask.

Banks spins around. "My birthday. For the first ever—it was my birthday. It's never mine and it's never been Maddox's."

"True," Maddox says. "I'll vouch for him on that. It'll give you a complex after a while."

Mom shakes her head. Eventually, the frustration turns to a chuckle.

Banks gives her his best smile—the one that works on most people. "Can I have them, though? Since we already got them?"

"I'll put them on your Christmas list."

"I just want you to know that the youngest child usually takes care of their elderly parents," Banks says, walking backward toward the door. "And that is me."

He turns to leave.

"Good," I shout. "I heard you have lots of experience with the elderly recently."

"Fuck off, Jess."

The door slams behind him. At the same time, Maddox gets up.

"I need to go," he says. "Ashley will be home soon, and I promised to take her out to dinner tonight."

"Good boy," Mom says.

"Later," I say.

"See ya."

The door shuts—quieter this time.

The house is still for once, an unusual occurrence for this place. Someone is always coming and going. It's my normal. I grew up with this. I'm used to it. But now I wonder ... will it be too much for Pippa?

Mom sits down beside me. "How's Pippa? Did you check on her?"

"Pippa was fine," I say. "I think she's just a little overwhelmed."

"I probably had a hand in that. I'm sorry. I didn't realize."

I grin at her. "You're fine. She's not used to ..." I search for the right word, but only one comes up. "She's not used to a family, I guess."

Mom sits back and looks at me curiously.

"She feels like no one has ever loved her before," I say.

"I hate to hear that she feels that way. That must be awful."

"I know. I want to find her parents and rip them a new asshole every time I think about it."

"How can we make this transition easier for her? What can I do to help?"

"We're probably going to have to ask her that. I just try to make sure she knows I'm always thinking about her. She's felt very ... invisible, I think? Maybe inconsequential? I don't know the right word. She agreed to move in with me this weekend, but I see her hesitations. I get it. But I want her to know that ... this is it. I think of her more than I think of myself. Maybe if she realizes that, she'll relax a little."

Mom nods. "She needs reminded she's loved."

I nod too. Clasping my hands together on the table, I take a deep breath. "Just for the record, she doesn't want to have kids."

Her brows shoot to the ceiling, and she visibly processes my statement.

"There are a lot of reasons," I say. "I think the biggest one is that she doesn't understand that love is infinite. Do you know what I mean? She thinks I could not love her one day, or that her kids may not love her. She's never seen how it works."

"Do you think she'll change her mind?"

I shrug.

"Are you okay if she doesn't?" Mom shifts in her seat. "If Pippa never wants kids, can you imagine yourself at my age without them? It's a real question, Jess."

I've thought about it a lot. I've played it out repeatedly in my head.

I wouldn't want to have kids with anyone but Pippa. But if she doesn't want them ... I don't want to be with anyone else either.

"Mom, it comes down to this. I love Pippa Plum because of who she is as a person. And this decision is a part of her. Would I like kids? Yeah. Is it the *make it or break it* question for me? No. Do I feel sad when I think about being your age without kids? A little bit. But when I think about standing in my kitchen and not having her walk in the door—I can't live with that."

I nod, my view getting hazy.

Mom stands and comes around the table, pulling me into a hug. "I love you, Jess. You are a good man."

"Thanks."

She lets me go. "I'm here for the both of you. You know that."

"I know."

"And I have an idea. I'm going to text you in a little bit because I have to find the name of it, but I think your dad got it at Brinkmann's in Sunnydale." She laughs. "I had to quit using it because he drove me nuts. He'd start in before I got out of bed and, I love the man, but enough. I get it."

"Do I want to know what this is? Because I love your love with Dad but I don't need details, you know?"

She starts to speak when a sound rustles from the kitchen. We look over to see Banks grabbing the chip box off the counter.

"Love you, Mommy," he says, slipping down the hallway. The back door pops closed.

I chuckle as Mom shakes her head.

"You know," she says, going back to whatever she was doing when I walked in. "Maybe not having kids is a good choice."

I laugh, give her a wave, and head home.

~

Pippa

"More, more, more—stop." Kerissa bends down to her wineglass and slurps the top down so it doesn't spill. "It's been a day. A week, really."

"What's going on?"

I haven't said a word to Kerissa about Jess. She's been such a good friend and listened to my work drama for the past few weeks. I've dominated the conversations.

It's time I repay the favor.

"On Tuesday, so two days ago, John told me he wanted to be with me seriously," she says.

I pull my brows together. "Who is John?"

She takes a long drink, downing nearly half the glass. "The mayor."

"Oh. I don't think you've ever said his first name in this context. Anyway, proceed."

She curls her feet beneath her. "He's all like—*I'm transferring you out of my office so we can be together. I really see a future for us. We just click.*" She lowers her chin. "Look, I know men can be full of shit, and I've played my fair number of games with them right back. But I believed this fucker."

Oh no. I grab the wine bottle and top it off.

"Thanks." She takes another sip. "So on Wednesday, yesterday, he takes me out to dinner in Lakely. Wined, dined and sixty-nine'd me."

I choke on my drink.

She pats me on the back as I sputter. "There's no better way to put it."

"Noted." I hold a hand to my chest and gasp until it doesn't burn to breathe anymore. "Keep going."

"I slept at his house last night. I left my fucking toothbrush there because, by all accounts, we were going to replay the last part of our night again tonight."

I nod, not wanting to imagine that visual.

"Then I get to the office today and get a text that says something like, 'Hey, it's been great but I'm getting back with my ex-wife so we need to cool things."

My jaw drops. "What? Are you serious?"

"Yes. I'm serious." Her eyes narrow. "I hadn't been out of his bed for *three, maybe four hours*, Pip. And he went from jizzing all over my face to getting back together with his ex-wife. What the fuck?"

I lean back and give her room to process. It's obvious she hasn't done that yet.

This won't permanently damage Kerissa. Guys are a dime a dozen to her. But she'll still need to wrap her brain around what happened and conclude he's a dick.

"And I wonder why I have trust issues," she says. "Actually, no, I don't. This shit is the exact reason I don't think soulmates are a real thing. Human beings are too skittish."

I remember our conversation about soulmates. She didn't believe in them then, and I did. She's more convinced than ever before she's right.

And so am I.

I wonder how much our beliefs impact the outcome. *If we go into the world thinking the possibility of love is there, does it up our odds that we'll find it? If we approach life with the attitude that we'll never find it, does that increase our chances that we won't?*

I grin. "Well, I'm not sure about that. But he's obviously not yours."

"Obviously. But next time, I'm taking things slower. I'm not going to be dazzled by sex and sweet nothings. It takes too much of a toll on me when it all falls to shit." She holds a hand up. "I'll be fine. This is a blip in my radar. But I'll still need to be pissed about it for a week, and I need to go buy a new toothbrush."

I laugh. "I hope the ex doesn't see yours on the counter."

"Honestly? I hope she doesn't, either. Clearly, I was a moment in his life. Maybe she is his life, you know? It would piss me off to think that something stupid I got caught up in ruined something that could've been good for her."

"That's a mature way to look at it."

She slurps her wine again. "Lesson learned. If a relationship has lasting potential, I'm not rushing into it. There's time. It's forever, right?"

My stomach tightens. "Right."

I force out the negative self-talk threatening to shove its way into my brain.

No, I'm not doing this. Stop.

"I can't imagine if I would've bought all the way in. Can you imagine how tricky this would be if I had dove in headfirst?" She shivers. "It would've been a nightmare. And for what? For it to fall apart? Slow and easy, Pip. That's the name of the game from here on out."

"We've done this for a week now. Maybe. But that's not really true, Pippa. Doesn't it feel like we've always done this—we just didn't know it? Like we were taking the long route to get here?"

My stomach curls, and I set my glass down. My face is hot from the wine.

"Okay, what do you have to tell me?" she asks. "How was the trip? How was Jess?"

She wiggles her eyebrows.

Suddenly, I don't know where to begin. I don't really *want* to start.

I'm so thrown off by what Kerissa has said even though I know it doesn't directly apply to me. Still, my pulse is racing, and I need to be calm and excited when I tell her. Otherwise, she'll start asking questions that I might not have the answers for tonight.

"It was great, and he was great." *He is great*. "I'm tired of talking about it, though. I've had everyone asking me about it today, and I just want to chill and watch trash television with my best friend."

She smiles at me. "Let's do it."

I flip on the television, and we pick a show. Kerissa becomes invested in the dish the chef is making from the get-go. But me?

I have too much to think about.

28

JESS

I tuck the small box I picked up from Brinkmann's on my lunch break into my pocket and jog up the walkway. There was a slight delay as I made sure everything was out of my truck before I came over. I want to ensure we can get as much of her stuff on this trip as she wants.

My knuckle raps on the door.

She pulls it open like she was waiting for me. *My girl.*

I wrap my arms around her and hold her as I close the door behind me. She nestles against me.

"How was your day?" I ask her.

She pulls away, grinning. "You have to ask? We texted all day."

"It's the polite thing to do."

She rolls her eyes, still smiling, and leads me into the apartment. Empty cardboard boxes are stacked next to the television. A box sits beneath her little bookcase with half of the books gone. I spy another box in the kitchen with items all around it on the floor.

"I like the look of this," I say.

"I thought you would." She heads into the kitchen. "Are you wanting to start moving stuff tonight?"

"We might as well, right? At least get some of it and then we can come over tomorrow with Maddox's truck and get more."

She takes a deep breath and looks at the floor.

The hair on the back of my neck stands up. *What's wrong*?

"I didn't have time today to get with my landlord," she says. "So I'm not sure what's going to happen with that. It might be a good idea not to move everything just in case."

"Why would that matter?"

She picks up a mint green colander. "If I'm paying for an apartment, I might as well get some use out of it."

My brows pull together as I try to make sense of this.

"Until I get out of my lease, I could just stay at your house sometimes," she says, lifting her gaze to mine. "And you could stay here too."

"Pip …"

She places the colander on the table—not in the box.

"What's going on?" I ask. "What am I missing?"

"Nothing is going on. Everything is great." She smiles at me, but something is slightly amiss. "I still love you and want to live with you. But maybe it wouldn't hurt us to take things a little slower. I mean, what does it matter if I officially live with you now or six months from now?"

"*Six months*?" I ask, my eyes popping out of my head. "What the hell happened today? I dropped you off yesterday, and things were one way. They seemed fine today. And I come here now, and it's like you're … *six months*?"

"That's the length of my lease. And it's not that long, really."

My head is ready to explode. "I've waited for you for fifteen years and just got you. Six months feels like a punishment."

"Jess, *no*. It's not like that."

"Then what's it like?"

I cross my arms over my chest as my heart threatens to pound its way out of it. I can't believe this is happening.

"Nothing has changed between us," she says. "I'm still madly in love with you. I still want things to be the same. I'm just saying that I have this apartment and—"

"No, what you're saying is you want to keep an out."

I wait for her to argue with me. She doesn't.

"Have you not listened to anything I've said over the past week?" I ask her. "You think you need to keep a way out of a relationship with *me*?"

"I don't mean it like that," she says, her eyes widening.

"I don't care how you mean it. That's what it is. We both know it."

"I'm trying to be practical."

"You don't trust me."

She sighs. "I know you're disappointed. And I'm sorry—"

"Stop it." My frustration begins to seep into anger as I see the trauma inflicted on her by her parents emerge. "I'm disappointed. Yeah, I am. *But not in you*."

Her chest rises and falls so much that I can see it from across the room.

"And don't apologize to me for this—for any of it," I say, emotions battling inside me. "You feel what you feel. But don't use me being disappointed to justify your fear. You don't get to think I'm disappointed in you, so it's okay to let the fear ball start rolling down the hill."

She grips the back of a chair.

"I'm disappointed in your parents. I'm disappointed in your brother. I'm disappointed in every man, every person who you've met along the way who has encouraged you to think that you should always keep a way out."

Tears fill her eyes. "I can't help it."

My heart splits into two pieces. The contents spill across the floor with the mixing bowls and measuring cups.

"Can I just have a minute?" She takes a napkin off the table and wipes her nose with it. "I'm sorry, Jess. *I'm so sorry*. My head is just spinning, and I don't know what to do. I do trust you. I love you. I love you so much." Her voice breaks. "But something in my head keeps screaming at me that I'm going too fast and I'm not looking at the big picture."

I have to earn her trust. It's the only way to show her this is different—we are different. "What are you asking me for?"

"Space. Just a little bit," she says. "Just for a little while."

I force a swallow and breathe deep. "You want space? I'll give you space. I told you I'll always give you what you want."

Tears flow down her cheeks.

I walk over to her and pull the box out of my pocket. I open it, take out the two black bands, and then set the box on the counter.

"When my mom told me about this, I thought she had something else in mind." I grin sadly at the memory as I pick up Pippa's hand. I lace my fingers through hers, watching our connection. "But this turned out better."

I slip the band over her wrist and fasten it.

"What's this?" she asks, inspecting it.

I put the other on my wrist and then tap it. The small circle on her wrist lights up, and it vibrates.

"Every time I think of you, I'll tap that," I say.

Her bottom lip quivers.

I hold her face in my hands and press my lips to her forehead. My eyes close, and the deepest breath exhales from my lungs.

This will work out. It has to.

I kiss her again and then step away. "All right. I'm going to go because you asked me to."

The words kill me to say. She flinches as she absorbs them.

Tell me to stay, and I won't go.

I give her a minute to speak—to tell me she doesn't want me to leave—but she doesn't.

"See ya later," I say and head to the door.

I wait for her voice. It never comes.

Tears fill my eyes as soon as I get in my truck. I give her apartment a long look before flicking my bracelet ... and pulling away.

29

JESS

"How many T-shirts does one man need?"

I pull a tote out from under a shelf in my closet. Sitting on the floor in the middle of the walk-in, I sort through a stack of shirts I didn't know I still owned. *I thought Banks ran off with all of these.*

On his five-foot-seven frame.

Despite my bleak mood, I chuckle.

Cleaning out my closet isn't something I thought I'd be doing at ten o'clock on a Friday night. But being here alone wasn't what I thought I'd be doing either. And that whole thing pisses me off.

Fuck her parents. Fuck her brother. Fuck them all.

How can people be so selfish and self-centered to make a person afraid to fall in love? How is that a thing? And how did Pippa turn out to be such a warmhearted woman after being raised in that toxicity?

I pause, holding a blue shirt in my hand. *Because she's amazing.*

I reach over and tap the bracelet. Then I toss the shirt in a give-away pile.

"Fuck my life," I say, sighing.

A purple Tennessee Arrows shirt that used to be a favorite one of mine peeks out from under a misplaced hoodie. I reach across the tote to grab it when a shadow crosses the doorway.

Eyes glued to the opening, I slowly move into a crouch.

"Hey," Banks says, poking his head around the corner.

I grab a shoe and chuck it his way. He laughs, easily missing it, so I throw another one for good measure.

"One of these days, you're going to get killed walking into people's houses," I say.

He winks. "Nah, I knew I was safe here. I went through all your shit while you were gone."

Bastard. "What do you want?" I ask, falling back on my ass.

"If I had known you were gonna throw shit at me, I wouldn't have brought you pizza." He holds a plate covered in foil. "You didn't come to Moss's, so I brought you leftovers."

Damn you, Banks.

I lean back on my hands and blow out a long, tired breath.

"Brooke said she texted Pippa, and Pip said she wasn't feeling well." He frowns. "I suck at math, but I put two-and-two together. Sorry, man."

This is his saving grace. This is the reason Banks can pull off the shit he does, but we all still love him. *The guy has a heart of fucking gold*.

"Thanks, Banks."

He flinches. "No Sparkles? *Wow*. You must be fucked up."

I grab another shoe and toss it toward him again. This time, he doesn't move, just laughs, and it falls a few feet in front of him.

"You wanna talk about it?" he asks. "If not, I'll put the pizza in the fridge and go ... somewhere else."

I don't want to smile, but I do.

He puts the plate on my dresser and then leans against the doorjamb. "Don't take this the wrong way, but I'm having a hard time figuring out what kind of problem you two had. When it was Brooke and Moss, it was easy. Moss has issues." He grins. "And when it was Ashley and Maddox, again—easy. Things get hard, Maddox stops.

But you, *my brother that's not in my wolfpack anymore*, I can't quite figure out how you fucked things up."

I try to glare at him. *I try*. But his shit-eating grin makes it impossible.

"Maybe I didn't fuck it up. Did you consider that?" I ask.

"I did. Because I know you. You like everyone to think you're an approachable asshole."

I lift a brow. "An approachable asshole? Really?"

"Yeah. Foxx is just an asshole. You'll still talk and engage me when I'm bored, but you don't want anyone to think you like it. You don't want to lose your edge."

"I assure you that I don't like coming home to find a rooster in my yard. Or your stickers everywhere. And I don't like when you take shit out of my pantry. Or my tools."

He holds a hand in the air. "We're getting off track. This isn't about me."

I roll my eyes.

"You don't fuck shit up, Jess. You're the most responsible one out of us. That's why you're Dad's favorite."

"I am, aren't I?"

He chuckles. "My point is ... where is she?"

I groan as I get to my feet. A pile of T-shirts is beside me, and another is by the door.

"What are you doing with those?" he asks.

"Donating them."

"To me?"

I shake my head and pass him. I grab the plate and take out a slice of pizza.

"Let me help you," Banks says. "Tell me your problems, and I'll tell you what to do."

"What on earth do you know about relationships?"

He grins cheekily. "I've been conversing with a lot of very experienced ladies as of late."

I choke on my pizza.

Although I don't want to hash it out aloud, because God knows

I've done it mentally a million times this evening, Banks has made an effort. At least it won't be just me moping in my head.

I tap the bracelet.

"To put it in its simplest terms—she's scared to be loved. Really, that's it."

He flinches. "I don't get it. Does she not want to be loved?"

"No, she does. It just ... makes her feel vulnerable. She doesn't know what to do with that. She associates someone 'loving' her as pain. And I just have to show her that's not what it's like here. I'm not going away. She can kick and scream and whatever she wants, but that won't change anything."

Banks grins. "You're all right. I almost take back everything I said about you."

I grin too. "That's okay. I don't take back anything I said about you."

Together, we laugh.

"Want to go to town, grab some beer, and sit out on the dock and talk shit?" he asks.

I know he doesn't really want to do that. We haven't drunk on the dock in years. But the fact that he's willing to do that for me—to take my mind off this—means a lot.

I grab him in a front headlock. "I might just kick your ass right here."

He scrambles, weaseling his way out of it. *Fuck, this guy is strong*. Before I know what's happening, we're in full-on wrestling mode in the middle of my bedroom floor.

30

PIPPA

"If you don't like my blankets, you can go home," Kerissa says.

I glare at her and pull the purple piece of fabric you can see through over my legs. "It doesn't even meet the definition of a blanket. This is a glorified sheet."

"It works. I don't have overnight visitors unless they're in my bed." She shrugs. "Wanna sleep with me? I cuddle."

"No."

I frown, thinking about the fact that I could be at Jess's right now. I could've been there last night and all day today. We could've spent our first Saturday together sleeping in. I bet he would've made me French toast.

My bracelet blinks for the millionth time today.

Every time it's gone off, I've tapped it back. I've even tapped it a couple of other times today too. But besides the tapping and a text message this morning that said *good morning*, I haven't heard from Jess. He didn't even reply when I said *good morning* back.

I asked for this.

I specifically *asked for this*. And he said yes to my request.

He said he'd always give me what I wanted.

Kerissa yawns. "I'm getting sleepy."

"Me too. But I don't know if I can sleep."

"Want me to stay with you at your house? I can sleep anywhere."

I frown. "No. I just didn't want to see the empty boxes anymore." I fake cry. "I ruined this, Kerissa."

"Doubtful."

"It's embarrassing."

"It's my fault," she says. "But I had no idea he asked you to move in with him, or else I would've been more careful with my word choices."

"This is not your fault. Not even a little. The responsibility of this life fuckup is purely on my shoulders."

She yawns again. "Cut yourself some slack. I'd probably freak the heck out if Jess Carmichael were worshipping the ground I walk on."

"Not helping."

"But, I gotta give it to you—you have some pretty good self-restraint and big balls to do what you did."

"Kerissa. *Not helping*."

"I'm giving you facts. That's what friends do. If you want friends to blow smoke up your ass, find someone else." She waits for a reaction, but all I give her is a glare. "I'll soften it up for you. You're smart. Witty. Gorgeous. You—"

"Stop."

"Fine."

I sigh, pressing my head against the pillow. Instead of meeting fluff, the back of my head hits the sofa. *I'm buying her pillows and blankets for her birthday.*

"I hate myself. That's the only excuse," I say.

Kerissa gets up from the other end of the couch and stretches her arms over her head.

"Nope. I think it's the opposite," she says. "I think you love yourself, as one should, and I think you've learned to protect yourself from things that hurt you. For example, I balk at passionfruit and toddlers. I've been traumatized by both. But you've been hurt by people using love as a weapon. Naturally, you'd build defenses."

I just stare at her. *Why does that make sense?*

"I'm no therapist or anything," she says. "But I would venture to say that you can't just rip down the walls you've built over your whole life. It'll take some time. But maybe you can think about it and be okay with not shouldering the whole thing yourself. That's all Jess wants, Pip. He wants you to trust him enough to let him help carry the load."

This coming from the girl who doesn't believe in soulmates.

"I'm going to bed," she says. "You can sleep with me if you want, like I said. If not, I'll see you in the morning, but I'm sleeping in. Kisses."

"Night, Kerissa."

She closes her bedroom door behind her.

Is Kerissa right? Have I learned to protect myself to the extent that I'll never be able to know love? Will I ever trust Jess with my heart?

Because I know I want to. But how?

How do I rip down walls that I erected to keep me safe from love —or a lack of it? Will I ever allow Jess to shoulder some of this shit? Why should I? Why should he?

I sigh, rolling onto my side—and not into Jess's arms.

What have I done?

31

PIPPA

"I'm going to figure out how to fix this today," I say, staring at myself in the mirror. "What are the mantras online that they have little kids repeat? I am brave. I am bold. I am beautiful. I am kind." I pause. "I am not a fool. I am not a coward."

I groan. *That got off track.*

There are bags under my eyes. I haven't cried over this situation until late last night. I think I was numb. But when I left Kerissa's in the early morning hours because I couldn't sleep and walked in the door, the sight of the boxes piled around my apartment reminded me of what I could be doing. And where. And with whom.

I've tapped my bracelet on and off all morning to no avail. Jess hasn't tapped me back. He didn't text me good morning either, and I was too much of a chickenshit to text him first.

I hate that I'm this way. Proud, fearful, and uncertain.

Ironically, the only thing I feel happy, content, and certain about is that I love Jess.

My phone buzzes, and I leap for it, my heart pounding in my chest. "Please be you, Jess. Please."

I glance at the screen.

Unknown: Hey, hey. It's Banks.

I add the number to my contacts and sit on the edge of the bed. Why is he texting me? Is something wrong? *Shit.*

Me: Hi.

Banks: I'll give you fifty bucks to stop tapping that bracelet.

Me: Why?

Banks: Because every time you hit it, Jess stops what he's doing and stares at it. Then I have to restart what I was saying, and it's super annoying.

Me: Okay …

I stare at the screen for a reply, but nothing comes.

"What in the world is that all about?" I carry my phone into the kitchen in case it goes off again. "Why would he just look at the bracelet? Does he not want me tapping it? Does he regret it today?"

My stomach churns. *Fuck.*

Panic rises from the depths of my soul and mixes with the bile in my throat.

I don't want to think that's the case, but it must be. He certainly hasn't tapped me back.

My knees weaken. I sit at the kitchen table and put my head in my hands, trying to sort my emotions so I can think.

I jump when my phone buzzes again.

Banks: You've never lived until you've risked your life. Just saying.

I laugh.

Me: What?

Banks: What's the worst thing that could happen to you? You could die. But how does that happen? Because Jess loves you to death? Poor you.

Me: Banks, I'm not sure we're on a close enough level for you to be saying this to me.

Banks: You've leveled up, fam. Congrats.

Me: You do realize that your brother's probably so frustrated with me that he can't see straight, right?

Banks: I have a sore rib to prove it.

Huh?

Banks: Whether you want to be or not, you're a Carmichael now. We've claimed you. So whether you and Jess fix your shit or not, Hi, sis. Don't forget me at Christmas.

I laugh, but my bottom lip quivers all the same.

Me: You're funny.

Banks: Whatever. See you later.

Me: Bye.

Banks: Hey, can you bring some pop? It was my thing, and I forgot.

"What the hell are you talking about?"

Me: ?

A knock raps against the door. I'm too busy deciphering Banks's text to think about it.

"Come in," I yell. "Honey, is that you?"

The door latches closed. I look up and my stomach hits the floor.

Jess stands in the doorway in a pair of dark denim jeans and a crisp white T-shirt. His hair is wet like he just got out of the shower. The cologne I love so much lures me to him.

"Hi," I say, my heart in my throat.

"Hi." He looks me up and down. "Why are you still in your pajamas?"

"We had a conversation about this. I like to sleep in on the weekends."

"We also had a conversation about this. Sunday dinners are nonnegotiable."

What?

My body stills as I look at this beautiful man. His face is calm; no games are being played. *So what does this mean?*

"Come on, Pip. We have about an hour before we eat, and I was hoping to get your opinion on my closet before we go."

"I ..." I furrow my brow. "Your closet?"

He walks across the room and sits next to me at the table. He folds his hands on top near mine but not touching them.

"Jess, I'm confused."

"About what?"

Is he serious? I don't know how to verbalize it.

Isn't he mad at me? Doesn't he think I'm a brat? Is he disappointed in me but pretending we're okay?

"You asked me for space," he says. "So I gave it to you—I'm giving it to you. I left you alone Friday night and all day yesterday. It about killed me, but I did it."

"But aren't you ...?"

He grins. "Aren't I what?"

"Mad at me?"

His grin turns into a chuckle.

"Don't laugh at me," I say.

"I'm not laughing at you. You're just too damn cute."

My cheeks flush as relief creeps through my body.

He leans forward. "I told you I'll give you what you want and what you need. You needed space. Cool. I mean, not cool—I hate it, but you don't always get everything you want in life."

I listen, afraid to speak.

"What did you think?" he asks, a smile flirting with his lips. "That we were over?"

Slowly, I nod.

His smile grows.

"I was afraid that it was over," I say, my words wrapped with emotion.

"This will *never* be over for me."

Tears flood my eyes.

"I don't understand how long it's going to take to make you believe that I'm here and I'm not going to leave—unless you tell me you don't want me." He reaches for my hand. "But I'm not going anywhere. Not without you."

I give him both of my hands. He squeezes them and rubs the tops of them with his thumbs.

"It's not over for me either," I say.

"Good. Because I'd really hate to take you kicking and screaming to dinner. I can't show up without you now. They may not even let me in."

My laughter feels good.

The tension in my shoulders melts away. My eyes ache, and the exhaustion I've been fighting slowly creeps in.

"What does this mean?" I ask.

"What do you want it to mean?"

"Don't answer a question with a question."

"It means whatever you're comfortable with as long as you know we're together. As long as you don't doubt *us*." He sighs. "Eventually, you'll associate love with happiness. I don't know how long it'll take me to get you there, but I will."

My heart swells in my chest.

Eventually, you'll associate love with happiness.

You're already doing it, Jess.

I stand and walk around the table. He turns to the side like he knows what I'm going to do. I sit on his lap and study his handsome face.

He's already been more consistent with his love than anyone I've ever known.

What's the worst thing that could happen to you? You could die. But how does that happen? Because Jess loves you to death? Poor you.

I giggle. *I'm quoting Banks now? What the hell is happening?*

"What?" he asks, wrapping his arms around my waist.

"Nothing. Just thinking of something Banks texted me today."

His jaw drops. "Banks texted you?"

I nod. "I don't know what to think of it, really, but we need to buy pop before we go to your mom's."

"Fucking Banks." Jess laughs, shaking his head in disbelief. "Does this mean you're going with me today? Or are we going to stay here and get inundated with calls and texts from my relentless family?"

I run my fingers through his hair.

My heart races. But the longer I think about it, the more certain I am.

"When do we need to leave?" I ask.

He pushes the side button on my phone and looks at the time. "Probably forty-five minutes at the latest. Why?"

"I need to do three things before we go."

"What's that?"

I smile at him. "I need to get dressed."

"Okay."

"I need to find some tape."

"For what?"

"So my stuff doesn't blow out of the boxes in the back of your truck."

His eyes light up. "Really?"

"Really."

He holds my face and brings his mouth to mine. It's desperate yet controlled, demanding yet gentle. It's perfect, just like him.

My tongue swipes his lips. He growls into my mouth. He cups my ass and stands, wrapping my legs around his waist.

He walks us toward my bedroom, our kisses growing frenzied. He tosses me on my bed.

"What's the third thing?" he asks, stripping his shirt over his head.

I toss my top at him. He snatches it out of the air and grins.

"The third thing?" I shimmy out of my sleep pants and toss them to the side. "This."

He removes the rest of his clothes and climbs onto the bed with me. Hovering over my body, he smiles. *God, I've missed that smile.*

It's only. Been a day, but when you think you're not going to see something again, that time feels like forever.

"I love you, Mr. Carmichael. And if you ask me to move in again, I'll say yes."

"Move in with me."

"Yes."

"Marry me."

"Ye—whoa, wait." I giggle as his grin deepens. "It really is too soon for that."

He kisses me softly. "Fair. I'll take what I can get."

I'm sure he already knows that he gets it all. He already has it all.

32

PIPPA

I've never seen a house so full of life.

"If you get overwhelmed, just say the word," Jess says as we step inside. "I'd hate to have a reason to go back to our house."

I look at him and grin. He winks at me, making me laugh.

My God, I love this man.

"Did you bring the pop?" Banks yells from the kitchen table.

Jess holds up two twenty-four packs. "This cost about fifty bucks, I'll have you know."

"I had no idea," Banks says, making it clear he absolutely knew that. "Hey, Pip."

"Hi, Banks."

"You made it," Damaris says, coming around the island. "I'm so happy to see you, sweetheart." She pulls me into a quick hug, kissing my cheek. "Do you like spaghetti?"

"Do I like spaghetti? Who doesn't?"

"Good point." She grins and heads back to the kitchen. "Have you met Ashley and Brooke?"

I wave at them. "I met Brooke at Honey's. But I've only texted with Ashley."

"Nice to meet you," Ashley says, cutting up vegetables and tossing them into a gigantic salad bowl. "We missed you the other night."

I ignore Jess's eye roll. "I thought something inside me was broken. But I'm all healed up now."

Jess scoffs, making me giggle.

"Moss is going fishing tonight. I'm going to watch girlie movies if you want to come over," Brooke says.

"Yeah, that sounds fun," I say. "Thanks for asking me."

"Pretty sure she's going to be busy tonight," Jess says, wrapping his arms around me from behind.

"We're getting you one of those fucking pillows," Maddox says.

My eyes go wide.

"Not *a fucking pillow*," Maddox says. "A pillow about fucking. It's in the living room. Jess got it for the parents for Christmas of all things."

Jess lowers his lips to my ear. "I can buy you a fucking pillow, though. Sounds like something we could get into."

"Look who's here," Honey says. She and another older woman come from the hallway. "It's a small world, isn't it?"

"It really is," I say, happy to see her.

"I heard you're moving out, and we won't be neighbors anymore," she says.

"True. But I'll still visit you."

"You better." She pats my shoulder as she goes by. "There's the man of the hour."

We all follow her gaze to Banks. He sits up as he sees Honey coming.

"Banks, you know your biggest fan, Gloria, don't you?" Honey asks.

Maddox snickers.

"Gloria, my girl," Banks says, getting up. "Good to see you, beautiful."

"You're the talk of the retirement center," Gloria says.

The room bursts into a fit of laughter. Banks struggles not to look embarrassed.

"I have that effect on women," Banks says.

"Ones that can't see very well," Moss says.

"Fuck off," Banks tells him.

"Ones that might lose their dentures when they're kissing him too," Jess says, earning a scowl and a middle finger from the geriatric magnet.

Gloria sits beside Banks. "I'm putting together a fundraiser, and I need your help."

"Shoot."

"I need you to be auctioned off."

His brothers howl with laughter. I look at Damaris. She's giggling too. When she catches me looking at her, she shrugs.

"There will be a bachelor auction," Gloria says. "It isn't for a while. A month, maybe two. But I know if I announce that Sparkles is being auctioned, it'll get us a lot of attention."

Her voice gets drowned out by the laughter in the room.

Banks cheeks turn red, but he refuses to back down. "Sure. Want me to take new photos to really bring in the crowd?"

"That would be great," Gloria says.

"I can't," Moss says, holding his stomach. "I can't do this."

Someone taps on my shoulder. I extract myself from Jess's arms and turn to see Ashley.

"Hey, Operation Couch is a no-go," she says softly. "We'll all be briefed tonight via text."

I snort. "Is it that big of a deal?"

Her eyes go wide, and she shakes her head. "You have no idea."

"Let's say grace so we can eat," Kixx says from the back of the room. He looks at me and smiles warmly.

The room quiets, and hats come off heads.

Kixx clears his throat. "Dear Heavenly Father, I want to thank you for this meal we are about to receive. Thank you for the family gathering here to enjoy it and the hands that made it. Thank you for bringing our new friend Gloria to the table to share this meal with us, and thank you, Father, for our Pippa. We are so grateful to be able to welcome her into our family. Amen."

A round of *amens* is said throughout the room. Then, like someone flipped a switch, it all comes to life again.

My heart swells as I take in this unruly, loving, amazing bunch of humans.

"Is this too much?" Jess asks quietly.

I stare up at his handsome face. "It's perfect."

"That's a shame."

"Why?"

"I wanted to take you home."

I stand on my tiptoes and kiss him sweetly. "You'll be able to take me home every night, my man."

He wraps his strong arms around me and holds me tight.

It's not this hug, in particular, that mends the ragged pieces of my heart. It's not the hundred times he's said he loves me today, and it's not the fact that he cleaned his closet out for me on the night we were apart.

Jess Carmichael is the first person to care to find the scraps of me that others have ripped apart. He'll never stop looking, never stop inspecting every crevice to find another piece to put back in place.

Because that's what love is.

Love is patient, kind, and forgiving.

Tender and aggressive. Sweet and spicy.

It's giving and taking. It's work but also free.

Love is the exhilaration and euphoria I feel when Jess touches me. It's the adoration and warmth that flows through my veins when our eyes meet. It's the safety, the power that he gives me by just being him—and by letting me be me.

EPILOGUE: JESS

"Did you like that?" I ask Pippa, pulling her onto my chest.

She laughs, pulling her sundress down, and smiles. "Did it feel like I liked that?"

"It tasted like you did too."

The past week has been amazing—perfect even. We have most of her things moved in. I offered to keep her apartment and pay the rent for her so she could have a place if she needed space. But she refused, canceled the contract, and had her stuff in boxes within twenty-four hours.

She's the one now attacking me as soon as I get home from work for dinner, sex, and then a hike or walk on the beach. Although it's not always in that order. There's usually a bubble bath in there somewhere too. But the best part of the day is going to bed with this woman. Holding her, listening to her breaths as she sleeps, knowing that she feels safe and loved.

Knowing she's here with me—safe and loved.

There was a wedding magazine on the coffee table this morning. When I saw it, Pippa smiled and said it must've been Brooke's. And maybe it was. But I'm not asking her to marry me—not for real—until she tells me that's what she wants.

Pippa is learning the realities of life with a large family … who frequently message, unexpectedly drop in, and check to see how she's adjusting to the Carmichael madness. I'm learning too, though. This woman has meant so much to me for so long that I'm determined to get this right. I'm attempting to go slow and be calm … and learning that maybe I'm more like my mom and Banks than I thought.

I'll never say that out loud.

"Are you happy?" she asks me, drawing a circle on my chest.

"Infinitely. Are you happy?"

"Yes." She smiles. "This feels really good, you know—and not just what you just did to me."

I chuckle.

"I didn't realize life could feel like this," she says. "I don't have to give up my peace to have companionship. Who knew they could go together? Except we're going to have to get rid of the bracelets. I see what your mom meant. It's nice but … not."

I plant a wet, loud kiss on her lips, making her giggle.

"What do you want to do today?" I ask.

She hums. "Maybe we could—"

"Are you guys home?" Banks yells.

Pippa and I groan.

"Oh, there you are," he says, stopping in the doorway. "Why are you on the living room floor?"

"Do you have a reason to be here?" I ask.

He studies us for a moment and then shakes his head. "Yes. I need paper and a pen."

Pippa hides her face in the crook of my arm and laughs.

"You walked into my house for that?" he asks.

"I'm sorry. I forgot to knock. Want me to go out and come back in?"

I want to argue with him or, at the very least, point out his ridiculousness. But that will take time, and I don't need him here any longer than necessary.

"Two things," I say. "First, Maddox's house is closer. Go there next time."

"They lock their doors."

Oh, for fuck's sake. "Second, the paper and pens are in the kitchen drawer by the straws and bread ties. But why do you need them in the first place?"

His eyes twinkle with mischief, and I know I'm fucked.

"So I have an idea and need your help," he says.

"No."

"You haven't even heard me."

"Don't have to."

"What is it, Banks?" Pippa asks. "Tell us so you can go home."

He opens his mouth like he's going to spout something off to her but changes his mind at the last second. *Smart move*.

"Okay, you have a skill at writing personal ads," he says to me. "I got a million calls when you put me on that site. Fuck you again, by the way."

"And ..." I ask, hurrying him along.

"And you were my last friend. Maddox is gone, Moss is gone, and now you're gone. I have no one. No one even wants me at their house anymore."

"You're being dramatic," I say.

"So?"

I stare at him. "Get to the point."

"I want you to help me write an ad for a best friend and a roommate."

Pippa cracks up laughing.

"I'm being serious," he says, stone-faced.

I sigh, turning my head to my girl. She giggles and kisses my cheek.

"Just do it and get it over with. Otherwise, he'll keep coming back," she says.

"She's right. I will," Banks says.

I groan.

"Do it," Pippa says softly into my ear, "and we can try out that fucking pillow you bought yesterday."

I move her off my chest and get to my feet. "Sparkles, I'm giving you ten minutes."

"Atta boy."

"I have some ideas," he says, following me into the kitchen. "Should I go with *in search of a best friend and roommate*? Maybe *best friend auditions*? Or I could keep it simple and say *I'm looking for a roommate*? I considered *couch for rent* or *be my friend*, but both feel desperate."

I stop at the table and look at him.

Oh, where to begin ...

I pick a headline and run with it, just so I can run upstairs to the woman I love.

The one who loves me back.

Finally.

She called it a fluke that I love her, but she was wrong. It was and is the easiest decision I've ever made.

Pippa Plum was made for loving, and I'm totally up to the task.

Forever.

Banks's book, FLAUNT, comes out in June 2023. Preorder available.

CHAPTER ONE - CRANK

If you've already read Flirt (Moss's book) & Fling (Maddox's book), and need another Adriana Locke book, may I suggest Crank?

It's a blue-collar meets silver spoon, small-town romance.

CHAPTER ONE
Walker

"I'm not taking you to the hospital."

Peck teeters on the edge of one of Crave's billiard tables. He sways back and forth, his sneakers squeaking against the cheap wood over the chatter of the patrons of the bar. "You don't think I can land a back flip off here?"

The truth is I'm pretty sure he could. My cousin has the reflexes of a cat. The problem is he also has nine lives, and I'm sure he's used up eight of them already.

"The question isn't if you can land it. It's how bloody the end result would be," I say, taking a sip of beer. "And I'm not trying to splint a head wound. Can you even do that?"

"*You* could. Look at my arm." He holds his left forearm in front of him, his watch catching the light from the new fixtures above. "This is some of your best work."

Memories of splinting Peck's arm with nothing but a belt, a bar towel, and a Playboy rush through my mind, as does loading him into the back of my truck for a quick trip to the emergency room.

"I really think I can do this," Peck insists, working his shoulders back and forth.

Downing another drink, hoping I'm good and hammered before Peck attempts this disaster, I look across the table. My older brother, Lance, is watching me as he brings an Old-Fashioned to his lips. We exchange a look, both of us waiting for Machlan to catch wind of Peck's antics and throw him out of Crave. Again.

"What's the worst that could happen?" Peck asks. "Another broken arm? I mean, I think I can get the rotation fast enough to not land on my head."

"I think it's your turn to take him to the hospital," I tell Lance.

He coughs, choking on his drink. "Yeah, I don't think so."

"Remember how hot that nurse was last time?" Peck asks, wiggling his brows. "Actually, that kind of makes me want to go for it now just in case she's on duty."

"She's not," Lance chimes in. "I think she was fired after the Hospital Administrator found her fuck-foundered in triage three the night of your broken arm."

"Peck! Get your fucking ass down." Machlan's voice rips through the bar, booming over the crowd.

Everyone quiets a few notches, not quite scared of my younger brother, but not willing to test his boundaries either. His reputation as a man you don't want to tangle with without a small army definitely helps his cause when it comes to managing his bar. Peck, on the other hand, just rolls his eyes.

"Just one jump, Mach! One. Uno. I got this." Peck gives Machlan his best shit-eating grin before looking at me and Lance. "If he throws me out, I'll be back in a couple days. Hell, he threw me out on Tuesday and I was back on Thursday for corn hole."

"I think that just means you're in here too much," Lance offers.

Peck starts to respond but his attention is redirected as Molly McCarter saunters by. The dim lighting does nothing to hide the exaggerated sway of her hips or the way she licks her lips as her sight sets on *me*.

Bracing for what may come out of her mouth, I fill mine with alcohol.

"Hey, Walker," she says, stopping at my chair. Her hands rest along the top rung, her fingertips sliding across the back of my neck. "Hey, Lance."

Lance tips his glass her way.

"I was thinking," she purrs, "my car is way overdue for an oil change. Maybe I could bring it to Crank sometime this week, Walker? Do you think you could *fit it in*?"

"I'm pretty full this week," I lie, ignoring her thinly veiled offer. "See what Peck has available."

A huff whispers through the air and she pivots on her heel. "Thanks anyway."

"I can get you in ..." Peck's voice drowns into the Crave chaos as he follows her towards the bar.

He tails after her, all but drooling, as she slides onto a bar stool. Her gaze flicks to mine, her knees spread just a little farther apart than a lady ever should. Then again, no one has ever called Molly a lady.

"Ever fuck her?" Lance asks, downing the rest of his drink as he turns back to me. "I've been tempted to a couple of times and did get a decent blow job one Halloween when she was dressed up in this nurse outfit."

"What is it with you and nurses?"

"Think about it: they're smart, make good money, work a lot so you have free time, and they're used to getting dirty," he smirks. "It's like a straight shot to my dick."

"And they're good with needles, have access to medicines that can make you lose your mind, and I've never met one who didn't have a warped sense of humor," I counter. "They set off my crazy radar."

Lance laughs. "Did that radar just start working? Because I distinctly remember you getting balls deep with some psychologically-challenged women. One in particular."

"Are you feeling froggy tonight? Because if you keep that mouth runnin' like that, I'm about to knock those glasses off your face."

I'm kidding. More or less. The problem is Lance knows it.

"Oh, go to Hell," he laughs.

"Already there, brother. Already there."

He takes his glasses off his face and places them on the table. "I usually look at your life and think I'd hate to have it. But after the day I had today, I'd trade you places."

"What? Did the high school kids refuse to learn about the American Revolution?" I laugh. "You have such a cush job."

"I'm a professional."

"A professional bullshitter, maybe."

He makes a comeback, but it's swallowed in the roar of the crowd as a popular song blares through the overhead speakers.

Crave, an old brick building along Beecher Street, is longer than it is wide, and pulses with the noise of the crowd and music. Alcohol ads, high school sports schedules, and a giant cork board adorn the walls. The latter is a good read and filled with letters and notes from one townsperson to the next. Affairs have been called out, coon dogs found, marriage proposals made, and entire conversations about who is working what shift at the factory have taken place on that thing. It's been a mainstay of the bar since our uncle founded it almost fifty years ago. When our younger brother, Machlan, took over Crave thanks to Uncle George's failing liver, he extended the wall of corkboards all the way to the door.

"That's new," Lance says, moving over one seat closer to me. Motioning to the phallic design made up of yellow rubber duck Christmas lights on the wall between the pool tables, he laughs. "Let me guess: that's Peck's handiwork."

"Naturally. Machlan wasn't thrilled, but Peck rallied the masses and they convinced him to keep it."

"It is nicely done," Lance says, chewing on the end of his glasses. "I can see the art in it."

"Fuck. I should've been an artist if that counts as art."

"Apparently things didn't go well with Molly," Lance says, twisting in his chair.

"She's never gonna give Peck a chance."

At the sound of his name, Peck walks through the front door. He stops just inside, the glow from the exit sign giving his mop of blond hair a pinkish hue.

Peck makes a beeline for our table, a look etched in the lines on his face that sends a ripple of concern up my spine. After growing up with him and then working with him for the last few years, I can read him like a book. Something is wrong.

"What's going on?" I ask, scrambling to my feet as he gets closer.

"Walker, man, you need to get outside," Peck says. "Someone just bashed the front of your truck."

"What?" I hiss, sure I misheard him. "Someone did fucking what?"

"Yeah, man. You need to get out there."

Blood ripping through my veins, I plow my way through the bar. Machlan lifts his chin, sensing something is off, but I shake my head as we pass. I know he loves a good fight, but this one is mine.

Lance is on my heels as we make our way through the crowd. "Who did you piss off now?"

"Someone who wants to die, apparently." My fingers flex against the wood of the door, the warm summer air slamming my face as I hit the sidewalk. "You sure you don't want to stay inside? I think getting into a street fight is against your teacher code of conduct."

"Fuck off," Lance chuckles. "I'll have Peck hold my glasses and I'm in."

"You, my brother, are an intelligent heathen."

"I'll take that as a compliment. I think."

The top of my black pickup truck comes into view, sitting beneath one of the few lamps lining Beecher Street. There are two people standing on the sidewalk next to my truck.

"Do we know them?" I ask Peck through gritted teeth.

"I promise you we've never seen them before."

"So it's not ..." Lance doesn't finish his sentence. "*Holy shit.*"

The two women turn to face us and I think all of our jaws drop. The first is tall with jet black hair and a strong, athletic build. It's the second one who has me struggling to remember why we're out here.

Long, blonde hair with faint streaks of purple and the brightest blue eyes I've ever seen, she assesses me in the hazy streetlight. She doesn't make a show of looking me over like most women do, batting their eyelashes like some damsel in distress. There's something different about her, a quiet confidence that makes her almost unapproachable.

Unapproachable, but still hot as fucking hell.

My gaze drifts down her ample chest, over the white lace fabric of the top that hugs the bends of her body. Cutoff denim jeans cap long, lean legs that only look longer next to the Louisville Slugger half-hidden behind her.

It takes a ton of effort, but my eyes finally tear from her body and to the body of my truck. Sure enough, there's a rip across the grill and a broken headlight that looks an awful lot like a slam from a baseball bat. It's nothing that can't be fixed in my shop, but that's not the point. The point is the disrespect.

"Either of you know what happened?" I ask, leaning against the hood. They remain silent. The only response is a dashed look between them.

Settling my scrutiny on each one individually, watching them squirm, I save the blonde for last.

"Did you see anything?" I ask, turning back to the tall one.

Her weight shifts from one foot to the other as she runs a hand through her shiny hair like we're talking about coffee or having a beer later. "Me? No. I didn't see a thing."

"Really? You were standing out here just now and you didn't see anything?"

"No," she smiles sweetly. "Nothing at all."

Peck steps between us and inspects the damage. When he turns around, he bites the inside of his cheek. "If I were a betting man, Walker, I'd say it looks like someone walloped Daisy with a baseball bat."

The blonde lifts a brow, something on the tip of her tongue that she holds back.

"You got something to say?" I prod.

"You named your truck 'Daisy'?"

Her eyes narrow, almost as if she's taunting me. That she has the guts to challenge me combined with those fucking blue eyes throws me off my game. "I did. Got a problem with that?"

"No. No problem," she says, twisting her lips into an incredibly sexy pout that I want to kiss off her goddamn face. "Just never met a man who named their truck after a flower."

"Me either. Now, before I go calling the Sheriff about this, I'm gonna give you two a moment to consider telling me what happened. And," I say, cutting off the blonde, "I'll give you a piece of information before you decide what to say. Doc Burns' office has cameras installed that will show everything. Just let that sink in a second."

Their eyes go wide as they instinctively move together into a protective huddle. The tall girl points to the blonde who responds with a frantic whisper. She's guilty as hell.

On one hand, I want to break her down and get inside her in ways she's never dreamed. On the other, I can hear my brain issuing an alert to back away slowly.

The longer they confer, the more time I have to watch. The blonde controls the conversation, the other deferring to her as they talk amongst themselves. It's hot as hell.

The light bounces off the wounded plastic of the headlight and draws my attention back to the fact that Daisy is damaged, and in all likelihood, one of these two did it.

"You really calling Kip?" Peck whispers. "He's not gonna do shit about this, you know."

"He might throw them in the back of his cop car and fuck their brains out. Especially the blonde," Lance whistles. "Can you imagine her in handcuffs? *Shit*."

The thought shoots a flame through my veins that catches me off guard. The vision of her bound up with one of these assholes at the helm irks me. Bad. "You two stay out of this. Let me handle it."

The sound of metal pinging against the ground rings through the air. The girls jump, the blonde leaping away from the aluminum bat as it rolls across the sidewalk and lands in the gutter with a flourish. Her eyes snap to mine, guilt etched across her gorgeous face. "It was an accident."

"How, exactly, does a baseball bat accidentally strike the front of my truck?" I ask. "Did it just hop over there and smash itself into my headlight?"

"Well," she gulps. "I ..."

"She was imitating her brother," the dark-headed one says. "So we stop using pronouns, I'm Delaney. This is Sienna."

"I'm Walker. That's Peck and Lance." I rest my attention on Sienna. She's leaned against the grey car, her arms crossed over her chest. "So?"

"I was swinging the bat," she says, "while Delaney puked over there and it slipped out of my hands."

"I think we're gonna have to see your swing," Peck chuckles.

Sienna rolls her eyes. "You do *not* need to see my swing."

Imagining her ass popped out, her body moving for our benefit, seems like a fair trade for the hassle of dealing with this tonight.

"How else do we know it was you? It could've been Delaney and you're just covering for her," I explain, loving the frustration on her beautiful face. "Gonna need to see the swing."

"No."

"Lance, call Sheriff Kooch."

"Wait," Sienna sighs. "It *was* an accident. I can cut you a check for the repairs but please don't call the police. I ... I can't have a record. You don't understand."

Looking away, it takes everything I have not to laugh. The plea in her voice is so damn adorable it almost makes me give in. Yet, she hasn't shown any remorse, and that's something I can't get to sit right.

Swiping the bat out of the gutter, I extend it to her. The air between us heats, our fingers brushing in the exchange. The contact is enough to have her eyes flicking to mine. The light above may be dim, but it's bright enough to see the way her lids hood, her lips part just barely as she pulls her skin from mine.

A zip of energy tumbles through my veins and I remind myself I can't tug on the bat and pull her into me. There's no way I can cover her lips with my own, sliding my tongue across hers, making her attempt at resistance to this proposed swing futile.

Instead, I step back.

"Batter up." Peck motions for her to go. "Let's see it."

"Are you really going to make me do this?"

"Did you really just smash the front of my truck?" I ask. "The answer is the same to both questions, Slugger."

Her eyes narrow, but there's a fire in them that turns me the hell on. She steps away from her friend, zapping all the power I held just a few seconds ago with the flick of her tongue. It darts out, rolling across her bottom lip as the bat comes over her head. Sticking her ass out, bending her knees, her eyes still locked on mine, she slices the bat through the air ... and stops it at the last possible second before impact.

It's everything I thought it would be.

"Any questions, fellas?" she asks, propping it up on one shoulder.

"I have one," I say, forcing a swallow, trying to redirect my thoughts. "If you could stop it that fast, then why the fuck didn't you do that the first time?"

"Very funny." She tosses the bat into the back seat of the car and crosses her arms in front of her again.

"Can I ask why you have a baseball bat to begin with?" Lance asks. "Do you belong to some softball league or something? If so, I just took a huge interest in women's softball."

Sienna laughs as Delaney's face turns red. "Delaney's car is like a scavenger hunt. You can find anything in there. So while she got sick, I just rummaged around in the trunk, found the bat, and fooled around." She looks at me, her eyes softening. "Are you going to be here for a while? I'll go home and get the money. I didn't bring my debit card with me tonight."

It'll cost fifty bucks to fix the damage and about an hour's time. Definitely not worth her going out of her way tonight. But it *is* worth making her come around again and say she's sorry. It might do her some good.

Might not hurt me either.

She clicks her tongue against the roof of her mouth, the motion driving me crazy.

"Come see me Monday morning at Crank. It's two streets over," I say, gesturing to the north, before I can talk sense in to myself.

"Smart," Peck whispers behind me, getting an elbow to the side from Lance.

Her jaw sets, a glimmer of resistance clouding her baby blue eyes. "I have plans Monday. I can try on Tuesday."

The nonchalant attitude cuts through me, like her fuckup is no big deal. I wasn't set on Monday morning, but I am now. "Monday or I call the Sheriff. Your decision, but make it quick. I got shit to do."

"Fine," she huffs. "Monday."

"Fine," I mock. "See you Monday morning."

We start back down the sidewalk, her gaze heavy on my back. I pause at the bumper of their car. "Peck got your license plate number, so don't think about not showing."

"I did not," Peck hisses, catching another elbow from Lance as their car doors open and slam shut.

"What the hell are you going to do with that?" Lance asks once we're out of earshot. "Because I have a list of suggestions if you need them."

As we get farther away, the air clearing of Sienna's perfume, I realize it's not suggestions I need. It's a heavy dose of self-control.

ACKNOWLEDGMENTS

First and foremost, thank you to my Creator.

Spending time with Jess and Pippa has been a treat. There have been so many people behind the scenes helping to keep the ball rolling while I was working, as well as giving me an assist in the writing process.

I write big, loving, slightly chaotic and shenanigan-prone families because that's what I know. That's what I have at home each and every day. For that, I'm eternally grateful. To Alexander, Aristotle, Achilles, and Ajax—sometimes your antics wind up in my stories. Thank you for making me laugh continuously every day. And to my husband—you will never know how much I appreciate you for everything, but maybe for my snack at two o'clock every morning the most. You nailed the nacho game this round.

To Rob and Peggy Patterson, I'm so proud to be a part of your family. Thank you for your calls and texts—and for always cheering me on.

I say it every time, but Kari March truly does the best cover design. She's magic and I'm so grateful that she understands what my gibberish-y ideas mean. I love you, Kari.

Hey, Tiffany—we did it again. I made you sweat a little with this one, but you never stopped believing in me. Your ability to stay calm when I start "doing the math" is ... well, it's pretty funny because I always wonder if you hang up the phone and panic. If so, you don't show it and, for that, I'm so grateful.

Kenna Rey came through in a big way for me with Fluke. Her

ability to frame constructive criticism in a positive way is outstanding. She's also a great friend. Thanks, Kenna. I appreciate you.

Anjelica Grace came in clutch! I don't know how you work in my chapters in the chaos of your life, but you always do, and you do it with a smile. I'm assuming you're smiling anyway. If not, don't tell me. Also, thank you for always making sure that there are enough hands to do all the things I say they're doing. That's the real work right here. Ha! Thank you for always answering my call for help.

Michele Ficht is one of my longest booklandia friends and also one of the most reliable, professional, thoughtful, and thorough people I know. I could list adjectives endlessly. Thank you for always being such a light and willing to help me polish a manuscript. I appreciate you so much.

Thank you to Susan Rayner, the woman that has beta read the most Adriana Locke books of anyone. Thank you for jumping in a document and reminding me that I know how to write a book when I forget. You're such a good friend and I adore you.

Lara Petterson is a blast of energy almost every morning. Her "Hey" when I pick up the phone always makes me smile. Thank you for our strategy sessions, encouragement, and friendship. I love you.

Big thanks to Overbooked PA, Brittni Van, for the excitement, encouragement, and energy she brings to every project. Sometimes we get off topic and our calls go off onto weird tangents, but we get there in the end. Ha! Love you, Britt. Thank you for everything.

I put out a call for music assistance when I was writing Fluke, and so many suggestions were given. But Sara Miller gave me not just her song choices to keep me motivated, but her entire playlist. That list got me through some hard scenes (pun intended). Tell your husband I appreciate him letting me borrow "the list". No one will ever know. *winks*

Marion Archer hasn't given up on me yet, and that surprises me a bit. Ha! Thank you, M, for your patience, love, and keen eye on my manuscripts. Your suggestions are always so helpful and your comments about laughing make me laugh! I'll get the correct use of hyphens one day, but probably not lay/lie or past/pass. Sorry.

A big thank you to Jenny Sims for working me in and for her patience when I forget to send the doc. *facepalm* I appreciate your attention to detail and thoroughness in making sure my document is the best it can be.

Mandi Beck and I finally got to write at the same time again! It's been a long (long) time coming. This made me think about writing our first books so many years ago. We had no idea what we were doing or what we were getting into—but wasn't it the best? Thanks for being my ride-or-die, candle-lighting, ready-to-clam-it friend. What would I do without you?

When I'm in the throes of being unsure I can pull a book off (every time), S.L. Scott fills my text messages with encouragement and reminders that I've done this before and can do it again. Her willingness to hop on a call and talk through a plot point or help me figure out why my hero feels a certain way, is invaluable. I love you, Suzie.

Jessica Prince is my writing partner. We meet on Zoom every morning and get our words in. Usually. Sometimes we just turn off our cameras and pretend to eat lunch. But what matters is that we show up for each other ... even when she has to text me a hundred times. Thank you for getting me in the chair, Jess!

Oh, Candi Kane PR—where do I begin? One day, I promise I'll give you all the things you need for cover reveals. I won't forget to send excerpts. And I'll give you ARCs early. I wouldn't count on getting all of that on the same book, but I'll work on it. Thank you for being so incredibly kind and professional and patient (even if your DM's are a little suspect—ha!).

Becca Mysoor (Becca Edits Things) was a tremendous help with getting all of the intricate backstory pieces together for Fluke. Thank you for sharing your gift and magic with me!

Thanks to Stephanie Gibson for always helping with Goodreads, keeping an eye on things at night, and for always being in my corner. And hugs to Kaitie Reister for the encouraging messages and energy in All Locked Up. I appreciate you!

And to you, my reader—I hope this book made you smile. I hope it gave you a little hope. I hope it made you believe in love. And, most of all, I hope you find your Jess.

ABOUT THE AUTHOR

USA Today Bestselling author, Adriana Locke, writes contemporary romances about the two things she knows best—big families and small towns. Her stories are about ordinary people finding extraordinary love with the perfect combination of heart, heat, and humor.

She loves connecting with readers, fall weather, football, reading alpha heroes, everything pumpkin, and pretending to garden.

Hailing from a tiny town in the Midwest, Adriana spends her free time with her high school sweetheart (who she married over twenty years ago) and their four sons (who truly are her best work). Her kitchen may be a perpetual disaster, and if all else fails, there is always pizza.

Join her reader group and talk all the bookish things by clicking here.

www.adrianalocke.com

Printed in the USA
CPSIA information can be obtained
at www.ICGtesting.com
LVHW032022161223
766414LV00039B/455

9 781960 355010